Penguin Books
Moreover, too ...

Prior to starting his 'Moreover ...' [column in *The Times*,]
Miles Kington was on the staff of *Pu[nch* for ten years, before which]
he had joined the musical group 'Ins[tant Sunshine', with which he]
plays double bass, and even before th[at he was briefly a reporter on]
The Times. This was immediately before leaving Oxford, where he
read French and German, starting in 1960. He was born in 1941. He
is also the author of *Let's Parler Franglais!*, *Let's Parler Franglais
Again!*, *Parlez-vous Franglais?*, *Let's Parler Franglais ... One More
Temps*, *Moreover ...* and *Nature Made Ridiculously Simple*, all
published in Penguins, and *Miles and Miles*.

Moreover, too...

Miles Kington

Penguin Books

Penguin Books Ltd, Harmondsworth, Middlesex, England
Viking Penguin Inc., 40 West 23rd Street, New York, New York 10010, U.S.A.
Penguin Books Australia Ltd, Ringwood, Victoria, Australia
Penguin Books Canada Limited, 2801 John Street, Markham, Ontario, Canada L3R 1B4
Penguin Books (N.Z.) Ltd, 182–190 Wairau Road, Auckland 10, New Zealand

First published 1985

Copyright © Miles Kington, 1985
All rights reserved

The author would like to thank *The Times* for permission
to reproduce material which first appeared there

Made and printed in Great Britain by
Richard Clay (The Chaucer Press) Ltd, Bungay, Suffolk
Filmset in Monophoto Sabon by
Northumberland Press Ltd, Gateshead, Tyne and Wear

Except in the United States of America, this book is sold subject
to the condition that it shall not, by way of trade or otherwise, be lent,
re-sold, hired out, or otherwise circulated without the
publisher's prior consent in any form of binding or cover other than
that in which it is published and without a similar condition
including this condition being imposed on the subsequent purchaser

Introduction

As everyone must know by now, *The Times* celebrated its bicentenary in 1985. It certainly came as a shock to me to realize that I have been writing the 'Moreover . . .' column for two hundred years, but time flies when you're having fun.

Having lived through the Napoleonic era, the spread of railways, the rise and fall of Oscar Wilde, the collapse of the Edward VIII coronation mug industry, the Falklands War and a new Napoleonic era under Mrs Thatcher, I am sometimes asked to what I owe my longevity. Quite simple. I have ignored public affairs and events of any kind. To be conscious of the milestones of history is to be conscious of the passing of time and quite honestly, casting my mind back over the last two hundred years, I cannot remember anything important happening at all.

To take a small example, there was a sinister rumour at *The Times* early in 1985 that the building was to be visited by the Royal Family. I promptly closed the door of my tiny office tight and put a DO NOT DISTURB notice outside, as there is nothing that interrupts a train of thought more than getting up and curtsying the whole time.

That afternoon I looked up from my typewriter and realized I was being watched from the doorway by a man. I stared at him hard, but he would not go away.

'And what do you do?' he said suddenly.

'I make the occasional joke and try and get it in the papers,' I said. 'What do you do?'

'Pretty much the same thing,' he said.

'I stare into space a lot.'

'So do I.'

'And I get asked a lot of stupid questions.'

'I know the feeling well,' said the man. 'Maybe we should change places.'

It was only later I realized that it was the Duke of Edinburgh. But the man is a good sport, and later in the year we duly swapped places for a fortnight. Some of his pieces are in this book, and I wonder if you can spot which ones they are.

Meanwhile, I am looking forward to the next two hundred years of 'Moreover...' Whatever momentous and earth-shattering things happen in those two centuries, be assured that 'Moreover...' will be there to ignore them, day by day.

A complete, rip-roaring, thunderous novel

CHAPTER ONE

'Waal, I ain't one fer admitting defeat,' said old Will Wordsworth, spitting with amazing accuracy at a daffodil near by, 'but this little ol' limerick's got me beat.'

'Blamed if I see how it works,' said Alf Tennyson. The young man stared moodily at the tiny object. 'It ain't like an epic at all. It's so tiny there ain't nothing to it – more of a lady's weapon if you ask me.'

'Talking about my invention?' said a long, cool voice.

They gasped and swung round. There, in the middle of the Last Chance Saloon, Henley-on-Thames, deep in the heart of shootin', rowin' and puntin' country, stood a stranger. They knew him from his long moustaches and the rhyming dictionary poking from one corner of his otherwise well-cut coat. Edward Lear!

'We was just saying, Mr Lear, that your limerick is mighty hard to handle. No offence, but ten dollars says you can't get it to work.'

'*A singer from out of El Paso,*' said Lear instantly, '*Got caught up one day in a lasso. When he finally got loose, From that darn pesky noose, He was no longer profundo basso.* You owe me ten bucks, gentlemen.'

After the stranger had departed, they sat and stared at each other.

'El Paso don't rhyme with lasso,' said Alf.

'Right,' said Will. 'But he still licked us.'

CHAPTER TWO

'They say "King" Lear's in town,' said Kid Swinburne. 'What's more, they say he's found a rhyme for Albuquerque.'

The poets gazed moodily at the bottle of hock and wished to heaven 'King' Lear had never been born. What use were their long drawn-out stanzas and etiolated similes against the quick-fire, rapid repeat limerick? It was plumb unfair. When the saloon door of the Paradise Inn, Stratford-on-Avon (bang in the middle of the Shakespeare ranch) opened, they didn't look round. They knew who it was. 'King' Lear.

'Anyone got anything to say to me?' drawled the King.

'Yes, I have!' declared young Cov Patmore, jumping to his feet. 'Take this, Mr Lear! *There was a young man of Dunstable, Whose morals were wholly unstable...*'

'It ain't Dun*stable*, kid. It's *Dun*stable. Get wise.'

Patmore slumped over the table, deeply wounded. Lear grinned wickedly.

'Well, gents, if that's the best you all can do ... Oh, and by the way, mirky, turkey and Circe, if you're looking for a rhyme for Albuquerque. Another thing. I'm working on a new model. The Chinese limerick. Be seein' ya.'

CHAPTER THREE

'Tell me one thing,' said grizzled Matt Arnold. 'How come we're all talking in this pesky accent?'

'To sell the whole story to the Yankees, they say,' muttered Bob Browning. 'By the way, I figure that Circe is no kind of rhyme for Albuquerque.'

'I believe you,' said Matt. 'Now all we need is someone who dares say it to his face.'

CHAPTER FOUR

They were all there for the shoot-out at the OK Corral. Bob Browning, with Liz Barrett begging him not to get involved, young Alf Tennyson, now old Alf Tennyson, Bill Thackeray, Ed Fitzgerald, 'Doc' Poe, Gerry Hopkins and Art Clough. All against the one man, 'King' Lear.

Trouble was, Lear hadn't showed up.

'Trouble is, he ain't showed up,' sneered 'Doc' Poe, whose accent did at least sound authentic.

'Oh yes, he did,' said old Alf Tennyson, pointing to the wall behind. There, written in big white paint, was the following message: '*They all came to the OK Corral, Fit to fight and plumb full of morale, But they hadn't the brain, To write a quatrain, Or a bar of an old Bach chorale.*'

CHAPTER FIVE

'You cain't rhyme "corral" with "chorale",' said 'Doc' Poe, coughing.

'I can,' said 'King' Lear.

CHAPTER SIX

'All right,' said 'Doc' Poe, 'but I bet your talk about the Chinese limerick was so much hogwash.'

'I like your nerve, Poe,' said 'King' Lear. 'So I'll tell you. You know the Chinese do things back to front? Writin' and readin' and that?'

'Ah've heard so,' said Poe.

'Then listen to this,' said Lear. *'In China, the limerick's wrong, A kind of back-to-front song. And this is the worst, The last line comes first, So there was a young man from Hongkong.'*

CHAPTER SEVEN

Edward Lear jumped into his bed, along with a dashing redhead. He had drunk so much whisky, he felt kinda frisky, so he ... (*That will do, thank you. – Ed.*)

The billion-year racket

'Cocker' Leakey, the distinguished but outspoken Cockney palaeontologist, should be a happy man. He is the discoverer of *Homo Millwallicus*, man's seven-million-year-old football vandal forebear. His book *Not Just a Pretty Skull* is still in the best-seller lists and he is busy making a new series of his popular BBC-TV programme, *If The Bone Fits*. His theory that Darwin got it back to front, and that monkeys represent a distinct advance on mankind, is rapidly gaining ground.

And yet today he is a slightly chagrined man because he has not been invited to join in the current series of palaeontological digs being organized by the police force in London.

'I'd have thought I'd have been the obvious bloke to have along,' he told me yesterday, as we reclined in the saloon bar of his local, the Skull and Trowel. 'Who knows bones better than me? Who knows London better than me? Who's better at the quick ten-minute interview on *Nationwide* than me? Well, stands to reason.'

What makes Leakey a mite depressed or, in his own words, as hopping mad as a prawn in a frying pan, is that he has recently made discoveries which he thinks the police would be very interested in. From a kneecap and a toenail found on his latest expedition, he has deduced that prehistoric man ran the biggest protection racket in history, ranging over Europe and most of Africa.

'Man's instincts don't change much over the years,' he explained, as he ordered another Olduvai Gorgeous, his favourite cocktail. 'I mean, when a bloke bashes a friend over the head and removes his valuables, the basic process is the same whether it takes place now or seven million years ago. And the same applies to the sex business as well. There's always been a sex industry as far as we can remember. But the question that historians have never asked is the one I've asked: *What did prehistoric man get up to when the little lady wasn't looking?*'

He thinks he has solved the age-old mystery of why we have found so many caves with prehistoric paintings, and what they were for.

'Sex arcades, that's what they were. A little bloke standing outside, no doubt, yelling, "Show's just starting! Frankest pictures this side of Africa! Only three sharp flints to get in." Well, it's the only theory that makes sense. All those middle-aged balding hunters trying to recapture their lost youth, they had to go somewhere, didn't they?'

Leakey's theory is that these caves represented one of the biggest sources of income of the era, and so naturally attracted the attention of prehistoric gangs of criminals. Cocker reckons that they moved around in groups of twenty or thirty, collecting protection money from the cave-runners, and duffing them up when they wouldn't oblige.

But why should today's police be interested in all this, fascinating and convincing though it is?

'Blimey, takes a while to get things through your thick skull, doesn't it? Talk about prehistoric journalists ... Well, this was the biggest protection racket in all of history and yet to my knowledge not a single arrest was ever made. So it's still an unsolved crime on police books, right? And without me, I don't see how they're ever going to crack it.

'Believe me, as soon as they announce that they're looking for a toe-nail about seven million years old to help them with their inquiries, I'll be round like a shot. No, on second thoughts, I'll get *them* round to the Skull and Trowel like a shot. Joe, another Corpse Reviver for the gentleman.'

Life begins at Trust House Forte

I have received an interesting query from Mrs Jean Lewis, in Hochdahl, Germany. Why, she wants to know, are there so many signs in Soho saying 'Live Topless Barmaids'? Are these girls replacing dead topless barmaids or what?

No, Mrs Lewis, it is the word 'live' that is changing. It is no longer the opposite of 'dead', it is the opposite of 'studio-recorded'. I have had several embarrassing experiences of chatting to topless barmaids in Soho clubs and realizing after ten or fifteen minutes that I had been talking to a video recording.

To avoid more confusion about what is live and what is not, I have prepared this small glossary of the new meanings of all life-related terms.

Alive: dead, as in the sentence: 'The craft of dolly-thatching is still alive in Rosemary Oliver's little shop in Covent Garden...' The word is usually qualified, as in 'very much alive', or 'alive and kicking'.

Animation: a technique whereby modern cartoon films on children's television can be rendered almost motionless; only the eyes and mouth of the characters move, and then rarely. There is, however, a great deal of talking and music.

Biography: an account of a man's life written at a time when it is too late to consult him about details. If details are subsequently invented, it is called a frank biography; if they are suppressed, the biography is said to be authorized.

Biological: obsolete, referring to the study of life itself; now, appertaining to the effect of washing powder on badly soiled laundry.

Life: 1. That which is, existence, the very stuff of being, anything which even David Attenborough cannot explain. 2. The ownership and maintenance of large quantities of dogs, logs, etc. as in *Country Life*, *Cheshire Life* and so on. 3. The theory that the only two important things in this world are being cheated by a shady firm and telling smutty jokes with a leer (cf. *That's Life* with Esther Rantzen). 4. The process of meeting all the people from your past who ever cheated you or told you smutty jokes (cf. *This is Your Life*). 5. Eight years spent in prison.

Lifebuoy: a large cake of red soap thrown to a drowning man.

Life-giving, life-enhancing, etc.: two of a number of terms applied to beliefs which turn normal, bright teenagers into zombies.

Lifeline: an Arts Council grant.

Lifestyle: something possessed by someone who spends all his time appearing on TV.

Live: music recorded in front of an audience a year ago. Also, a TV show which was recorded and edited yesterday so that all the human mistakes and lapses have been removed.

Live-in: sharing a house for tax reasons. Cf. the song by Cliff Richard, 'Live-in Doll'.

Lively: 1. Misprint for 'likely', as in *The Lively Lads*, 'not bloody lively', etc. 2. Dead, as in 'the lively arts'.

Liver: a fabulous bird which lived beside the Mersey and died of cirrhosis.

Living: 'Life is for the living' – a phrase much used at funerals.

Quick: able to move fast across a zebra crossing. Cf. dead.

Revival: the inability of theatre managements to find good new dramatists. NB: a Shakespeare revival is always called a reinterpretation.

Undead: film term applied to a ghastly apparition that refuses to go through the normal dying process so that it can reappear in the sequel.

Vital: an artist who has no ideas but lots of energy is said to be vital.

Vivacious: able to keep absolutely still in front of a camera, with no clothes on, as in 'Lovely, vivacious Jacqui Quiff is a student of hairdressing. You get top marks from us, Jacqui!'

The best of bad taste

A passing fuss was caused a short time ago by the publication of a book of riddles, edited by Kevin Crossley-Holland, which contained two jokes about Lord Mountbatten in the worst possible taste. Whenever I hear that something is in the worst possible taste, I immediately suspect that I am missing something funny, so I took steps to find out what the offending riddles were: imagine my chagrin when I found out that they were both quite familiar to me, having been told to me by my children over a year before.

The only funny thing, in fact, was the sight of grown-ups working themselves into a lather of indignation over the juvenile sense of humour. Children love black humour – in my schooldays it was the newly imported sick jokes from America that were all the rage – and it is only when they mature that they become toffee-nosed and obsessed with good taste, in other words when they start denying the way people really think and talk.

Good taste breaks out all over the place. It broke out in Kilburn not so long ago when the council tried to outlaw the telling of Irish jokes, and were greeted by a storm of merriment from all right-minded Irishmen. I learnt all my best Irish jokes from a book published in Dublin, though of course they weren't jokes against Irishmen – they were jokes against the people of Kerry, who perform the same fictitious function there as Tasmanians do in Australia or Belgians in France.

And it broke out again when Tony Banks of the GLC tried to insist that the London Marathon could only take place if twenty or so disabled competitors were allowed to wheelchair themselves in the race itself. Organizer Chris Brasher quite rightly pointed out that a running race is a running race, and that the last thing runners want is to find themselves falling over wheelchairs, though in the prevailing spirit of good taste he had to put very tactfully the notion that people in wheelchairs, however worthy, were not runners in the true sense.

Now, it is one of the axioms of humour that the best jokes about minorities usually come from the minorities themselves. The funniest Catholic jokes I know were told me by Catholics. I remember with great pleasure George Shearing, the blind pianist, telling Roy Plomley on *Desert Island Discs* of his stint in an all-blind orchestra and of the night, just before curtain-up, when one of the saxophonists yelled: 'Stop! I've lost my glass eye!' If you've never seen fifteen blind musicians on their hands and knees looking for a glass eye, said Shearing wryly, you haven't seen anything.

Another wonderful blind pianist, Eddie Thompson, once told me that one of the saddest moments of his life came when he achieved a great ambition, and got to drive a dodgem car at a funfair. No sooner had he started than the proprietor turned him off with the words: 'I'm not having a blind man on my dodgems; you might bump into somebody.'

But the best of all blind jokes came from Stevie Wonder, the blind and black American singer/composer, who was once asked (or asked a million times, knowing interviewers) if blindness had hampered his career a great deal.

'Well, it might have been worse,' said Wonder. 'I could be black.'

But when I heard of Tony Banks's good taste, I couldn't help thinking of Douglas Bader on the *Michael Parkinson Show*. It was a fairly mundane show, as I remember, but the light came into Bader's eyes when they started on sport for disabled people.

'You haven't seen sport at its most furious till you've seen wheelchair basketball,' he said. 'It's probably the most exciting game in the world. And the dirtiest. Their wheelchairs are pitted with dents and marks where they've run into each other at full speed in an attempt to commit mayhem. I saw a game in Canada recently which I still remember with awe, because both sides had taken against the referee, whom they considered to be far below standard.'

'And what happened?' said Parkinson.

'They ran him over,' said Bader promptly.

I wish Bader were still around to comment on Tony Banks. He would, I feel, probably support Mr Banks's insistence on having wheelchair athletes in the main marathon itself, on the grounds that a wheelchair athlete may not actually be able to win the race, but he could do an awful lot of damage.

And I wish I could hear Mr Banks's reply.

The tea-break job

'Thieves who spent three hours breaking into an iron safe at a company near Bristol found only some tea bags and sugar' – The Times

Chairman: I think you all know why I've called this meeting.
Board: We certainly do, sir.
Chairman: Anyone not know why I've called this meeting?
Simpson: Yes, sir. I don't know why, sir.
Chairman: It's about the safe, Simpson. You've heard about the safe?
Simpson: Yes, sir. But it's only a few tea bags and some sugar. I don't see why we need a board meeting to replace a few tea bags...
Chairman: God give me strength, Simpson. Let me explain it to you. When a safe is broken open and the thieves make off with tea and sugar, the question the firm has to ask itself is not: Shall we replace the tea and sugar? What *is* the question, Simpson?
Simpson: Ummm... Why wasn't there any milk in the safe, sir?
Chairman: No, Simpson, the question is: *Where has the money gone?*
Managing Director: Could you perhaps explain the situation for us all, Chairman?
Chairman: Certainly. Listen carefully, Simpson. Two days ago, there was £30,000 in that safe, but no tea and no sugar. When the thieves were caught, they had tea and sugar on them but no money, and they had no time to dispose of the money. Therefore the money had disappeared before the thieves arrived. Only people in this room have access to that safe. I wonder if anyone of you would like to say anything?
Managing Director: Perhaps it would help if we found out who put the tea and sugar in the safe.
Chairman: Perhaps so. (*Silence*.) Well, I'm waiting.
Simpson: I've remembered now, sir.
Chairman: Yes, Simpson?
Simpson: You remember the meeting we had on Monday? When you asked for more efficiency and less time-wasting? And you said that people drank far too much tea around the place and that we could save both money and time if we only kept the tea under lock and key?
Chairman: I'm still waiting, Simpson.

Simpson: I think what I'm trying to say, sir, is that I put the tea and sugar in the safe. I left the milk out because it might go off.

Chairman: And you took the money out?

Simpson: Yes, sir. Well, I thought that anyone going in there for a teabag might be tempted by the sight of so much money.

Managing Director: Can you remember what you did with the money, Simpson?

Simpson: Let me think ... Yes, I swapped it.

Managing Director: Perhaps you could explain ...

Simpson: I put the money in the tea caddy, sir. It stood to reason that anyone looking for tea would know it was in the safe now and would come for the key.

Chairman: You. Put. The money. In the caddy.

Simpson: Yes, sir.

Chairman (*into intercom*)**:** Miss Berry, could you bring the tea caddy in, please? *No, I do not want a cup of tea!* Just bring the caddy in, nice and gently.

Managing Director: I think it's only fair to say that without Simpson's prompt action, we would be £30,000 poorer.

Miss Berry (*entering*)**:** Here's the caddy, sir. The money's quite safe in there, sir. I've been keeping an eye on it. (*Leaves.*)

Managing Director: So I'd like to propose a vote of thanks to Simpson.

Chairman: Seconded. And I'd like to propose he is then fired.

Simpson: Seconded. I mean, look here, sir.

Chairman: Let me make a note of that ... Why are there never any blasted pencils when you need one?

Simpson: Ah. Well, sir, do you remember the other day you said that people got through stationery at a scandalous rate? And that somebody ought to lock away the pencils?

Chairman: All right, Simpson. Just tell us where you put the pencils ...

Simpson: Well, sir, you know the very big safe where we normally keep the secret designs? Well, sir ...

Of Brahms, the man, I sing

The notion that classical music is a stuffy kind of art received a severe knock this last week when the *Radio Times* informed its four million readers that Brahms, when young, had earned a living playing the piano in brothels in Hamburg. This came as a shock both to the pop fraternity, who thought that only the Beatles ever got started in Hamburg, and to jazz fans, who were under the impression that only Jelly Roll Morton got started in a brothel.

Morton, who had a diamond set in his teeth, played champion pool, pimped, claimed to have invented jazz and had a long-running rivalry with Duke Ellington, was actually a pale character when set beside Brahms. It is often forgotten that Brahms, too, claimed to have discovered jazz, though this was due to a misunderstanding for which he was not responsible.

It happened in the cotton fields near Budapest one day, when Brahms was out for a walk, trying to dream up another trick to play on Wagner – the Duke Ellington of his day. He gradually became aware that the workers in the fields were singing alluring and dangerously exciting rhythms as they turned the cotton into drip-dry tunics for the Imperial Court. Brahms's fingers snapped and his eyes sparkled.

'Hey, what do you call that kind of music?' he asked one of the singers.

'What do we call dat music?' said the man thus addressed, played by the young Louis Armstrong. 'Why, we calls dat music jazz!'

This was a mischievous invention on his part, as they actually called it Hungarian folk music, but he reckoned that the young man with the mane of white hair and huge grey beard would fall for it. He was right. Hastily establishing that the folk tunes were not in copyright, Brahms turned them into concert display pieces and played them in brothels all over the world. At the end of the programme he would slam the keyboard lid shut, jump up and shout: 'And that's jazz!'

As nobody knew what he was talking about, they prefered to call it Hungarian Dances, but either way, as they put it back in the cotton fields, they done stole our music again.

Brahms was always secretly disappointed that the stuffed-shirt audiences didn't show more reaction, and he would often break off in the middle of a piece and observe drily to the listeners: 'This place *is* licensed for dancing, you know.'

Brahms liked to be in tip-top physical shape, mostly because he was waiting for the promised twelve-round contest against Wagner that the latter seemed afraid to turn up for. 'I'll get that Hun, By the end of round one,' Brahms used to taunt him. 'Just get me in the Ring with Wagner,' he boasted to friends, 'and I'll eat him for coffee break.' Once the threatened fight did actually take place, but, unbeknownst to Brahms, Wagner had hired Bruno Walter, the Bavarian Mauler, to take his place. Brahms only found out the truth after twelve gruelling rounds which the judges scored six to Brahms and six to his opponent, with Brahms winning the encore on points.

'Just typical of Wagner,' growled Brahms afterwards, 'to send in a dep for a big gig.' He later got his own back when he thrashed Wagner at snooker in the big Bayreuth Finals, sixteen frames to three, and went on to meet the Russian champion, Tchaikovsky, whom he always considered rather too effete to be a really good snooker player.

Brahms was a larger-than-life character who had diamonds set in all the white keys of his travelling piano. Before he breezed into a new town, the place would be plastered with posters saying: 'Brahms is coming! All pianists are requested to leave town for their own safety.' And then the great man himself would arrive, in a white suit, surrounded by bodyguards and attended personally by the Abbé Liszt. The first thing he would ask on arrival was the address of the best brothel in town, and there he would sit for hours, strumming at the piano those old tunes he had learned back on the Danube levées and maybe accompanied by the singing of the madame (played by the young Billie Holiday). Then he would proceed to the concert hall and, in his own words, knock 'em in the aisles.

At the end of his life, when he was fat and heavy, he opened a bar in Vienna and became a bit of a nostalgic bore. I prefer to think of the Johannes Brahms with his razor-crease suits, his rakish straw hat and the slim cheroot, thrashing hell out of the eighty-eight ivories and leaping into the audience to pummel any critic he spotted writing something adverse about him. Men still talk about the time he beat up three reviewers *and* issued four proposals of marriage during a performance of his first piano concerto, without missing a single note.

Forget about the BBC celebrations. Let's go out tonight and get drunk in his memory.

Those toe-tapping tax people

'The Inland Revenue is planning to include some swinging new legislation in the Finance Bill which will take effect from April, 1984' – The Times.

'Hi, cats!'

The door of the Tax Planning Department opened, and in came Tex Walters, his fingers snapping and his hips swaying slightly, in time to the old Artie Shaw record playing in his skull. Artie Shaw. What a guy. Married twenty-seven times and still solvent. What a tax adviser that guy must have.

'I've been cooking up a groovy little number for the Finance Bill. Think you're going to really dig it, Sid. What say we define holiday caravans as second homes and tax the hell out of them? That should clear up the traffic jams in the West Country.'

Mr S. Wedderburn, the Sid refered to, sighed as his colleague clicked and snapped his way to his desk. Why had God sent a born-again hep cat to share his hitherto quiet life in tax planning? Mr Wedderburn liked calm, serene, *structured* legislation. It will come as no surprise to learn that he was a lover of Mozart.

'It is no part of our duties, Tex, to sort out traffic problems in the West Country or, indeed, anywhere. We are here to devise ways of raising revenue and discouraging avoidance.'

'Oh, don't be a square, Sid. We're here to put a bit of jive into taxation, hot it up a little! That's what I always say.'

Mr Wedderburn fingered his Glyndebourne tickets as a reminder of the sane world. Tex didn't hear; he was trying to get some papers into a rubber band too small for the purpose.

'Why don't they give us some proper-sized bands?' he grumbled.

'That's the regulation size now,' said Mr Wedderburn.

'Well,' said Tex, twinkling at him, 'I wonder if the big bands will ever come back?'

Mr Wedderburn arrived early the next morning for some peace and quiet. It was no use. Tex was already there, pounding away at his honky tonk typewriter.

'The joint is jumping,' he sang to himself. 'Come on cats, and put on VAT – the joint is jumping! Oh, hi Sid – I came in early to work out details of next month's party.'

Mr Wedderburn's heart sank. He had forgotten that Tex was organizing the Inland Revenue's first-ever Jazz Band Ball. In a weak moment the head of department had agreed to let Tex go ahead with a departmental party.

'I've fixed up two swinging little bands to appear. The New Tax Evaders and the Quintet du Hot Club de Jersey. Should be a real wow! Have you asked Miss Asquith if she'll partner you yet, Sid?'

Mr Wedderburn's mouth opened and closed. He hadn't even dared to ask her yet if she wanted to go to Glyndebourne. Miss Asquith worked in Tax Replanning. She had a weakness for Mantovani, but otherwise she was all right.

'I've asked Sue to come with me,' said Tex, not waiting for an answer. 'Should be a real gas. Hey, did I tell you I'd had this really wild idea for taxing mistresses of company directors? That should put the cat among the pigeons. It don't mean a thing, if I don't wear a ring...'

'You'll be interested to hear, Tex, that I have asked Miss Asquith if she would do me the honour of accompanying me to the Ball. She has said yes.'

Tex did not look at all interested. He did not look as if he had even heard. He was studying a note on his desk, and groaning. 'I don't believe it. Sue says she won't come to the party with me. Oh, that really brings me down, man.'

In his distress, Tex found himself mixing idioms from quite different eras, but it was no use. Sue had really turned him down. Sue, the darling of the department, the blonde post-Doris Day dream teenager with the freckles and fresh look. He buzzed her to come in and give him an explanation.

'It's true,' said Sue defiantly. 'I've been asked by Steve. I'm going with him.' Tex looked at Sue, speechless. For the first time, he noticed that she now had spiky hair coloured yellow, pink and black.

Steve was a new recruit to the department. He was, in a word, neo-punk. His clothes were torn artistically and the message on his T-shirt read: 'TAX-SNIFFING OK'.

'Hey, Steve,' said Tex. 'Have you got eyes to steal my gal? That's not cool, Dad.'

'I don't give a stuff what you fink,' said Steve, staring at him with dead eyes. 'Sue's with me now, right, OK, right? Well, OK. You're yesterday, Tex. You're nowhere.' With one sweep of his arm, Steve knocked the typewriter and other impedimenta off his desk and sat down to do some work. Mr Wedderburn sighed. Suddenly Tex and his swinging ways seemed old-fashioned and rather nostalgic. He wondered what Miss Asquith would think of Steve. Not much, he feared.

Will Tex win Sue back? Is Steve planning some dread neo-punk legislation? How would Andrew Lloyd-Webber tackle the knotty problem of company car allowances? What will Miss Asquith do when Steve asks her to dance? Don't miss the next gritty instalment!

Unusual jobs: no. 1

People who work professionally as broadcasters, TV personalities or simply as superstars are allowed to claim the clothes they buy for appearances against tax. Gary's job is to check their claims. It's as simple as that.

Dressed in a lemon yellow jacket, open white shirt, pale grey trousers and a medallion hanging against his chest, where it has created a pale patch in his suntan, Gary operates from an anonymous office in Mayfair. All the locals think it's an MI5 headquarters, but that's just a front.

'The medallion is, too, actually,' says Gary. 'It's a two-way radio with which I keep in touch with base. In this job you have to keep your wits about you, move fast, move silently.'

But why does an Inland Revenue officer have to keep radio contact with base?

'This business is all computerized now, you know – we're way into the information technology age. Look, I'll show you. Here's a claim from a well-known film star for ten suits, bought for ten chat shows, total cost £1,400. But here in our memory bank we've got video details of all ten of those chat shows. I just call up the requisite footage, take a look and what do I see? I see that he wore the same suit for all ten. Shabby grey worsted, with the left cuff button missing after the first five shows. So we disallow his claim and countersue him for false tax returns.'

Gary spent two years at the East Molesey School of Fashion and Male Cosmetics before entering the Inland Revenue, so he knows what he's talking about. He really wanted to be a TV personality himself, but unfortunately his grey-streaked hair makes a stroboscopic effect on camera; still, he enjoys using his expertise.

'Here's another claim we had last week. Famous entertainer, has his own TV variety show, does about six changes of costume during the show, sent in a claim for £2,000 worth of clothes. I've run his last season through the viewer and I reckon that at a conservative estimate he used up at least £5,000 worth of clothes – one little glitter number is worth £800 alone. Atrocious taste, mark you, but valuable.'

So that's all right, then?

'No, no – we sued him for filing false returns as well. People don't seem to realize that underestimating your allowance is just as illegal as overestimating it. We're hard but fair here. Well, hard, anyway.'

The hardest case they had recently was that of a freelance political journalist who claimed £500 against a beautifully embroidered Afghan jacket which he claimed to have bought in Kabul, and wore for a TV discussion on Afghanistan.

'Some sixth instinct told me he wasn't telling the truth. Oh, he had a receipt all right, but you get a feeling in this trade for when someone isn't coming clean. So we sent an investigator out to check up.'

The Inland Revenue actually sent a man all the way to Kabul just to check one receipt?

'Two, actually. There was someone on breakfast TV who claimed her Afghan slippers against tax. Anyway, our bloke got there and sure enough my hunch was proved right. The bloke had bought the jacket at Yussuf's tailor's shop all right – *but he'd got it for £36 during Yussuf's Mammoth Winter Sale*, and bribed Yussuf to fiddle the receipt.

'And that wasn't all. When our investigator got back, he claimed £660 for himself against buying protective clothing for the overland trek into Afghanistan. Well, that was foolish. We all knew he was a keen rock climber and had the stuff already. Of course he was drummed out of the Revenue and had his epaulettes torn off. And *then* he tried to claim for the epaulettes. Some people.'

And how about Gary's yellow jacket, grey trousers...?

'Oh, sure, I'll claim for that. Interview with *The Times*. Got to look my best. Uphold the Revenue image. I wouldn't bother claiming for your get-up, though.'

Oh, why not?

'Correct me if I'm wrong, but didn't you wear that suit for a brief appearance on *Late Night Line-Up* in 1968?'

Ready tuned and insured

'You can get an upright piano for just over £1,000. And that's not bad when you think you are buying something with 5,000 parts' – Mary Baxter, Piano Publicity Association.

The scene is the forecourt of Sid's new and used pianos, a large repair and tuning depot just off the North Circular Road. The manager, who is wearing a sheepskin jacket and a badge reading 'Schubert's Unfinished and I'm Not Feeling Too Great Myself', is standing there wiping his dusty hands. A customer comes up to him, pushing an old upright.

Customer: Sid?
Manager: He's not here.
Customer: Do you know where he is?
Manager: No idea. He died in 1947. We kept the name for tax purposes.
Customer: Ah. Well, if you're in charge, I wonder if you could have a look at my piano. I'm having a bit of trouble with it at speed.
Manager: Sure. Just park it over by that yellow Bechstein and we'll give it the once over at the weekend.
Customer: I'd be grateful if you could have a look now. I need it this evening.
Manager: All right, squire. (*He opens the top and hits the keys once or twice.*) Blimey, I'm not surprised you've been having trouble. When did you last clean the return mechanism?
Customer: Well, I . . .

Manager: Got to keep the return mechanism clean. When it gets dirty, it starts to stick and then you can't get those repeated notes, know what I mean?

Customer: So it's just the return mechanism needs cleaning, is it? That's a relief.

Manager: And these hammers are worn. Oh dear, oh dear, oh dear. Worn? They're more like cotton wool on a stick than hammers. And look at these strings. Oh deary, deary me.

Customer: Is it bad then?

Manager: Bad? I'm not saying it's bad. I'm just saying that considering it's an old Carl Schumann piano, made in Dresden seventy years ago, you're lucky it's still going at all. What do you use it for?

Customer: Beethoven, mostly. Though I quite often relax with some boogie-woogie.

Manager: Well, there you are then. That stuff really punishes a piano.

Customer: It's very quiet boogie-woogie.

Manager: Boogie-woogie? I'm talking about your actual Beethoven. He's murder on a little old upright like this. Quite honestly, squire, it's hardly worth mending this lot. Know what I'd do? I'd put in a factory reconditioned frame and new set of strings and hammers. I could do it for £600, sir.

Customer: £600!

Manager: We'd reline the pedals and put in a new sustainer as well, of course. All in the price. And top it up with new varnish.

Customer: It's almost like buying a new piano...

Manager: Now you're talking! By complete coincidence, I have here a wonderful upright, only one previous owner, a little lady who stuck to Mozart all her life and never went faster than moderato, straight up! Only just gone on sale. Bound to be snapped up by the weekend.

Customer: But I only came in to get a quick overhaul, not a whole new piano.

Manager: Suit yourself, mate. You want to push on with the old one, that's your privilege.

Customer: Well... how much are you asking?

Manager: £1,100.

Customer: *£1,100*, for this old thing?

Manager: It's got a beautiful response, this machine. Nice tuning, lovely action. Tell you what, I'll make it £1,050. Couldn't bring it lower without bankrupting myself.

At this point the assistant manager comes over and joins the discussion. He remonstrates angrily when he finds that the manager is prepared to let it go for just over £1,000. The manager says he's sorry, but he's already given his word to this gentleman. The assistant manager storms off furiously. Later that evening he and the manager dine out on salmon and champagne to celebrate the sale of a piano that only cost them £170.

Summer, these days

Ah, summertime! And the living is difficult. I don't know about you, but I planted this packet of courgette seeds the other day. The instructions were quite explicit. 'Place seeds in ground and stand well clear, because immediately there will be a bang, a flash and a blaze of courgette plants with bright yellow flowers and a crop of zucchini (that's Italian) which will make your mouth water. Why not also try our marrows, fat peas, black-eyed beauties and raven-haired signorine from the *mezzogiorno* (that's Italian too)?'

Well.

You know me.

Try anything once.

I put the seeds in the ground, retired to a safe distance and then I must have dropped off, because two days later there was still absolutely nothing to be seen except a little note reading: 'Thanks for the seeds. They were delicious! From your garden birds.'

It was then that the words of my old Italian master came into my mind. 'You know the trouble with you English? You never complain! Mama mia – if I was teaching lessons so boring as this in Italy, I would have the class down on me like a ton of straw. But you, you always sit there and take it ... Where do you think you're going, Kington?'

Yes, suddenly I had decided I would take his advice. I would be the first person who had ever written to a seed packet! *Madre de Dios* (that's Spanish), I would not take this lying down. So pen, paper and vitriol, and ... 'Dear Fratelli Seed Packet of Compost Magna,

25

nr Woodbridge. I have tried your courgette seeds and I say the hell with your courgette seeds. In future, I shall stick to baby marrows from the market and remain, yours faithfully, an ex-customer. PS The same goes for your purple-cheeked aubergines. Or melanzane, you Italian *poseurs* (that's French, by the way).'

The result was dynamic.

Five minutes later there was a glamorous knock at the door.

There stood a Ravenna-haired beauty wearing nothing but a simple black dress and a card which said: 'Hi! I am Giuletta, your Fratelli Seed Packet representative. What seems to be the trouble?'

'No trouble at all,' I said, brushing myself down and opening a bottle of Soave Bertani in one smooth movement. 'Come on to the patio and sit down, tell me all about yourself, I love Italian films personally, if it's too hot why don't you, um, undo a cuff button or something? Oh, and sorry about the bomb site, but I've been trying to grow zucchini there.'

'Ah, you speak Italian?' she said, her eyes growing wide, then narrow, then oblong with just a hint of tarragon and basil. 'I have always wanted to meet a man like you!'

'Really?' I said. 'Then what about Tarragon and Basil?'

'They are nothing to me,' she said hotly, 'but you, you are...'

'Yes?'

'You are different,' she said, fingering my threadbare grammar school jacket through which the ballpoint pens showed like emaciated ribs. 'You have ideas. You have *intellektualismus* (that's probably German).'

'Really?' I said. 'Gosh, you sound like my old Italian teacher, Mr Locatelli!'

'Locatelli?' she said, her eyes widening then narrowing, then going over to the hard shoulder. 'But he was my father!'

C'est un petit monde, as the Americans erroneously say. Either way, Giuletta moved in with me and for a short season we entwined together like two vines hoping to produce at least one great bottle. She taught me all she knew about vegetables, seasonal, the care of, and in return I told her the mysteries of English grammar. I did but see her parsing by, and yet I love her till I die.

'I must have off now,' she said, when summer was ended.

'You must *be* off,' I corrected her.

'Yes, yes,' she said. 'You will mention my firm in *The Times*, will you not, oh Kington? Fratelli Seed Packet of Compost Magna, nr...'

'Yes,' I said.

This pamphlet has been paid for by the British Board of Vegetables, and is published by Mills & Bean.

Take-over time

A message to readers of *The Times*.

Do you sometimes get a bit uneasy when you start reading a page of this newspaper and find it is a huge advertisement in a takeover campaign? When someone called Thomas Lonrho is appealing to you not, for heaven's sake, to sell your share in P & O to the House of Tilling? And you haven't heard of any of them, and wouldn't sell your shares to them either, judging from the kind of ads they put in *The Times*?

We at Moreover House intend to put a stop to that.

How? It's quite simple. We are making a takeover bid for the Monopolies Commission. This is a small but powerful organization in London which could, if it wanted to, put a stop to all this takeover nonsense. At the moment we believe its efficiency and profitability are way below capacity, and that its management would benefit powerfully from our expertise.

Under the stewardship of Moreover Holdings, the Monopolies Commission could make a whacking great profit by accepting commissions direct from all firms involved in mergers. Our message to shareholders in the Monopolies Commission is: **Accept the Moreover bid!**

Moreover would make a mess of it.

That is the message from the Monopolies Commission.

All right, so Moreover Holdings are a thrusting new group who have already taken over part of *The Times* newspaper. They have hugely successful enterprises in Hongkong, Singapore and Moscow, as well as a thriving hot-dog stand in the Cayman Islands. They have sole worldwide rights in General Galtieri's writings.

So what? They are also a fly-by-night organization whose methods have attracted the attention of the police in such places as Moscow,

Hongkong and Singapore. The public health authorities in the Cayman Islands have twenty prosecutions pending. And General Galtieri's works are considered to be a fake by none other than Lord Dacre.

Run properly, Moreover could be a credit to British business. That is why the Monopolies Commission is, for the first time, making a takeover bid.

If you own Moreover shares – **sell out to Monopolies!**

Oh, dear, oh dear.

The Monopolies Commission really has got its knickers in a twist, hasn't it? Did you ever see anyone so scared in all its life?

What it needs is someone grown up to run it. And that means Moreover Holdings.

On the day we take over there will be unlimited salmon for everyone. That's a promise. Stand by us and we'll stand by you. **Don't accept the Monopolies bid.**

A message from Monopolies.

Blimey, so they're offering bribes now, are they? A free lunch if we get taken over. Could you really trust a shady, corrupt outfit that made offers like that?

Here's what we say to Moreover shareholders. Accept our bid, and we'll give each and every one of you a small company of your own to play with. We have more than a few left over from previous cases.

Can't say fairer than that, can we?

A final message from Moreover.

Money isn't everything, you know. The quality of life counts as well.

And talking of private life, we have some *very* curious information about the lifestyle of the people who run Monopolies. Red hot, some of it. Not the sort of stuff you'd like to get out.

So remember: if the Monopolies bid is successful, Moreover Holdings will not be afraid to spill the dirt.

This is a blackmail attempt by Moreover Holdings, the group that nobody messes around with.

A message to Moreover Holdings and the Monopolies Commission. This take-over battle is now closed – Ed.

Steamdaze

I was once brought to a standstill in the late 1960s by an *Evening Standard* placard headline: NUDE POLICE SWOOP. In order to deal with the vision of unclothed policemen wheeling and soaring out of the sky, and swooping on some poor innocent (until proved guilty) victim, I had to come to a physical halt in the street. It was then I noticed the missing colon – NUDE: POLICE SWOOP – and could pass on peacefully once more, since which time I have not been brought to a stop by any *Standard* headline. Not, that is, until last Monday, when I read the message: LONDON STATION FOR SALE.

It wasn't until that moment that I realized deep down, that I had always wanted to own a station. This is probably because for four years, between the ages of about six and ten, I lived in a station. I went home to sleep and for meals, and I must have gone to school, but the rest of the time I lived in the station, simply because it seemed the best possible place in the world.

It was called Gresford; it was a country station and it had everything. It had a level crossing, it had a bridge, it had a signal box and it had buckets hanging up marked FIRE. Behind the station there was a steep hillside with woods which sprouted bluebells in spring and bracken in summer. The other side there were water meadows which specialized in lady's smock and cowslips and through which the River Alyn flowed, though I never found out where to. It had a notice asking passengers to shew their tickets at the barrier, and I often wondered why they had to shew them and not show them. It wasn't till I was grown-up that I realized railways like using words that nobody else uses, such as 'alight', 'commence' and 'terminate'.

Gresford also had trains. I leave mention of them till last because, although at the time I thought I was there to see the trains, I realize looking back that it was the station I loved. I didn't want to be an engine driver when I grew up; I wanted to be a stationmaster.

The line it was on was the main Great Western from London to Birkenhead, and Gresford is just beyond Wrexham, on the last bit of Welsh foothill before the rich Cheshire plains are reached. Why my English father wanted to live in Wales I never found out, but the result is that, although I had a Welsh childhood, I shall never be able to write about it like a real Welshman, not being one of the tribe, and not being called Gwyn or Thomas or both. The next village over the hill had the real Welsh name of Llay, and the Gresford lads had a long-standing rivalry with the Llay lads, but I never felt really involved.

Someone at Gresford station, one of the porters, I think, liked gardening and the main platform had lovely flower beds which one year entitled them to sport a plaque saying: 'Best Kept Station of the Year in...' Denbighshire? Britain? The world? It was also a base for pigeon racing. Now and again the stationmaster would lug a big basket full of pigeons off a train and leave it lying on the platform. You could hear them making soft noises inside. Where have they sent us this time? Gresford? Never heard of it. *Wales?* How the hell do we get home from Wales?

Then the stationmaster would re-emerge, checking his big turnip watch, and at the very dot of the very hour would open the basket. The pigeons would launch forth as if inaugurating the Olympic Games, circle above the station once or twice, feel the cold air coming down from the Welsh hills and shoot off in the direction of wherever they lived, apparently unworried by the thought that as soon as they got there they would be put in another basket and sent off again. Occasionally the stationmaster would find one rebellious pigeon skulking in the bottom of the basket and kick him out, then leave the station to me and the flowers. And the trains. The Castles, the Manors, the Halls, the 0–6–0s, the pannier tanks – ah, what engines they were in those days.

The curious thing is that for 99 per cent of the time there were no trains at all. One was always waiting for the next one. And why not? The whole point about being in a station is just being in a station. The one that has just come on the market, Marylebone, is a little big for my needs but now that I know that's what I want, I can wait.

A moral tale for our times

Edward Whipsnade was a model citizen. He always drove on the left and invariably stood for the Queen, though she had never stood for him. He rendered unto God those things which were God's, and unto Caesar those things which were Caesar's, which caused the tax people no end of trouble. So when he went on holiday, he decided to let the police know so that they could keep an eye on his place. He popped into the little local police station and there spoke to a man whom we shall call Constable Addison, as that is the name by which he liked to be known.

'I am going on holiday in the first two weeks of August,' said Edward Whipsnade. 'I have many valuables in my house which a burglar would like to get his hands on. I wonder if you could...?'

'Of course, sir,' said Constable Addison. 'Just give us your name and address, and the exact position of these valuables, with the whereabouts of the receipts, if possible.'

'How can that help you?'

'It will save time,' said the constable mysteriously.

Mr Whipsnade did as he was requested. And there, gentle reader, our story might have ended were it not that he had made one small significant error. He had said he was going on holiday in the first two weeks of August. This was a slip of the mind. He was in fact going on holiday in the *last* two weeks of the same month.

And thus it was that early in August Mr Whipsnade came home from a Wagner evening and entered his house to find a man on the sitting-room floor putting his valuables into a neat pile, preparatory to taking them out of the French windows. The man gasped. This was as nothing compared to the gasp Mr Whipsnade gave when he recognized the man as Constable Addison.

'What are you doing?' said Mr Whipsnade sternly.

'Just checking, sir, just checking. I was passing the house when I remembered your words about being on holiday, so I thought I'd cast an eye on your valuables. May I ask, by the way, why you are not on holiday? It is an offence to deceive the police by wilfully staying at home after announcing your absence.'

Ordinarily Mr Whipsnade might have blushed and gone straight to bed, but a man who has come straight from a Wagner evening is a very different kettle of fish.

'I feel you are up to no good, Constable,' he said. 'Stay where you are while I call the police.'

At this, the so-called constable burst into tears and explained everything. He was not, it seemed, a policeman at all but a member of a gang of unscrupulous burglars. They had set up a fake police station in this residential part of Kensington so that wealthy householders would report their holiday times to them. The 'policemen' would then gently deprive the rich residents of their videos, jewellery, Matisses and other goodies.

'And give unto the poor, I suppose,' said Whipsnade, surprised at his own sharp irony.

'No, sir,' sniffed Addison. 'We was going to sell the stuff and blue the proceeds on Crazy Spartan in the 2.30 at Newbury on Saturday. It's a sure thing.'

This placed Mr Whipsnade in a quandary. On the one hand he had enough evidence to send Addison down for a very long time. On the other hand he knew, as a leading racehorse owner, that Crazy Spartan would not in fact win the 2.30 at Newbury, but that the race would unexpectedly go to French Rocket. He would himself have backed French Rocket heavily, except that he was for the moment rather short of funds.

'I have a suggestion,' said Mr Whipsnade slowly. 'If you and your syndicate come in with me, I can give you some rather surprising information about the race of which you speak.'

And so it was that 'Constable' Addison rose from being a common thief to become an expert connoisseur of the turf, and that Edward Whipsnade started on the spiral of crime and deception which was to drag him down after five years to being an OBE and a Justice of the Peace. His new life would leave him no time for Wagner at all. I am sorry to say that he never missed it.

The birth of Mills & Bang

Men prefer facts while women prefer feelings, Rachel Billington once wrote; that is why the former read books about war and the latter read fiction, romantic or otherwise. And in her book *Animals In War* Jilly Cooper confessed that, although married to a publisher of 400 military histories, she had read fewer than half a dozen of them. 'In the same way that men spurn novels, particularly romantic fiction, women tend to avoid war books, as being an exclusively guts-and-glory male province.'

When two of our leading woman writers combine to express the same thought, I tend to treat it as received truth. And then my mind wanders to the next question beyond, which is: if it is really true that there is a sharp divide between men's war books and women's romance, is there not some way in which I can make vast sums of money out of this discovery?

From there it is but a short step to the formation of a new publishing house which will issue novels for men *and* women – romantic military fiction! Moreover's new imprint, which is to be called Mills & Bomb, or perhaps Mills & Bang, will shortly be flooding bookstalls with the initial titles, of which details now follow.

To Call Him Sir, by Angela Distaff

When Robin joined the platoon, he had already heard the stories about Sergeant Withers. Tough, cynical, sadistic, they said. And yet there was some soft pool of hurt concealed in the sergeant's eyes, which told Robin that there was an altogether more complex person tucked behind those sergeant's stripes than the world knew of. 'So you're bleeding Robin-bleeding-Darlington-Smythe, are you?' the sergeant said at their first meeting. 'Well, we'll have those bleeding hyphens knocked out of you before you can say hunt ball.'

The tears clustered hot on Robin's eyelashes beneath the whiplash of these cruel words. How I hate him, he thought. Yet before the war was very much older, the two men would find themselves mixed up in a circle of passion, carnage and ammunition shortage which would change both of them ineradicably.

Jungle Johnny, by Elena Samson

Major-General Bridget Yates, of the Women's Royal Air Corps, was used to interrogating prisoners. But there was something unusual about the man they brought in one day – his crinkly laugh-lines, perhaps, the proud, untameable look in his eyes or even the way he refused to speak no matter how hard she lashed him with her handbag. When he turned out to be Johnny Kapok, the famous roving American reporter, she had an uneasy feeling that their paths were to cross more than once in this hell without food or good cosmetics that women call war.

The Mountain Flower, by Iris Forage

A recce in war-torn Afghanistan was just another job to ace TV cameraman Max Winton, or so he thought. But he had not reckoned on a meeting with petite, sparkling Ludmilla, a runaway refugee from the occupying Soviet forces.

'You can hang around with us if you like,' said Max gruffly, 'as long as you don't mind carrying the spare camera and the batteries. And don't imagine you'll be getting a slice of our overnight allowances, my little Russian doll.'

'Of course not, Max,' said Ludmilla, playing with his ear-ring. She had not met men with ear-rings before, especially ones inscribed 'BBC News Cameramen Do It Overnight'. 'Tell me, do you think I could get a job with your Central Office of Information when we get back to Britain?'

We? The COI? Back to Britain? Max thought of his boss at Wood Lane. Would he understand if he returned with a Russian crew member? More to the point, would his wife Theresa? Max decided there and then to ditch Ludmilla at the first opportunity. Little did he realize how signally he would fail, or indeed that there was now a tiny bug fixed to his ear-ring.

Other titles in preparation: A Third World War Romance, *by Jean Hackett;* Belfast Beauty, *by Della Driscoll;* Yomping into Passion, *by Petra Stanley; etc., etc.*

Unusual jobs: no. 2

'My face has appeared on twenty or thirty books, and always as the author. I've been a famous thriller writer, a self-sufficiency expert, a professor of semantics, part of the *Sunday Times* Insight team – you name it, I've been it. With a blonde wig, I've been the occasional Mills & Boon-type authoress.

'Why? It depends, really. Sometimes it's because the author is genuinely shy and retiring, and hates to have his picture taken. Of course, shyness is an inverted form of vanity. Have you ever noticed that the one person in a group who runs from the camera is the one most obsessed with their appearance? Funny, that. Anyway, the publisher always likes to have a photo on the back, so they get me in.

'Then there's the best-selling author who doesn't like to be recognized in public. So he doesn't want his mug staring out of a million paperbacks, does he? People coming up to him and saying: "Your characterization was really ropy in chapter eight, you old fraud." They write a little clause in their contract saying they must not be pictured on the cover, so again they get someone like me in.

'But quite honestly, the main reason is that so many authors look so naff. They simply don't look the part. You buy a heart-stopping, sexy, thrill-a-minute book, and you don't want a bloke staring at you who looks as if he couldn't defend himself against a poodle, do you? Or, if he had to kiss a girl, always find himself kissing her nose? So, rather than put a picture of a wet civil servant on the back, the publisher sends for me. No boasting, but I'm semi-rugged, semi-sensitive and that's good for trade.

'Authors are lucky in that they generally don't have to appear in public and even when they do, people don't twig that the bloke on *Russell Harty* looks nothing like the bloke on the book. It's different if you're a performer. Like, if you're a singer, you can't sing behind a screen. Well, Elton John can sing behind a toupee, huge specs and a grand piano, but even so you can see bits of him.

'That's why I admire Barry Manilow so much. To have gone so far with a face like that. And songs like that. And, let's be honest, a voice like that. If he'd been an author, no publisher alive would have dared to put his face on a book.

'I think if the public found out how many of their favourite authors were really publishers' models, they'd feel cheated. But I don't see it as cheating. To my way of thinking, I look *more* like many of my authors than they do. To put it another way, people often don't look like themselves. Have you seen the faces on the election leaflets? Hello, I'm your friendly Labour candidate and all that? Terrible, terrible. They usually look more like Jack the Ripper or Ivan the Terrible.

'There's a new trend among publishers to choose authors for their looks. Let's get someone who's going to look smashing on the back of the book, they say. No names, no pack drill, but they sign up Jackie this and Jilly that and Pat the other, just for the glamour.

Well, what I want to know is this: can they write as well? I'm only asking.

'Incidentally, Mr Kington, I hope you don't mind my asking, but who've you got for that picture at the top of your column? Because – and no offence meant – he doesn't do a great deal for it. What you need is someone semi-rugged, semi-sensitive, yes, like me.

'On second thoughts, you ought to do a Richard Boston. Remember that? When he was writing a regular piece for the *Guardian* he used to complain about his mug-shot, so one day the subs stuck in a picture of Telly Savalas. The readers loved it. Next week they used a picture of Elvis, after that one of Brigitte Bardot, but then the editor stepped in and said it would have to stop. Great pity, I always thought.

'Know who I think would look good at the top of your column? Brahms. Brahms as a young man. Why not try it just once? See what people think. See if they even notice. Believe me, I think it would work and I should know. I'm doing myself out of a job, after all.'

A complete airline novel

Air travel is divided into two separate bits. There is the journey proper, which gives you time to read a Harold Robbins or Robert Ludlum novel. Then there is the bit when the plane stops, everyone stands up and nothing happens for ten minutes. Here is a tiny novel to fill that ten minutes.

The Gazebo Effect, by Sidney Aston

Harry knew, as soon as he got off the plane, that there was something wrong. He should have been met by a black Mercedes to whisk him off to a secret destination in the hills to meet with the mysterious Krotzky. There was no sign of it.

'I don't suppose you've seen a black Mercedes hanging around, have you?' he casually asked the airport official on the tarmac.

'There was one about ten minutes ago,' the man said through his dark glasses, 'but it whisked someone off the previous flight. Going to a secret destination in the hills, I expect.'

Damn, thought Harry. They picked up the wrong man. He felt very alone.

'Need a lift into town, feller?' a voice asked. Harry sighed. It was the talkative fat American he had sat next to in the plane, the one who kept chatting up the stewardesses. The kind of American who thinks that life is one long business convention.

'All right,' Harry said unwillingly. 'I was going to be met, but...'

Half an hour later he was speeding towards the city, sitting behind a chauffeur. The American next to him was talking, talking... Suddenly Harry felt an enormous tiredness overtake him. The American's face became very big, his mouth opening and closing like a sea anemone. He had been drugged, thought Harry. That cup of coffee at the airport had tasted funny at the time, but he had put it down to the local brew. As he reached for his Zametta .55, he lost consciousness.

'Feeling better?' a voice asked. Harry opened his eyes. The big American was looking down at him, and he wasn't smiling any more. There was a gun in his hand. It was Harry's.

'I'm Krotzky,' the American said. 'You were expecting to meet me.'

'Then what were you doing on the plane?' Harry asked baffled.

'I wanted to take a good look at you first. I wanted to see if you were the man we needed for the job. I think you are.'

'What job?' Harry asked crossly. 'I have a job already. I am the European rep for a British firm of fancy mustards. I thought I had to meet you about the Yugoslav franchise.'

'Your employers know nothing about this job,' Krotzky said. 'This is a much bigger set-up. Can't you guess?'

Harry thought of all the novels he had ever read on aeroplanes.

'You're going to smuggle drugs in mustard seeds?' he said. The man shook his head. 'You're going to bring Hitler back from South America? You're going to kidnap Mr Reagan? You're going to steal a Russian nuclear weapon? You're going to melt the polar ice caps and flood Guildford?'

'You've been reading too many airline novels,' Krotzky said smoothly. 'No, no, it's just a simple little assassination which could affect the course of world history drastically.'

'That's ridiculous,' Harry said. 'How could a little middle-aged man like me, with glasses and not much chin, help to change world history?'

'You're the only man who can,' Krotzky said. 'I don't know if anyone has ever told you, but you are the spitting image of General Jaruzelski. Put a uniform on you, and nobody could tell the difference.'

'I still don't understand. Who's going to be assassinated?'

Krotzky smiled. It was not a nice smile.

'You are,' he said.

He leant forward, holding a syringe. Harry made a sudden galvanic effort, leapt from his seat and clasped the handle of a door in the far wall.

'I wouldn't if I were you,' Krotzky said calmly.

Harry opened the door and rushed out. It wasn't till that moment that he realized he was in another plane, 15,000 feet up. Harry knew, as soon as he got off the plane, that something was wrong.

If you're still standing in the plane, go back to the start of the novel and continue.

Hitch-hiking: you write ...

Is that scruffy figure at the motorway entrance a fascinating companion for a ride or a threat to your life? Some points from your letters.

From the Bishop of Outer Manchester

Sir, I have only twice in my life picked up a hitch-hiker. The first time was as a theological student thirty-five years ago, when I gave a lift to a young man on the A1. I was rather nervous as I had some valuable church silver on the back seat. On the other hand, I felt it was my duty as a Christian.

I am afraid to say that on a lonely stretch of road the youth pulled a knife on me and forced me to get out. He took my vintage Austin car, leaving only the silver which he thought was my luggage. Since then I have never picked up another hitch-hiker until last Thursday when I decided that my fear had gone on long enough and I gave a lift to a very respectable-looking middle-aged man travelling to Leeds.

Imagine my amazement when, during our conversation, he suddenly said: 'That Austin of yours had a really clapped-out gearbox.' It was the same man again! Before we got to Leeds he pulled a gun on me and took my new Audi. Luckily, he let me keep my suitcase, which contained several million pounds in aid for the Third World.

From Mr J. Plugg

Sir, One of the most notorious tricks of hitch-hikers is to put an attractive girl by the side of the road. When an unaware driver stops, four or five men jump out from behind the hedge and get in too. For this reason I never pick up girls. Last week I stopped to give a lift to a scruffy bearded student and six ravishing blondes jumped out from the trees. I drove on immediately, conscious of my narrow escape.

From Viv, Debby, Rhoda, Sharon, etc.

Sir, We are six ravishing blondes who do a lot of travelling up and down the A4 as we are a dance troupe. Will the motorist who gave a lift to our choreographer please return him at once. Thanks.

From Lord Sprocket

Sir, I am the last surviving remnant of a family which has lived in Rutland for 400 years. Driven by loneliness I gave a lift to a young hitch-hiker last month and upon chatting to him discovered that he was the grandson of my great-uncle Harry who emigrated to Australia and was thus my sole heir! Who says that giving lifts to people cannot pay off? Later in the journey he pulled a gun on me and relieved me of my brand new BMW. If he should read this letter, I would like him to know that I have disinherited him.

From J. Wentworth-Chestnut

Sir, the first time I gave a lift to a hitch-hiker I was so nervous about being assaulted that I kept a knife handy about my person.

Sure enough, he suddenly made a threatening gesture but, being prepared, I was able to overpower him. It then transpired that he was not threatening me at all, simply reaching for his cigarettes. But as I had overpowered him I felt I had to go through with it and proceeded to rob him of his worldly possessions. I now regularly pick up and rob any hitch-hiker I can find. Not only does it give me a useful income, it gives me a chance to meet people of all walks of life.

From Sir Dougal Chambers

Sir, as the head of a large corporation I never give lifts to hitch-hikers, and I leave the driving to my chauffeur, Harry. Unfortunately, Harry has a predilection for giving lifts to people, and earlier this week I found myself in my own car with six dancers, a bishop who had had his car stolen, and a young man who had had everything stolen by a kindly driver. In future I have decided to travel by train, where at least you can have some privacy.

Answer me, somebody

We are often told that science will solve the great problems of our times sooner or later. What we are never told is who is going to solve the little problems of our times. In case any such authority does exist, I would like to list some of the small mysteries that most worry me.

● Why is it impossible to design an airport trolley or a supermarket trolley that goes straight?

● Why is it that we wash our faces with warm water and our teeth with cold water?

● Why are jazz performances always prolonged by the desire of every player in the group to play the last note even though they know the drummer will always win at the end?

● Why do dog-owners cry out: 'He won't hurt you', just as their animal leaps on you and plants its teeth in the nearest available limb?

● Why do we never see signposts on the road reading, 'Slough and the East' or 'Hatfield and the South'?

● What do engine drivers do during those long, unexplained stops in the middle of the country?

● What is the secret of design that enables teapots to dribble tea down their spouts on to the table instead of into the cup?

● What do firemen on engines do now there are no fires?

● Why is a man with an overdraft said to be borrowing from the bank whereas if he has a healthy account it never occurs to the bank that they are borrowing from him?

● Why is the most commonly asked question in Britain ('How are you?') one that nobody ever wants the answer to?

● Why are the objects attached to hotel keys now so big and heavy that it is impossible to get the key to the room let alone lose it?

● Why do men wear ties?

● Why are things more expensive in duty-free shops than in real life?

● Why is white wine called white wine?

● Why are pornographic films labelled 'adult'?

● Why is the *Sun* called a newspaper?

● Why is anything ever called the best thing since sliced bread?

● Why does perforating a sheet of paper with a line of holes make that paper harder to tear, especially along the line of holes?

● Why do the British always go to look for the sun when there is most sun at home?

● Why do butchers and fishmongers always close early and bicycle shops and chemists always stay open late?

● Why do British Rail's guards announce the destination of trains just after they have started, at a time when the information is at its least useful to anyone?

● Why do British Rail porters at main-line stations always end up with trolleys marked 'For passengers' use only'?

● Why do lists like this always end up criticizing British Rail even though the writer is a keen railway fan?

A Central American primer

Why is Central America so important to the US?
Because if it wasn't there, there would be nothing joining North and South America.

Would that make a difference?
Sure. It would mean that Columbus would have sailed straight through the gap and discovered India, as he meant to. The Indians would all be speaking Spanish, the United States of India would be the most powerful country in the world and Delhi would be the headquarters of American football.

Would that be so bad a thing?
Yes. The Indians are far too small for American football.

I see. Meanwhile, why are the Americans so worried about Nicaragua?

Nicaragua represents a terrible threat to the US. The Nicaraguan Navy has encircled the US with its mighty warships, they are infiltrating the US with Mexican 'freedom fighters' and now Nicaraguan marines are on 'manoeuvres' in nearby Canada. This can only mean one thing.

War?
No, the infiltration of the US by thousands if not millions more Spanish-speakers. There are now so many Hispanics in the US that President Reagan starts his speeches with the phrase: 'My fellow Americans and illegal immigrants...' The trouble is, only about 50 per cent of the population understand what he says. There are some programmes on public TV that no English-speaking American can understand.

Such as?
Coronation Street, Billy Connolly Live, Minder...

But surely Spanish is a noble and ancient language?
Not the way Hispanics speak it. Their language is a sort of street Spanish.

Is American English proper English?
It sure as hell ain't nothing else.

Why is Nicaragua trying to encircle the US?
The Nicaraguans are trying to force the Americans to hold free elections. You see, although the American Constitution allows for the election of anyone as President, the position in practice is quite different and presidential office is held only by millionaires who can spend a fortune to get in. They want to get Americans to introduce democracy.

What is the Central American system?
To become elected as President and *then* become a millionaire.

But surely they all get assassinated or shot at or have to resign?
I think that's the US you're thinking of.

Why is President Reagan sending so many advisers and the like into Central America?

I believe the intention is to teach the people to speak English so that when they arrive in the States as illegal immigrants, they won't be adding to the language problem.

I don't want to sound pessimistic, but doesn't this all sound like a Vietnam situation?
The only real similarity between Vietnam and Central America is that Dr Kissinger has been put in charge of both. If his previous policy is anything to go by, this means that he will probably end up bombing nearby states, as he did with Laos and Cambodia.

Which states?
California, maybe. Or Texas.

How will this help the situation?
It won't really. But it will give a lot of pleasure to people in New York and Washington.

Are you serious?
No – *estoy fuliando*.

How's that?
A bit of street Spanish. *Fuliar* – to fool around.

Why are you picking up street Spanish?
Well, as with Vietnam, you can never be sure which side is going to win.

More from Mills & Bang

The response to the creation of our new publishing house, Mills & Bang, was remarkable – all titles were sold out within days of hitting the bookstalls, and *Yomping into Passion* appeared briefly on the Cross-Channel best-seller list.

Now, Moreover Enterprises Ltd is proud to announce a further selection of Mills & Bang novels – the novels that are as tough as old boots yet as soft as a first kiss!

Cavalry Tulle, by Yolanda Dubbin

Debbie felt the wind streaming through her hair as she kicked Marmaduke into a gallop. How good it felt to be on her favourite horse once more, the soft turf of the downs beneath his hooves and the English Channel twinkling in the sun, way, way in the distance. Her memories of Oscar seemed just a bad dream.

Suddenly she became gradually aware that another rider was closing in to meet her. Crossly, she reined in and waited for him to arrive.

'I'm sorry,' said the newcomer affably, 'but this is private property. Restricted, you know.'

'To whom, may I ask?'

'Members of the regiment. Captain Bruce Derwent at your service.'

'And I,' said Debbie coolly, 'am Major Deborah Merryweather, newly joined to the regiment.'

Derwent's face changed. But before he could bring himself to salute her, a shot rang out and whistled past them. Quick as a flash he had leapt from his horse, bundled her from hers and rolled them both into a safe position in the grass.

'Who's trying to kill us?' she gasped, thrilling strangely to the touch of his uniformed arm.

'Nobody. It's an army firing range. They could kill anybody. By the way,' he said, his mouth not six inches from her perfect ear, 'I believe you know my best friend, Oscar Threadgold. Major,' he added reluctantly.

Oscar! His dark handsome face came before her, with its twisted smile. Then she looked at Bruce's sandy open features. How were their destinies to be intertwined?

'Perhaps you could put me down now, Captain,' she said icily.

A Man's Girl, by Grenada Pinn

'Sorry to bother you, sir,' said the sergeant, 'but I'd like to have a word about Private Simple.'

'What's the trouble?' said the captain.

'Fact is,' said the sergeant, 'I think Private Simple's a woman.'

The captain drummed his pencil on the desk.

'Extraordinary thing to say, sergeant. What makes you think so?'

'Difficult to pin down, sir. The way he walks. The extra large battle tunic. The tendency to use lipstick and shave his legs.'

'Does he pull his weight otherwise?'

'Absolutely. Best soldier in the platoon.'

'Then I wouldn't worry too much, sergeant. We need all the good men we can get, even if they are women.'

Damn, thought the captain. They're on to Yvonne's and my little scheme. It was only as the door closed that the captain realized there was something odd about the sergeant. He was wearing high-heeled shoes. Were their destinies to be intermingled in some strange way?

Free Fall Love, by Alberta Smithwick

Rowena, flushing, went hot and cold. She felt limp. There was a roaring in her ears. Not surprising, as she was half-way through her first-ever parachute jump.

'I say!' said a voice. She looked round. There was a man in the air near her. 'I say, I'd open your parachute if I were you!'

How stupid of her. She pulled the ring and the huge white canopy opened above her. The man smiled and put his thumb up as he floated away. She hated him instantly, and yet there was something about his warm crinkly eyes that told her their destinies would, given half a chance, be on the same downward path together.

Other titles coming soon: One Girl's Resistance, *by Jean Hackett*, NATO Nancy, *by Marcia Hastings;* Passion in the Pay Corps, *by Briony Hanrahan; etc., etc.*

Tough justice

We have already read about trials of men who removed yellow clamps without asking the police's permission, but today we have something worse: a man who is accused of removing a double yellow line. 'Moreover ...' *is proud to print exclusive extracts from the trial.*

Police witness: ... was painted on the road in 1980 by William Carstairs, a road-painter. It was the property of the Metropolitan Police. On 14 July, I observed that a section of it was missing.
Counsel: Where was it?
Police: I don't know. It was missing.
Counsel: Where was it missing from?
Police: Sears Roebuck Road, W1, sir. Under the car belonging to the defendant, registration number SHE1K.
Judge: A curious number.
Defendant: I hire it out a lot to Arabs, sir. It looks like SHEIK. They love it.
Judge: Quiet! You will get your turn in a moment.
Council: No further questions.
Clerk: Call the defendant.
Defendant: Here I am, sir. That was a short moment, to be sure.
Judge: Quiet!
Defendant: I'm sorry. I was under the impression that it was my turn to ...
Judge: You speak when you are asked questions.
Defendant: That seems fair. Fire away.
Counsel: You are Seamas Daldy, of somewhere in Kilburn, and an Irish citizen?
Defendant: I am that.
Counsel: What is your profession?
Defendant: In Ireland I was a motor dealer, sir, but I heard that there were any amount of openings on British TV and radio for bright men with Irish accents, so over I came. Sadly, things have not turned out as I hoped, and I am now forced to run a car hire firm with a turnover of many millions of pounds. Still, it's not the same. Not that I envy Terry, of course.
Counsel: Quite. And on 14 July you parked your car in Sears Roebuck Road, W1, on a double yellow line?
Defendant: No, sir. I parked my car there, but there was no double yellow line.
Counsel: I suggest to you that you found the double yellow line when you arrived, that you scraped away the yellow line and then parked in the space thus formed! (*Silence.*)
Judge: Well, Mr Daldy? Answer the question.

47

Defendant: He hasn't asked me a question, sir.

Judge: (*Consulting notes.*) True. Would you like to ask him a question, Mr Chambers?

Counsel: Did you scrape away the yellow line?

Defendant: No. (*Sensation in court.*)

Counsel: (*Breezily sarcastic.*) Are you asking the court to believe that the authorities had painted all of Sears Roebuck Road except the bit you wanted to park on? Are you seriously suggesting that a space the size of a car had specially been left? Do you want us to think that William Carstairs, road-painter, had left a gap for artistic effect? Can pigs fly? Is the moon made of cheese? What porridge ate John Keats!?

Judge: All right, Bill, steady on. You're too old to get rattled by the Irish.

Counsel: I'm sorry, Colin. Things haven't been too easy recently. What with the wife leaving me, the children taking to drugs and Barbican Puzzle losing the 2.30 at Newbury, I've been under some stress.

Judge: I understand. I had a couple of hundred on Barbican Puzzle myself.

Defendant: A no-hoper. You should have had your money stacked on Glue Sniffer, like I did.

Judge: Quiet in court! This is intolerable.

Counsel: Mr Daldy, the court has heard the police witness describe how the whole street was covered in a double yellow line. It has also heard you say that there was a gap in the double yellow line large enough for you to park in. Who do you honestly expect the court to believe, you or the police?

Defendant: Me.

Counsel: Yes, well, fair enough. Still, I think you ought to offer some explanation of this gap in the yellow line, don't you?

Defendant: It strikes me that so far the court has concentrated entirely on the absence of a double yellow line beneath my car, and has assumed that because it wasn't there, it must have been removed.

Judge: What other possible explanation is there?

Defendant: There is another theory that has not even been considered by the court so far, and that is that the yellow line was there all the time – but was not visible!

Counsel: Could you explain that?

Defendant: There is nothing easier than to buy a roll of black sticky tape and to spread it out over the double yellow line in such a way that it entirely covers the paint and looks like a bit of road, pockmarks and all.

Counsel: So that's what you did!

Judge: So that's the way it was!

Defendant: Not at all. You merely asked me for another explanation and I have given you one. I neither removed the yellow line nor covered it up. However, there is yet another theory...

Judge: Great stuff! I love theories. It's facts I can't handle.

Defendant: I would like to call a witness.

Judge: Defendants can't call witnesses, not if they're already in the witness stand.

Defendant: We can in Ireland. Call William Carstairs! (*After a bit of shuffling, Mr Carstairs fits on to the witness stand with the defendant.*) You are William Carstairs, a road-painter?

Carstairs: I was then.

Defendant: When?

Carstairs: In 1980, the year you are going to ask me about, when I painted Sears Roebuck Road end to end with a double yellow line.

Defendant: Could you tell the court how you arrived at your work?

Carstairs: I drove there.

Defendant: And where did you leave your car?

Carstairs: In Sears Roebuck Road, of course. It was the only free street for miles.

Defendant: Did you paint yellow lines under your car?

Carstairs: No, I left it till later, so that when I moved the car – oh, blimey! You're right! I clean forgot to go back and paint that bit. Stone me!

Defendant: And there, gentlemen of the jury, you have it. The yellow lines were not removed by me *because they were never there in the first place*. In fact, I myself went back the next day and painted the lines in, voluntarily. Alone of all the yellow lines in London, that short stretch is not the property of the Metropolitan Police; it belongs to me.

Judge: If I have got this straight, a man stands here accused of taking something which was never there, and even if it had been there, it would have been his own property. Who says that British justice is not the most wonderful in the world? Case dismissed!

Clerk: My Lord, we have just had a message from the outside world. It's from the BBC, and they say that one of their employees, a Mr

Henry Kelly, is not feeling well. They ask if the defendant is free to stand by to replace him...
Defendant: Lord be praised! It's my big break! Hallelujah!

Mills & Bang march on

The success of Mills & Bang, Moreover Enterprises' new imprint which satisfies both male and female fantasies, seems unstoppable. The secret of these tender, thunderous novels is that they are as soft as an eyelash, yet as uncompromising as a kick in the shin with an army boot.

Accordingly we present to eager readers a small run-down of new titles on our list.

Horizons of Love, by Gwendolen Fastnet

High in the skies over Dorking the Spitfire and Messerschmidt twisted and turned, each trying to gain ascendancy over the other. 'Hurricane' Kate, at the controls of the Spitfire, had already shot down twenty Huns, yet she knew that this time she had an opponent worthy of her.

'Got you now!' she whispered, as she turned and banked towards the sleek shape of the German plane. But all she saw was empty sky. Glancing back over her shoulder, she saw with horror the Messerschmidt coming down at her out of the sun. There was no way she could escape now. With resignation, she patted her hair into shape and closed her eyes.

'We'll meet again, Weiss nicht where, Weiss nicht wann,' said her radio softly. She opened her eyes, just in time to see the enemy cockpit flash past and a cheery face wink at her. Johnny von Arnsdorf! The one they called the Handsome Hun. How she hated him. Horribly humiliated, she realized that he had just spared her life.

'I'll get you, Johnny,' she vowed. And so indeed she would, but she never suspected that it would be as Mrs Johnny von Arnsdorf, after twists and turns of fate that would leave history breathless.

The Silken Sands, by Trudi Blessed

'We do not normally take women in the Foreign Legion,' said Major Pierre Danois. He paused, regarding the way her trim figure fitted into the uniform. 'And yet, in your case ... I presume you are joining to forget a great and tragic love?'

'Not at all,' said Joan briskly. 'I am looking for adventure, a hard life and a bit of a sun-tan.'

Adventure came sooner than she thought. That evening she was pinned in a corridor of the fort by an unshaven Yugoslav recruit called Yukovic, who smelt of cheap wine. His hands started to explore her uniform.

'I have never had a girl from Guildford,' he leered.

'Nor will you, laddie!' sang out a voice. It was Alec, the cheery Glaswegian she had met earlier. But before Alec could move, Joan had kneed Yukovic in the groin, chopped him to the back of the neck and kicked him twice expertly as he sank groaning to the floor.

'This fort needs cleaning up and I aim to see it gets done,' said Joan clearly as she strode past the open-mouthed Alec. Behind a hidden screen Major Danois smiled and twirled his moustache. He would break this little desert beauty before long, he thought, which showed how little he knew about girls from Guildford.

The Hot Summer Campaign, by Wendy Thrumb

On the retreat through Greece in front of the advancing Germans, Captain Leonard Tasker felt strangely protective towards the 3,000 men and 2,000 mules under his command. He also felt strangely protective towards Xenia, the proud Greek peasant girl who had attached herself to the company, even though accommodation was desperately hard to find for her.

'Hope you don't mind me mentioning it to you, sir,' said the old sergeant to him one day, 'but the men are beginning to talk about the way that girl sleeps in your tent at night.'

'Heavens,' said Leonard, flushing. 'Surely they don't think there's anything...'

But Leonard's loyalties are sharply divided when Xenia, out foraging for yoghurt, is captured by the Germans. Should he continue the retreat without her, or turn and fight them for possession of the girl whom he finds so inexplicably fascinating despite not being able to understand a word she says? A taut epic of revenge, pursuit and military incompetence, with many riveting details about mule maintenance.

Coming soon: S A S Sally, *by Lavinia Spittle;* No Funeral for Lucy, *by Gloria Platoon;* Snipers Beware, *by Frieda Wellington;* The Platinum Blonde Captain, *by Kitty O'Trench; etc., etc.*

Fighting talk

The other day I overheard an American saying: 'Give me a shot of Scotch,' and it occurred to me yet again to wonder why, although we can almost always understand what Americans are saying, they often say things in a way we never would. Part of it, I think, is due to the violence inherent in the way they phrase things. There must be something satisfyingly melodramatic about asking for a shot or slug of whisky rather than a glass or a wee dram, as if every act of drinking was a small piece of personal combat.

I've also heard Americans asking to be hit with a drink – 'Hit me with a shot of Scotch,' they plead. When the deed is done and the glass lies there empty, they don't say the drink is finished; they tend to say it is dead. Let me freshen it up for you, they say, leaning towards your dying glass, completing the violent scenario with the image of a tiny United Nations helicopter flying in to revive a drink with the necessary injection.

All very picturesque, but a bit over the top for British tastes.

That's why I found myself slightly disturbed by that poster designed to get us to eat more eggs which showed a massive teaspoon about to demolish an inoffensive egg. 'Go smash an egg,' it shouted, but the only effect it had on me was to make me want to lock my eggs away in the bank for fear of breaking them. We each have our little ritual for breaking and entering boiled eggs, but smashing them is not one of them. It's a bit off. Not quite on, actually. It's not exactly, well, British.

I suspect that because of our non-violent way of talking about violence, other nations are taken by surprise when we actually go to war. The diplomatic furrowed eyebrow and tut tut noises of the British give no hint of the opening shots to come – Argentina certainly seemed taken aback by the sailing of the Task Force.

What I would like to know, getting back to the Americans, is whether their talk is as violent when they are talking about violence as it is when they are talking about pouring drinks. Is Ronald Reagan, to mention the most obvious example, just shooting a line when he squares up to the Russians or is he really looking for a fight? And if it is just bluster, as I suspect, just a bit of American chest-thrusting and jaw-jutting, do the Russians know this? And if not, will someone please tell them.

My calm confidence that Mr Reagan is not in fact squaring up for a showdown is only soured by my memory of an incident in his autobiography. In his college days Reagan had to earn his summer vacation money by working as a lifeguard at a large swimming pool. He reckoned that during that time he saved nearly a hundred people from drowning, of whom not one ever thanked him. Many, in fact, had turned on him and been angry because he had made them look like fools, which had taught him one lesson in life: nobody is ever grateful for being rescued.

I think Mr Reagan is wrong there. In fact, Mr President, if you happen to be reading this, I am willing to commit myself now to being grateful if you save our lives in the future. I don't think I'm totally alone in this. Many Britons feel the same way. We'd all be, you know, really quite grateful, not to put too fine a point on it, actually.

The suitcase of the future! That's what we are offering you today.

Moreover Laboratories have been working on the problems which afflict travellers of every class, race and sex and we believe we have come up with something which is as far ahead of the normal valise as the word processor is ahead of the pencil.

People who prefer pencils to word processors may stop reading here and get back to their knitting by candle-light.

Firstly, what is the great problem attached to suitcases today? Not packing; they are easy to pack. Not unpacking; you simply open them and the contents fall all over the place. Not even identifying them; a traveller knows his own case as a mother knows her child.

No, the trouble is *carrying* them. They are simply too damned heavy.

Ah, you will say, but modern suitcases now have little wheels so that you can push or pull them along.

Ah, we will say, but have you ever met a suitcase whose wheels worked properly? Don't you find that, rather like airport trolleys, they always go off to one side? Fall over? Or set up such vibrations that they career away out of control, or refuse to take corners and take you to a part of the airport you have absolutely no wish to visit?

(This, we regret to say, is partly the fault of the customers, who when buying a suitcase never ask for a trial trip. When you last bought a piece of luggage, did you insist that it was filled with heavy objects and towed round the shop? Of course you did not. Any more than, when you last bought a jug or teapot, you asked for it to be filled with water to see if it poured properly.)

In numerous tests in the Moreover Laboratories we have found that the main reason for unsteady behaviour in wheeled suitcases is the fact that the suitcase is free-wheeling. Anything that is towed, be it trailer, caravan or suitcase, is inherently unstable, as you will know if you have ever pulled anything like that behind you. Even a golf trolley will misbehave from time to time, no matter how good your handicap.

What all these unstable things have in common is the lack of motive power.

The answer was simple. Give suitcases motive power!

Thus was born the Motorized Moreover Suitcase. Using a simple four-wheel drive one-gear motor, the Moreover Motorized Suitcase moves along at a steady 4 m.p.h., which is about the same as human walking pace. It is driven by battery, so it is almost silent. The weight of the machine, very little in any case, is counterbalanced by pockets of lighter-than-air helium built into the lining.

The one problem created by this revolutionary suitcase is steering. The solution is again revolutionary. We have put a small seat on top of the case and a steering-wheel at the front, so that the owner actually sits on his case and drives it along!

Instead of lugging or tugging, hauling or manhandling your suitcase, you can now for the first time ever take it for a spin. Those endless corridors at Heathrow are no longer a nightmare – they are a miniature race-track. And the de luxe model can actually go upstairs, thanks to the extra caterpillar tracks fitted.

The super de luxe model has done away with all labelling problems. Instead of a label-holder, there is a small inbuilt computer which you programme afresh each time you travel, with the correct new read-out.

The new Bagmobile, as we call it, needs no licence, as it is not being driven on a public thoroughfare. We anticipate that demand for this wonderful new device will be very heavy, so make sure of yours now. Send off your order immediately, together with a cheque made payable to Moreover International.

The retail price has not yet been finalized, so leave the amount on your cheque blank for us to fill in.

Send away now. You won't regret it.

Unusual jobs: no. 3

Banks do not like their customers raiding their own account more than once in a day. In order to stop them going from branch to branch, cashing a £50 cheque at each one, they used to have a page at the back which the cashier stamped with the date. Then they replaced this with another page containing a mini-calendar of the whole year, and every time you cashed a cheque, the cashier put a small cross on the date to prevent re-use.

It then transpired that unscrupulous customers, or at least customers who needed about £55, were eradicating the ink cross and cashing more cheques the same day. To counter this, cashiers started putting an ink cross on the date *and then puncturing the date with the pen*, to make an unreusable hole.

To counter this, people are now going to Darren to get the hole mended.

'I've always been in the loop-hole business,' says Darren. 'Admittedly, this is the first time I've actually been mending loop-holes – usually I just find them and get through them. Then somebody plugs them up. Then I find another one, and so on.

'First interesting job I had, years ago, was helping out a friend on British Rail. He worked in one of those travelling buffets and had been reducing the amount of coffee that went into each cup of coffee. To pocket the extra revenue? Could be, squire, could be – I never asked. Maybe he just disapproved of British Rail coffee, or was worried about the effect of caffeine on his much loved patrons.

'Anyway, British Rail introduced a pre-sealed cup with a fixed amount of coffee in it, which seemed to plug that loop-hole. So he came to me for advice. Easy, I said. Collect the used cups, wash them and fill them with cheapo coffee you've bought yourself. That worked for a while till British Rail tumbled to it and introduced a kind of cup that couldn't be reused after boiling water had been poured on it.

'What? Oh, after that, we worked on a way of making coffee without actually boiling the water, and so on it went. The point was, I got interested in the idea of having a battle of wits against the big companies – it made life interesting and provided me with a small income. I've devised ways of making rail tickets reusable, getting free phone calls from call-boxes, doing interesting things with restaurant receipts, you name it.

'This bank caper's a new one on me, though. Bit of a tough nut to crack, really. Oh, I don't mean the technique. Matching the paper and mending the hole is no problem, or even just inserting a whole new page. The problem is why anyone should want to bother. I mean, it's not as if you're going to get enough extra £50s in one day to make yourself rich. The only thing I can think of is that people are afraid of Poland.

'You know? There are all these rumours that the banks have lent so much to Poland, Mexico and the other places where the Pope keeps going, that there's nothing left in the kitty, and people are afraid that if they try to withdraw their money in bulk, the banks won't let them. So they're reduced to doing it in multiples of £50, as often as possible. Well, that's my theory, anyway.

'This is only a side-line for me, by the way. Most of the time these days I'm working on parking problems, and traffic control. Well, for instance, I've devised a parking ticket which you put *on* your car when you park it, to keep the wardens away. I've invented a rubber parking meter which you put on the pavement when you park, and right this moment I'm rushing out an inflatable look-alike yellow clamp.

'I'm a very fair-minded bloke, though. I work for the police as well, when they need me. Oh, yes. For instance, it was me that came up with the idea of putting cardboard replicas of police cars on those little police ramps beside motorways. You'd be amazed how a cardboard model can bring people's speed down.

'I'd appreciate it, by the way, if you didn't mention my connection with Old Bill. Wouldn't like my customers to think I was mixing with the wrong crowd.'

What's in a name?

I discovered recently that my name has got on to a mailing list which is being sold left, right and centre to providers of services that they consider essential. I know it's the same mailing list because although they have got my address right they have got my name wrong, and they always address me as Kington Miles, or Mr K. Miles.

In this guise I have been approached by the Old Vic, *Time*, *Newsweek*, the *Wall Street Journal*, a business travel firm and several organizations who are pledged to improve my business methods. I have not taken up any of their offers yet, as I read far too many newspapers and magazines already, and my business methods are too hopeless to be sorted out by any outside agency, probably because I spend far too much time sitting around reading magazines and newspapers.

My failure to do business with them is also rooted in my strong feeling that it's not *me* they are talking to. 'In your business you need to make many rapid decisions, based on a smooth organization...' 'When you have to fly abroad as often as you do, it's essential to have international air schedules at your fingertips...' 'It's vital in your line of business to know the state of the market and latest money movements...'

This isn't me. I don't have an organization. On the rare occasions when I fly, I leave everything till the last moment and panic my way through. Knowing the latest market movements wouldn't make the slightest difference to my life – I think I own a share, but I can't remember where I've put it. And when the French franc takes a dive, it does so with me politely looking the other way, pretending not to notice it and usually succeeding. So who are they talking to?

Kington Miles, is the answer. He isn't just a reversal of my names – he's a new person. This bloke Kington Miles is fast becoming an *alter ego*. Every time another piece of mail arrives, I have to resist the urge to forward it to K. Miles, though as he is obviously out of the country most of the time on vital business it probably wouldn't get to him immediately.

I see him as a keen whizz-kid, just into his forties but still youthful. He's the kind who arrives last in airport lounges but always gets on to planes first. He carries an armour-plated, Heathrow-proof case, which he is constantly opening to take out a few precious documents, on which he proceeds to make a few pencil marks.

Things haven't been easy for him, of course. He has had to work very hard to become so much richer than I am. But now he is one of the jet business set, and takes his own headphones everywhere with him, so that he can plug into the plane's in-flight entertainment without paying extra each time. His only regret is that they don't have a channel devoted to the latest market movement; I fancy that he listens to country music instead, his one aberration in a well-ordered life.

He is, in short, not exactly the sort of person I would like to have as a friend, though he probably doesn't have many friends, only opposite numbers, colleagues, contacts and golfing or squash partners. He knows about the insides of cars, the wires at the back of record-players, the best years of Burgundy and all the other things that I forgot to learn about and probably never will now.

The only thing that comforts me is the thought that he, presumably, has started getting post addressed to Miles Kington. Post that worries him. Things like obscure jazz catalogues from America, copies of the *Spectator* (which never mentions market movements), newsletters from bicycle shops, invitations to book launches and royalty statements from New Zealand for £5.60. Letters from readers objecting to his shaky command of English.

And although he consoles himself with the thought that somebody somewhere is just transposing his names, he must think of me sometimes as a real person, a sort of disorganized, distrait, dishevelled *alter ego*. Occasionally he must even be intrigued by the thought of me, though I fear deep down I am not at all the sort of person he would like to have as a friend.

Autumn leaves from Mills & Bang

Mills & Bang – the imprint that appeals to men *and* women. Yes, our list of new novels which combine military daring and mad romance, battle orders and *billets-doux*, has proved a runaway success this summer. Here to greet autumn is another handful of unforgettable yarns that combine the daring of men with the love of women.

Passion on Parade, by Samantha Browne

It was half-way through the Great War, and the General Staff were in a quandary. They feared the Germans a bit. They feared their French allies quite a bit. But above all they feared Captain Drusilla Salmon.

'No man's land?' she had cried, when she first arrived. 'No woman's land, more like! If a woman had been in charge of this place, it wouldn't be in this kind of a mess.'

She had a point, the General Staff privately admitted. The area between the German and the British lines had not been well maintained and could do with a bit of a wash and a brush-up. But they weren't prepared for Captain Salmon to organize a series of squads to go out at night and completely reorganize no man's land. Craters were filled in, barbed wire cleared away, the whole area re-seeded, until it looked not unlike one of the better municipal parks in Cheltenham.

'Trouble is, we're meant to be fighting a war, not redecorating

France,' said the General Staff, and they sent their youngest member, Colonel Chambers, to talk to her. 'My darling,' said Colonel Chambers, for he already knew her better than the General Staff suspected, 'we are very grateful for all your housework, as it were. But tomorrow night there is to be a general advance, so keep your squads well clear.'

'There will be no advance over *my* no man's land!' thundered Drusilla. God, how well khaki suited her hair, thought Chambers. 'Tomorrow night my men are putting out white benches and starting on a nine hole pitch 'n' putt course. That's final.'

Will the British Army advance? Will Colonel Chambers win her over? Will Captain Salmon be tempted to tip off the Germans in order to prevent the advance? A nail-biting story.

Beneath a Far Flag, by Rusta Lahbi

When Knut, a corporal in the Danish Army, is sent out to the Middle East as part of a UN peace-keeping contingent, he thinks of it as just another chance to get a sun-tan. When Lala, a nurse with the Indian peace-keeping contingent, is sent to the Middle East – which she quite understandably thinks of as the Middle West – she sees it as part of her mission to heal, as she has a sun-tan already. But a chance meeting in a wine bar inflames them both with passion.

'When this terrible peace is over,' says Knut, 'I will come back to your teepee and live with you.'

'I think you are thinking of Red Indians,' explains Lala. 'I am the other kind, from India.'

While Knut is working this out, Lala meets Jean-Louis, a sergeant with the French peace-keeping force and the only man she has ever met who can successfully explain structuralism to her. Torn between the blond Nordic beauty of Knut and the fiercely honest mind of Jean-Louis, she thinks of committing suicide by walking down the main street of Beirut. Then she has a better idea: she will get Knut and Jean-Louis to fight a duel.

Before the duel can take place, however, she meets Louise, a radical feminist with the CIA murder squad attached to the American peace mission, who persuades Lala that she is only acting out a stereotyped role wished upon her by Jean-Louis and Knut. They decide to run away together. Unfortunately, the night before the elopement Lala meets an Italian translator called Danilo, a rather effete wimp attached to the Red Cross, and she is seized by an uncontrollable urge to mend his socks. Just finishing the last pair at dawn, she sees from the window Knut and Jean-Louis marching out for their duel.

Nothing dentured

The failure rate of a marriage is not always the unmitigated tragedy it is made out to be. Every cloud has a sunny side up, and, every time a couple separates, a small cheer goes up from the toothpaste industry, which knows that the partner who is banging the door on the way out will make a chemist's the next stop.

'A happy couple shares a tube of toothpaste,' says a spokesman for the tooth trade. 'An unhappy couple buys one each. It's as simple as that. What is bad for marriage is good for toothpaste, and what is good for toothpaste is good for Britain. It's as simple as that.'

The spokesman for the industry is none other than our old friend Adrian Wardour-Streete, who is now in charge of the new pressure group, Dentifrice for Divorce. Sales of dental care goods have shot up in the last twenty years, just about keeping pace with the rise in divorce, and although they in no way wish to condone marital breakdown, they are absolutely overjoyed every time somebody walks out on somebody.

'Look, sweety,' says Adrian, 'people who are going through a split often feel they have no one to turn to. They're absolutely wrong. We at Dentifrice for Divorce are here to cheer. That's why we're setting up what we think is the world's first combined dental hygiene and social readjustment counselling service. Our dental mental course.'

To the outsider it seems as if Dentifrice for Divorce is not just brightening up the act of separation, but actively encouraging it. This suspicion is heightened by some of the slogans being planned for a forthcoming campaign, such as: 'Walk out on him – and take the paste with you!', 'Brush that man right out of your teeth' and 'Going away? Take the tube!'

'Well, yes,' concedes Adrian, 'it does seem at first sight that we're trying to make the world full of separated people each with their own tube of paste, though don't let's forget tins of tooth powder, that's very important too, especially as you can knock a full one over and have to buy a new one immediately, though of course we rely just as much on the people who squeeze tubes from the middle and throw away an unused bottom end. I'm sorry, what was the question?'

It's this sort of failure to listen to each other which causes so much marital breakdown, according to Dentifrice for Divorce, and in their white, gleaming flawless premises in Upper Left Street you can be sure of finding a sympathetic hearing all through the day. At night you can phone in your problems and hear a comforting voice talk you through your last brush of the day, or actually go round and use their all-night service-till to withdraw a fresh brush and tube of paste.

'There's something very therapeutic about brushing your teeth,' enthuses Adrian. 'It shouldn't be just a chore – it should be fun, an experience, a reaffirmation of life and hope.'

But what happens if his separated customers get so much confidence from the brushing ritual that they move in with someone else and share again?

'Actually, our records show that a second-time-round bonding tends to be a two-toothpaste bonding. Both sides are mature enough to be loyal to a brand and they usually stick to it.

'No, the market we have to crack now is the newly-weds. It might seem impossible to persuade a couple who share everything, even a bath, to branch out toothpaste-wise. But if we go heavy on the his 'n' hers approach, we might just make this big breakthrough. We're going to attempt this by introducing new role-playing flavours. We're going to get away from boring old spearmint and produce roast beef, tobacco and malt whisky for him, sherry, Turkish delight and cologne for her.'

But surely toothpaste is meant to get rid of the taste of food? Why combine food with toothpaste?

'Hey, I think you may be on to a great idea there! Nutritional toothpaste! For people in a hurry. No time to eat *and* brush your teeth? Do both at the same time with Lunchbreak Toothpaste...!'

From an idea by Keats

Autumn! Season of mists and mellow tum-ti-tum! Now heavy hang the keats in the hedgerow, while on the shelley strand the last deck-chairs are being put away for winter. Sir, sir, there's a dead politician in this deck-chair! What shall I do? Leave him where he is, lad – they'll come and get him when they need his vote. Yes, it's back to the Commons, back to the House, where some men are men and some are a mouse, with star parts waiting for people with nous (lyrics by Thatcher, music by Strauss). The part of Cecil Parkinson will be played by Norman Tebbit. Other parts are as follows: one part Grenada bitters, one part wormwood, one part gall. I thought gall was divided into three parts? Think what you like, lad, but I tell you this: the warning lights are going on all over England, and we shall not see traffic doing more than 40 m.p.h. again in our lifetime. Curse this fog, captain – I can't see a single thing on the motorway. But wait a moment, what's that over there? Is it one of ours? No – it's German! It's a Mercedes-Benz with all the latest attachments – we haven't a hope! Cones to the left of them, cones to the right of them, on rode the gallant five hundred into the valley of motorway mania, into the freezing fog where many are cold but few are frozen. Say what you like, you can't beat the dependable old Austin Mitchell, as seen on television. Now fades the Robin Day, becoming knight, and leaves a sudden darkness on the screen, so I must go down to Channel Four and see the old movies I've never seen, *Mourning Becomes Electra*, *Death in the Afternoon* and *All about Eve*, and now it's close-down again. Lighting-up time is at 4.48 and I've run out of cigarettes. Most of the fields in England have now given up smoking and stubble lies dark and heavy across the landscape, a five o'clock shadow, a carbon copy of the real thing. O to be browning abroad, now that autumn's here! Cynthia and I have decided not to go skiing this year, owing to the recession, so we're taking one of those bargain breaks, in a motel near Swindon. Yes. Quite unspoilt. They have a fancy dress ball in Ye Olde Tudor Disquo on Saturdays. I'm going as a politician and Cynthia's going as my secretary. Wonderful fun. Then we put out the Do Not Disturb sign and see if we can recapture that old black magic, it's got me in its spell, that old black magic, right here in the motel. If you were the only buoy in the world and I was the only gull, I wouldn't come and perch on you. But I must go down to the see again (as the Bishop said to the actress) and do a lightning tour of the clergy – 30 Revs. per minute! April in parish, summer is called but autumn is chosen, if autumn leaves can winter be far behind? Yes, the old cycle of the seasons, now with a flat tyre and the front light gone, but what the hell, Sturmey-Archer, what the hell, once a lady always a lady. Personally, I can't see what all the fuss is about; once you've seen one dead tree, you've seen 'em all. Autumn has branches everywhere, stiff and stark against the sky, red clouds at evening, shepherd's pie. Sarge, we brought this bloke in for being alone and palely loitering. He's got this banner with a strange device, or what we call an offensive weapon. Well, throw the book at him, then – personally, I'd suggest the *Oxford Book of Autumn Verse*. Under the spreading chestnut tree, the village drunkard heaves. The chestnut tree is stark and bare, but the drunkard is covered in leaves. News at Ten, Autumn. Now back to the studio. Over and out.

Anatomy of an interview

Q. What is an interview?
A. An interview is an encounter between an unknown person and a famous person, for which the unknown person gets paid but the celebrity does not.
Q. Why should a celebrity undergo this ordeal?
A. To keep in touch with the public while only having to meet one of them. To put straight mistakes made by the previous interviewer. To publicize a book or film. Because he has been told to.
Q. What does the interviewer get out of it?
A. An autograph for his children.
Q. What does it mean when an interviewer says: 'He paused and thought deeply before replying?'
A. It means the celebrity is trying to remember the answer he always gives to this question.
Q. Does he always give the same answers?
A. Yes.

Q. Why?
A. Because he is always asked the same questions.
Q. How does an interviewer prepare for an interview?
A. He looks up cuttings of previous interviews with the celebrity to see what kind of questions have been asked before.
Q. And then?
A. He asks them again.
Q. What if the interviewer actually does ask different, new questions?
A. The celebrity pauses and thinks deeply, then gives the same old answers.
Q. What is the question most often asked in interviews?
A. 'What sort of difference has fame made to your private life?'
Q. What is the answer to that question?
A. 'It means I have to suffer interviews by odious little nerks like you.'
Q. Does he actually say that?
A. No. He says: 'I have very little private life, but I owe everything to the public, and never resent their intrusion.'
Q. Does the celebrity manage to correct mistakes made by previous interviewers?
A. Yes.
Q. Does this make him happy?
A. No. A new interviewer always makes new mistakes.
Q. What is the difference between a good interviewer and a bad interviewer?
A. A bad interviewer, when writing his piece, always mentions where it took place. 'As we took tea together in the Ritz', or 'Sitting in his elegant work-room, hung with Hockneys', or 'From his hotel bedroom overlooking the Thames'. This gives the false impression that the interview will somehow be different from other interviews; a good interviewer would not give this impression.
Q. Are there any other kinds of interview?
A. Yes, the *Radio Times* interview. This always takes place during the actual production of the star's programme, as if to create the impression that the interviewer is talking to him during the white-hot moment of creation.
Q. And is this the impression created?
A. No. We get the impression that the star is too busy to see the interviewer.
Q. How does the interviewer describe the celebrity?
A. As smaller than I had expected.

Q. What do celebrities most like talking about?
A. Their new books or films. But they find this difficult.
Q. Why?
A. Because interviewers prefer talking about their old books and films.
Q. How long does an interview take?
A. About an hour less than the interviewer contrives to suggest.
Q. Why do so many interviewers end: 'And there, regretfully, I had to leave it'?
A. Because he is being kicked out.
Q. Why?
A. Because someone else is waiting to interview the celebrity. And there, regretfully, we shall have to leave it.

Christmas is coming, God save us all

However much we like Advent calendars, there is something very old-fashioned about them, something which doesn't quite correspond to real Christmasses. So for all of you who like little windows, but don't like pictures of teddy bears and red-breast robins, here's a brilliant new idea – a Christmas check-list!

Simply tick off each of the following Christmas omens as you see them. When all the boxes are full, it's Christmas time.

☐ An article by Kingsley Amis on hangovers, and the uselessness of trying to cure them.

☐ A reminder that it is now too late to post Christmas cards abroad.

☐ A message from the BBC that you can see more than a hundred feature films over the Christmas period if you have nothing better to do.

☐ A man from the Weather Centre saying that we are unlikely to have a white Christmas this year, but we can always dream about it.

☐ Bing Crosby on radio doing just that.

☐ The first Christmas card from someone you wouldn't dream of sending a card to.

☐ A search for gloves which reveals only three in the house, none of them matching.

☐ A horrendous traffic jam explained by the surly taxi driver as being caused by all those blasted people come to see the Christmas decorations.

☐ The sudden realization that all the Christmas trees left in the shops are less than a foot high.

☐ The first Christmas card from someone whose address you have lost.

☐ The general air of foreboding and doom at work, caused by the approach of the office party.

☐ A cheery article about mulled wines and hot punches, which you cut out and put with all the articles you have cut out at previous Christmasses.

☐ The first Christmas card from a relative abroad to whom it is now too late to send a card back.

☐ The first TV trailers for Christmas specials, made by TV stars who have already finished the programme and are now lolling in the Bahamas.

☐ An encouraging article saying that Beaujolais nouveau is now even better to drink than when it first got here, and that the stampede to drink it on the day of arrival was only a publicity gimmick by the importers. The article does not mention that it, too, is a publicity gimmick by the importers.

☐ The first TV news item on Christmas at Greenham Common.

☐ The first Christmas card from an illegible signature.

☐ A belated decision to go out and buy a Christmas tree less than a foot high, only to find that they have all been bought by Japanese bonsai tree enthusiasts.

☐ The first ice on the inside of the bedroom window.

☐ The first feature about young British novelists saying which pop-up books they have most enjoyed in the last year.

☐ A premature leak about the Queen's Christmas broadcast, revealing *either* that she is addressing the unemployed directly this year, *or* that Barry Manilow will make a guest appearance.

☐ An announcement by British Rail called Special Christmas Services, announcing that there will be no trains on Christmas Day.

☐ The sudden memory that the big box hidden away for the children said on the lid, 'Batteries not included'.

☐ A realization that the only calendars left in the shops feature either kittens or parts of Scotland coloured bright yellow and blue.

☐ The gradual replacement of all scheduled TV programmes by trailers for Christmas programmes.

☐ The appearance of the first TV news reader with a piece of holly on the desk.

☐ The total collapse of the television set two minutes after shops close for Christmas.

Casual is as casual does

Jack Ivy liked occasionally to buy a copy of *Practical Tattooist*. He didn't know why. He had no interest in tattooing and didn't want to get tattooed. He just liked the pictures, he supposed, in the same way that he occasionally bought books of photographs. He was what the trade calls a casual buyer.

The trade hates casual buyers, because they muck up marketing surveys. One week a magazine puts on circulation and nobody knows why, so they get a marketing survey done. The survey reports a year later that it was due to seasonal factors or in other words they haven't the faintest idea. But it's because of people like Jack Ivy, who go around casually buying magazines one week and not the next. How irresponsible can people get?

In the case of *Practical Tattooist*, however, things were different. It was a specialist monthly imported from the US which sold nine copies in the United Kingdom every month. When Jack Ivy decided to buy his casual copy the sales went up to ten, and there was rejoicing in the offices of Magimport. 'Sales are up by over 10 per cent!' they would cry. 'It's the big break-through!' The next month sales would slump back to nine and there would be gloom at Magimport, with all leave cancelled. How could they plan for the future with all this uncertainty?

What nobody realized, least of all Jack Ivy, was that he bought the *Practical Tattooist* only when it had a flag on the cover. Mermaids, eagles and ships he ignored, but there was something stirring and romantic about a flag billowing across a man's chest which forced Jack's hand into his pocket to extract the necessary £1.50.

One day a new magazine appeared called *Flags and Banners* No. 1. It had a free, giveaway tricolour taped to the cover. Jack trembled when he saw it and forgot all about *Practical Tattooist*. '*Flags and Banners*, please,' he said to the salesgirl. As a matter of interest, the nine regular buyers of *Practical Tattooist* were also flag freaks, and they too switched to the new magazine. Several people were laid off by Magimport, when sales slumped to nil.

The odd thing was that *Flags and Banners* was not destined to have a No. 2. The proprietors of the magazine had noticed that first numbers of new periodicals always did very well, so they had decided only to print first numbers. By the time *Flags and Banners* had hit the bookstalls it had already closed down, and they were working on the first number of *Small Room Beautiful*, the first ever de luxe magazine devoted to top people's lavatories, and probably the last.

Meanwhile, things were desperate at Magimport and the manager had decided on a desperate gamble.

'I've got a mate,' he told the assistant manager, 'who specializes in driving away vans that don't belong to him, then selling the contents. Well, last night he took a lorry loaded with Scotch, only when he got home he found he'd nicked the wrong one and he'd got 5,000 pop-up toasters on his hands. He can't get rid of them.'

'What's this got to do with magazines?' asked his assistant, not unreasonably.

'Simple. We're going to tape a free giveaway toaster to the front of all our magazines. It'll be the first time anyone's ever given away something valuable, and it'll cost us nothing. We can't lose.'

Next month *Practical Tattooist* had soared to its highest ever sales of eleven, and to their dying day Magimport believed it was because of the toasters. It wasn't. It was because *Flags and Banners* had folded, the nine regulars had returned to the fold and two extra copies were sold in error to customers who thought they were getting *Household Gadgets for Men*. Meanwhile Jack Ivy had casually bought *Socialist Weekly*, which had a tattered Chilean flag on the cover that week...

(Many readers have rung up demanding to know what on earth this story has to do with Christmas, or indeed anything. It's quite simple. A subscription is the best Christmas present you can buy. Don't be a Jack Ivy. Don't cause heartbreak to people like Magimport. Purchase a subscription to *Moreover* now! Every day, Monday to Friday, only 23p. And there's a free gift with it every day – *The Times* newspaper! Thank you.)

My friend Barlow

Introducing the mastermind

'In my experience,' said my friend Barlow, 'BBC commentators don't know what they're talking about.'

We were watching Wimbledon at the time. Some over-trained athlete had just leapt in the air, blond hair quivering, and batted the ball down across the net so fast that no line judge had had time to fault it. 'A backhand slam, probably the most difficult shot in tennis,' said the purring BBC-2 voice. Then Barlow had made his remark. Then we begged him to elucidate.

'The most difficult shot in tennis,' said Barlow, 'is the underarm right-hand volley between the legs, undertaken while you are holding a wine list in the left hand and endeavouring to select a vintage.

'The last and indeed the only time I played this shot was in 1963 at Cannes, at a little restaurant called Jojo's, which only had about six tables but which oddly had its own tennis court. I was in the mixed doubles. It was not an ordinary mixed doubles, as I was playing with another man against two English girls.'

A bit unfair, we commented.

'It certainly was,' reminisced Barlow. 'We were 1–6, 3–6, 3–5 down in the third set. At that moment the waiter came out to say that our table was ready, and asked me to select a wine. No sooner had I taken the wine list than the ball came flying at me, my partner yelled "Yours!" and I executed the shot I have already described.'

With what results? we inquired.

'Good and bad. Good, in that it was a winner, the tide of the game turned and we won in five sets. Bad, in that the wine I chose turned out to be a very ordinary Fleurie and the chef had gone home before we started eating.'

Any further questions were superseded by a commotion from the TV. One player had landed a ball near the line, and the other had told the umpire that if he did not change his decision, he would disembowel him. 'This is a call that will be talked about for many a long year,' said the BBC-2 robot.

'In my experience,' said Barlow, 'no line call is ever talked about for more than five minutes afterwards. The only exception I know to that was a line call which was made in the Nairobi Open in 1959 and is still furiously discussed in parts of Kenya.'

We begged him to tell us more.

'One of the finalists was Simon Edgeworth, an absolute cad but a fine player. His opponent was some health fitness fanatic doctor from Scotland. Well, the Scot hit a deep shot down the line to him in the final set which Simon couldn't reach, so he calmly took hold of the line – we used real lines, not chalk – and *pulled* it towards him, so the ball went out, not in.'

Was this not against the rules?

'Oddly, no. When the rules had been made, they hadn't bargained for people like Simon. He got the point, later the match, and later still the Scots doctor's wife. Kenya was a bit like that, you know. Finally, the doctor strangled Simon one night. With the same line, curiously enough. That's why they still talk about it.'

'My goodness!' interrupted BBC-2. 'Has anyone ever seen two chaps throw themselves about on a tennis court like this pair?' There were obligatory shots of two men lying prone on the turf.

'I have, as a matter of fact,' said Barlow. 'Did I ever tell you of the time I was involved in the All-Jersey Championships, in 1968? There were two chaps against us in the doubles who chased for everything, as if possessed. Finally they both made a dash for one angled slam going way out of court, and crashed into the bushes. Not knowing the local geography, they did not realize it was a cliff-top court and both tragically fell 300 feet. But, and this was the extraordinary thing, one of them managed to hit the ball in mid air.'

With what result? we asked breathless.

'The ball came back on our side and proved a winner. It had been match point to them so of course they won. It is the only tennis title that has ever been won posthumously.'

We looked at each other silently. Then we leapt on Barlow and tied and gagged him so we could watch the TV more comfortably.

Barlow bounces back

My friend Barlow is a bit of a wine buff. That is to say, he keeps things in his cellar which cannot be touched for ten years, like a man with very slow-growing mushrooms. Some of his wines are so long in the maturing that he sees them being inherited by his children, and I believe he goes to his solicitor to alter his will whenever a certain year turns out to be disappointing.

Above all, he is the kind of person who, in a restaurant, peruses the menu listlessly but goes through the wine list in scholastic silence, broken only by the kind of noises made by a university tutor wading through an essay: sharp intake of breath, grudging agreement, tut-tutting noises and a guttural version of 'Yes, but...' He then turns to the assembled company and says: 'What does anyone feel like?', a sure sign that he has already decided what wine could be fit and proper.

The only time I have ever seen Barlow go through a menu with excitement but a wine list listlessly was when we ate in a Chinese restaurant in Buxton. Buxton has some very fine features – good caves, nice opera house, splendid Festival and spa water which bubbles out of every hole in the ground and was once being marketed in bottles with the snappy selling line of Bux Fizz. But on this particular occasion it was food that we needed, and, as Buxton's one really good restaurant was full, we went to the Chinese establishment. We ordered our food and Barlow then started going through the wine list, with all the enthusiasm of a man doing his VAT returns.

'Wines in a Chinese restaurant are always terrible,' he told us. 'I don't know why it is, but they always are. They never seem to bother. I mean, this lot...' He gestured hopelessly at this lot. 'Oh well — what does anyone feel like?'

'You tell us,' we told him.

He ordered a Châteauneuf-du-Pape 1978. It arrived, already opened. He tasted it. Well, at least it wasn't corked.

'It's very bad form to bring it to table already opened,' he told us, as we whooped our way through the sliced beef, black-eyed beans and shredded chicken. 'Waiter, could I see the cork?'

Respectfully, we watched the cork being brought on a small tray. Barlow inspected it and pronounced the bottle recently opened. We hoped he would pick up the cork with his chopsticks and nibble it. He failed us.

'All right if we go on drinking, Barlow?' we said. He nodded. But he grew no more animated.

He kept sipping the wine in a puzzled sort of way, as if it were asking him questions his winebuffmanship had not equipped him to answer.

'Out with it, Barlow,' we cried at last. 'What's wrong with it? Did they tread the grapes upside down? Does it come from the unfashionable end of the vineyard? Shall we get the waiter to show you the corkscrew he used? Do you think the butler did it?'

'Oh, you may laugh,' he said moodily, 'but I happen to think this is a very, very good wine. And I can't make out why. Let's order another bottle to see if it's any worse.'

Another bottle was brought, the waiter showed Barlow the cork and we all held our breath. Disaster. This bottle was just as good as the last. We tried a third one over the vitrified toffee apples and lychees. In vain did the waiter shower Barlow with more corks. The wine was getting better and better.

It was only at the exit from the restaurant that Barlow suddenly cried out with delight.

'I've got it!' he said. 'I know why they serve good wine here! You see, Chinese restaurants know nothing about wine, so they just buy a selection at random the year they open. This restaurant obviously bought far too much in 1978 or 1979, when they started business, and they're still serving the same wines *which have matured to perfection*. They have no idea what good stuff they have, which is why it is all so under-priced. They are serving good wine *through sheer ignorance*.'

A wine buff, in other words, is someone who can invent a theory to fit any unexpected set of facts. I hadn't the heart to tell him that on the menu it said: 'Established 1969'.

Barlow ahead

There were four of us at table. Myself, my friend Barlow, the Duc de Cointreau and the Marquesa de Quimbal, relaxing after another day's energetic play in the Commoner/Gentry Tennis Tournament. Over coffee and cigars, we were discussing the best Bloody Mary we had ever tasted and the Marquesa was waxing enthusiastic – I think waxing is the only word one could use to describe what she was doing to enthusiastic – over one she had tasted in Greece.

'Do you know the island of Bupa?' she was saying. 'It's still one of the last unspoilt islands in the whole of the Aegean. You get the ferry to Sciatica, then get one of the slow island boats to Edmundoros, and take a rowing boat across to Bupa. When I first went there they had never seen an Englishwoman before, and when I left they still hadn't.'

The Marquesa is, of course, Spanish.

We rattled our brandy glasses a little, as a signal to get on with her story.

'After a journey of some five hours, or half a mile, on mule, we arrived at a little village whose name I never learnt and went thankfully into the shade of a small bar, with tamarisk, oleander and Greek rhubarb growing outside. There, I was poured a Bloody Mary such as I have never had before or since. I could not clearly see everything the barman did, but he put into it celery seeds, one coriander leaf, Tabasco, Cretan garlic, tomato juice made from Tunisian tomatoes and a herb I could not identify. It was wonderful.'

'Molle,' said my friend Barlow.

'Pardon?' we said.

'Molle,' said Barlow. 'It's an aromatic Peruvian leaf. A touch does wonders for a Bloody Mary. When I was on Bupa, I advised the barman to try some. I'm glad to learn that he is still following my advice.'

I broke the ensuing silence by saying that I had never tasted a Bloody Mary better than the one I had had on a sunny Sunday morning on Sixth Avenue in New York, low down by Greenwich Village.

'Sixth Avenue is dull when it's cloudy,' I said, 'but on a warm day you might almost imagine yourself in Florida.'

'Florida is full of tottering geriatrics,' said the Duc de Cointreau.

'So is Sixth Avenue on a Sunday. They have all gone out, hale and hearty, to buy the Sunday *New York Times*. Bowed down by the weight of this monstrous encyclopedia, they stagger home having heart attacks and seizures at every corner, ageing before your very eyes. There is nothing more delightful than sitting with a Bloody Mary and a snack which now escapes me, watching them.'

'It was Eggs Benedict,' said my friend Barlow.

'So it was,' I said. 'But how did you know?'

'I was there with you.'

'But you were not there,' said the Duc de Cointreau quickly, 'when I had the best Bloody Mary of all time, staying with my dear friends the Lord and Lady Gabardine. They have a small shooting lodge with ninety-six bedrooms not far from Perth, and invite a few friends up when the last of the tourists have been shot or scared off. There it was, in 1972, that their butler Murdoch served me a crimson concoction which took him half an hour to make. Would you believe, *mes amis*, that it was flavoured with heather?'

'What genus?' said Barlow.

'This heather,' said the Duc, ignoring Barlow but sweating a little, 'is grown in a garlic bed, thus acquiring its characteristics. The Tabasco he uses has a single strand of tarragon immersed in it. And the ice with which he cools the heavenly drink is taken from the bed of the Ardblair Loch, brought hence by a sweet and dimpling Highland lass.'

'Louise,' said Barlow.

'By all that is holy, how did you know that?' said the Duc hotly.

'Would you expect a gentleman to tell you?' smiled Barlow.

'Of course not,' said the Marquesa sweetly,' but won't you tell us about the best Bloody Mary you have ever tasted, Barlow?'

'Certainly,' said my friend. 'When I make a Bloody Mary, I take a 10 oz. glass of Waterford crystal...'

With a unanimous cry we rose to our feet, pelted Barlow with cigar stubs and filthy napkins, and went off for an early bed.

Barlow gets his comeuppance and fails to notice

The Chinese would enjoy watching my friend Barlow. Apparently they prefer sports involving delicacy, technique, coordination and nerve to sports requiring simply strength and stamina. My friend Barlow is very good at that kind of sport – darts, snooker, bridge, shove ha'penny and wine-fancying are just some of the ones he is good at. I know, because he has thrashed me at all of them, though never in front of a Chinese audience.

He may also be good at bezique, cribbage, dominoes, poker, snakes and ladders, and hoop-la. I don't know. I have always avoided encounters with him at these games, but I suspect that he is good at anything which you can play one-handed, leaving the other free to hold a glass. He himself modestly puts down his skill to the seven or so years he spent training to enter the medical profession. I think it's seven. Maybe he added another two on for practising games.

The curious thing is that when I first met him at university he was engaged in an outdoor sport, namely sprinting. This is an activity so repugnant to his basic urges, not to mention his anatomy, that I am not surprised he gave up after beating the twenty-second barrier for the hundred yards, but during his brief sprinting career I noticed that he had evolved a technique which I don't believe anyone else has ever tried; he contrived to give the impression as he came up the track that he was not last in this race but first in some other race altogether.

Twenty years passed and I never saw him play an outdoors sport again, unless you count his brief career as a bowler of googlies so unpredictable that they deceived the bowler more than the batsman. But he used to refer mysteriously to the fact that he was a member of Rye Golf Club. Now, Rye is the sort of place which takes its golf seriously and I could not imagine that Barlow's golf, if it was anything like his sprinting or cricket, would pass the auditions, nor could I think of a reason for his wanting to join.

The reason turns out to be suitably Barlowesque. The hospital to which he is attached has an annual golf match between the staff and students which is staged at Rye. For some time the staff were so superior to the students that they put my friend Barlow on the team as an act of mercy to the other side. Then the students began to improve and Barlow was dropped. But they forgot to cancel his membership.

And two months ago Barlow and I found ourselves in Rye for the Rye Festival, and it came to pass that we both got out our golf clubs from the cellar, and I have now seen Barlow playing golf. As with sprinting, he has developed techniques which are probably new to the game and I wish to record them as a footnote to golf history.

1. He does not believe in hitting the ball very far. He says that this makes the ball harder to lose, and also that the more strokes you take, the more fun you get out of it. A golfer who goes round in 65 is not getting value for money, says Barlow.

2. He prefers the rough to the fairway. All the bunkers are on the fairway, he says; you're safe in the rough.

3. His favourite club is the putter. I don't mean that he is better at putting, merely that he takes a putter as soon as he is within a hundred yards of the green and tries to putt on to the green, for which purpose he is forced to emerge from the rough. He too is the only golfer I have ever seen who is often still not on the green after his first putt.

4. When under great stress, he tends to place the ball where he thinks it should have gone. On one hole he was trying to putt on to the green from twenty feet. The ball went up the bank, nearly reached the green, then rolled back into the exact position it had come from. He hit his next shot without having moved from his last shot. It rolled back about three feet away. He picked it up and put it in the place to which it was becoming accustomed.

5. After each hole he said to me, before marking his card: 'Well, what shall we call it?' By this he meant that if he had taken eight for the hole, he would prefer to write down five. 'But nobody is going to see the card, Barlow,' I said.

'You never know,' he said mysteriously. If Richard Nixon had covered his traces like Barlow, he would still be president.

6. Although I outplayed him in every department of the game we still found, when we came to check the cards, that we had halved the match. I still have not worked out how he did this one.

A fowl Christmas

There is a picture hanging in the Photographers Gallery in Great Newport Street called 'Christmas Dinner, South London, 1982'. It shows a poor woman and two children eating nothing but sausage and beans, and when I saw it I felt as depressed and guilty as you do after reading the *Guardian*, which of course is exactly what I was intended to feel. It never occurred to me at the time that less than a week later, at Christmas Day lunchtime, I would get much less to eat than that, and that nobody would feel sorry for me.

Things started pretty well. We had gone to stay with my brother in Devon – four of us, four of them, very domestic, no trouble with the washing up rota, etc. He lives on top of Dartmoor. If any of my readers is reading this in the prison nearby and decides to escape later, he will see my brother's house near enough if he heads eastwards. Anyway, supper on the first evening was all local produce – oysters and mussels from the River Dart.

Have you ever opened oysters? I never had. What you do is insert a knife and twist it, and a little flake of shell comes off. Then you put the blade in somewhere else, twist it again, and another fragment of shell comes off. Then you stick the blade in deeper elsewhere, twist it more sharply and the blade comes off. Then, when you have run out of knives, you apply small hand grenades to one end of the oyster. This just about does the trick, and after about two hours you have a dish of open oysters and a wrecked kitchen. The oysters were delicious. There weren't a great many per person, but we still had Christmas lunch to look forward to.

The next day, Christmas Eve, we had wild duck for supper. Have you ever plucked a duck? I never had. What you do is sit with the duck on your lap and pull the feathers out until you are surrounded by a pile of down 2 ft high. This means you have almost completed one wing.

It is astonishing, by the way, that ducks, who spend most of their lives flying around, do not build up mighty wing muscles in the way that ballet dancers have thighs like balloons or tennis players have one hand four sizes larger than the other. But I regret to report that under all those feathers a duck wing looks as puny as a garter with the elastic gone. Perhaps ducks fly with their stomach muscles. Perhaps they walk everywhere these days. You have time for thoughts like these when you are plucking ducks, which takes two hours the way I do it. The duck was delicious; there wasn't much meat but we still had Christmas lunch to look forward to.

With Christmas Day only hours away, my brother and I realized we hadn't seen much of our families yet. We'd been too busy breaking and entering the larder. And now we had to wrap our presents. Have you ever wrapped a present? I had, but you wouldn't think so to look at me. I do it with a roll of sticky tape in one hand and a roll of sticky tape in the other. And the technique I use reminds people of someone trying to get the feathers back on to a wild duck.

The only thing of note that happened before we finally got to bed was that my son was very ill. The only thing of note that happened during the night was that the two girls became very ill. The only interesting thing that happened on Christmas morning was that everyone else felt very ill, and by midday it was like being in the House of the Dying.

We did try to open our Christmas presents. Have you ever tried to open Christmas presents when your strength has sunk to below the strength of sticky tape? It's not easy, especially when you finally rip open the parcel and find that you've been given something edible.

Actually, it wasn't half a bad Christmas Day after all; when the sick people are in a majority, it's the few healthy ones who feel the odd men out. We all crept around feeling sorry for ourselves and totally revelled in it. We speculated endlessly on whether it was the duck or mussels that caused the trouble. We switched off the Queen's broadcast after a couple of minutes because she looked so disgustingly well fed, unless of course it was the colour control.

In fact we felt incredibly virtuous when all eight of us got through the hours of Christmas daylight without touching a single solid. I think all I ever had for Christmas dinner, South Devon, 1983, was a cup of hot Bovril. My brother took a photograph of me doing it. We are sending it to the Photographers Gallery, Great Newport Street. You'll be able to see it there next year.

Unusual jobs: no. 4

'It's a funny thing, but a scriptwriter who can handle divorce, punch-ups, betrayal, depression or anything bad like that often finds it hard to deal with death. So when a character has to be written out for one reason or another, they send for me, and I write the scene or episode. I sometimes feel like the public hangman.'

He looks very well on it. George Damson has been killing off people now for fifteen years, armed only with a typewriter, and he has enjoyed every minute of it. Sometimes it's because the actor involved has had an unfortunate court case, sometimes it's because he has died and very often it's simply because he wants to leave the series, but whatever it is, he has to be bumped off somehow.

'Usually I don't know the character involved very well, so he or she doesn't mean much to me, whereas to the resident scriptwriter it's a close friend. Not to mention a cushy billet. I remember one character in a television series who had to be got rid of because the actress wanted to emigrate – a real Tartar, a boarding-house landlady who gave everyone a hard time and was consequently the most popular person in the show.

'Well, the permanent scriptwriter refused to kill her off – he really loved her, because it's much more fun writing slagging-off dialogue than anything else – and when he heard that I was being called in, he went mental. He started turning in scripts in which all the *other* characters were meeting a horrible end. Couldn't use them, of course. We even had a meeting one night in which somebody seriously suggested bumping off the scriptwriter. Reality and fiction tend to blur after a while.

'What? Oh, the actress solved everything by having a fatal heart attack. Though I sometimes wonder if the TV company wasn't behind it.'

What's the best way of disposing of unwanted characters?

'Off-stage, unfortunately. Car crash or accident abroad. The other characters hear the news, stagger around a bit. "My God, how awful, oh no, I can't believe it." Same as Greek tragedy basically, except the Greeks did go on about it. More than we do. Personally, I'd prefer to have a few on-screen deaths – spectacular collapse at party, harrowing suicide, savaged to death by Rod Hull and Emu, that sort of thing – but the public can't take it. Usually the actor isn't available by then, anyway.

'What I'd really like to do is use a few of the deaths that happen in real life, blokes found dangling from Blackfriars Bridge, people struck by lightning on clear days and so on, but I can't. Know why? Because people wouldn't believe it, that's why. Funny old thing, death.'

Isn't his job peculiarly modern and sadly in tune with our times?

'No way. It's one of the oldest jobs in the world. I bet Shakespeare got someone in to deal with Falstaff, because he couldn't bear to do it himself. And think of Sherlock Holmes, who not only had to be written out but written back in again, due to popular demand. I sometimes have to do that, make characters emigrate to America or run off with someone, in case they're needed back later. Like in the Bible.'

Pardon?

'Well, this may sound irreverent, but the most famous rewrite case of all time is none other than Jesus, who was written out of history on Friday and written back in again on Monday. I'm not saying it didn't happen. In fact, I'm pretty certain it did happen. Coming back again because you're the Son of God has probably got to be true because no scriptwriter could get away with making that up. If I were called in to get rid of someone in *Crossroads*, for example, I'd think twice about saying he was the Messiah and was going to be called away on other business.'

Yes, quite. Has George got any unfulfilled ambitions in the writing-out field?

'I'd like to have been called in by the Labour Party to help ease out Michael Foot. What a botch they made of that.'

Tales of old Soho

'Visit one of the last live strip-tease shows around!' says the sign in Brewer Street, Soho.

'Personally, I blame the video games,' said old Mo Kanary. 'They're staying at home to play Spice Invaders, or whatever it's called. They're too lazy to seek out live entertainment.'

'Personally, I blame the violin menders and pasta-makers,' said old Alf Deadwood. 'All this area is being taken over by trendy craftsmen. Hand-made bicycles. Second-hand books. Graphic bloody artists.'

'Do you know where the Sexy Pigalle used to be?' said Mo. 'Know what they've got there now?'

'No,' said Alf. 'Something to do with silkscreens, I expect.'

'A games shop,' said Mo. 'Chess, and snakes and ladders, and dominoes, all hand-carved by women with long hair and wholemeal clothes.'

'Remember Sue the Snake Girl?' said Alf.

'No.'

'She had an act based on snakes and ladders. She climbed up this ladder with a python called Stafford Cripps, and got it to take all her clothes off. Very classy, it was. She kept the act going for, oh, ten years or more. She used to go on holiday when the python hibernated or something, then come back. Anyway, one day the ladder collapsed under her and she broke a leg, and do you know what?'

'No,' said Mo.

'That snake was so popular with the punters that next week it went on by itself! Got a great big round of applause. You don't get loyalty like that with people today. If people want to see a snake they stay home and watch bleeding David Attenborough with a bleeding boa constrictor on the telly. Rotten snakes, too. Did you ever see a boa constrictor taking David Attenborough's clothes off!'

'No,' said Mo.

'Well, then,' said Alf.

They were sitting in the saloon bar of the Pimp and Nickel, one of the last of the old Soho pubs. They sat here every day, having the same conversation. The next step was for Mo to blame Westminster Council.

'Personally, I blame Westminster. Cracking down on the dirty film places. Well, all right, but then *we* get it in the neck as well, and we were Art. Remember Mary the Amazing Model?'

'No,' said Alf.

'She used to enact scenes from famous paintings, all nude of course. There was one called the *Judgement of Paris* I used to enjoy, where she did amazing things with apples. And the *Death of Nelson*.'

'That's not a nude painting.'

'It was the way she did it. "Kiss me, Hardy!" she used to cry. That was the signal for the blackout.'

'Culture, that's what it was, culture. Artistic. Lots of lads, down from the north, football game or something, it was the first time lots of them had seen a naked woman. They got a good introduction. Artistic. Something to remember.'

'One day she did a painting called the *Flight of Icarus*. She broke her leg, too.'

'You had a lot of legs broken in your place, my old son.'

'Yes, well, you've got to take risks in live art, haven't you? Do you remember Fifi the Flying French Girl?'

'Yes,' said Alf, 'I married her.'

'Oh yes,' said Mo. 'So you did. Sorry.'

They both fell silent, thinking back to the great days of theatre. It was generally about this point that the conversation came full circle.

'Personally, I blame the video games,' said Mo.

'Out,' said the barman.

From Tales of Old Soho, *Moreover Publications, only £15 – all right, two quid to you, squire.*

Down among the sweating palms

This year, have a holiday to remember! Only from Moreover Travel! Two weeks on the lovely Iles de Brochure!

These palm-fraught islands are only thirty-six hours from Heathrow. How do you get there? Easy. You just jump in a cab and say: Take me to Heathrow!

No, but seriously, the Brochure Islands are a dream come true. Surrounded by water on all sides, they represent the kind of holiday you thought you'd never have. Swimming, drying, getting sand between your toes, losing your towel – these are just four of the many activities available. Or if you'd rather just sit on the beach and stare morosely into the distance, that can be arranged, too.

The Romans called these islands the Devil's Rocks. The Crusaders came this way, but did not stop. The Portuguese landed in 1567 and left behind the curious structure known to this day as Costa's Grill. In the eighteenth century the French gave it to the British, who did not want it and gave it back. Now, left behind by history, the Iles de Brochure are a quiet haven where you can eat yourself silly or dance the conga, if that's your idea of a good time.

Native Brochurians speak English, French, Dutch and German, or Swedish for a slight surcharge. During the day they wear plain hotel workers' uniforms, but they exchange these in the evening for their native costumes so that they can sing and dance spontaneously in the residents' dining-room or on-stage in the Garden Barbecue. Their many native folk songs, such as La Cucuracha or the Blue Danube, have been put on a long-playing record which you may purchase in reception.

The Hotel Moreover is the most luxurious on the main island, Paella, but there are many others to choose from, ranging from five-star to one-star. The grading is as follows:

***** Television in every room, receiving programmes and that night's video film.

**** Television in every room, receiving programmes.

*** Television, black and white, in every room, receiving programmes only in Brochurian.

** Television in every room receiving only radio programmes.

* Television in the next room.

There are cars on the islands, but most people prefer to use the horse and buggies, which will take you to the interior of the country, down to the beach or wherever the horse feels like it. Once a year the Iles de Brochure erupt in a fantastic Fiesta de Cabriolet, in which the buggies are decorated with flowers and flags, everyone dances in the streets and all wine is free. This occurs just after or just before your holiday.

For breakfast, either you use your own bedroom kettle to brew instant coffee with biscuits, or you make your way to the breakfast lounge, where the staff will be pleased to serve you instant coffee and biscuits. Lunch is a come-as-you-please affair of salads and cold meats and so is dinner. Dress, of course, is quite informal, though we try to discourage leisurewear within the hotel itself.

If you wish to get away from the hustle and bustle of the beach life, we can recommend a trip into the interior by horse and buggy, taxi or simply on shanks's pony. The contrast is startling; gone are the luxurious palms and putting courses of bright green – instead a gaunt hot landscape made up of native rocks and scrub, reaching a height of some 367 metres at its highest. Here you will find small, unspoilt villages, with old Brochurian ladies ready to sell you cold drinks and cups of tea, as they have done from time immemorial.

The cost of all this? An unbelievable £2! Yes, that's all it costs to send for the Moreover leaflet and browse through it at your own leisure. It's the holiday of a lifetime – and you can enjoy it in the comfort of your own home!

Moreover Travel. The vacation that's tailored to your pocket.

Just send us £2. You don't have to do anything else.

Believe us, there's nothing else you can do.

Royal rendezvous

You may have read in the newspapers that Prince Andrew has got a new girl-friend. You probably thought to yourself at the time: I see that Prince Andrew has got a new girl-friend. Or perhaps you thought: I wonder if there's any proper news in this damned newspaper. What you almost certainly didn't realize is that behind such a brief announcement lies an exhausting amount of royal ritual and ceremony, which must always take place the same way.

It starts with the age-old exchange between prince and proposed girl-friend, which goes like this.

Prince: Willst thou be my girl-friend?
Girl: I willst.
Prince: Dost promise to be discreet? To smile at the press? Not to stand around in thin dresses with the light behind?
Girl: I dost.
Prince: Canst come and see my Mum some time next week?
Girl: Canst.
Prince: I now pronounce us prince and girl-friend.
Girl: What about the bit about my not selling your letters to the press?
Prince: There won't be any letters. I've learnt my lesson.

The prince then takes his new girl-friend to see his mother at the Palace. There is a rather touching ceremony at the entrance.

Guard: Who goes there?
Prince: The prince.
Guard: The prince and who?
Prince: The prince's girl-friend.
Guard: Advance, girl-friend, and be recognized.
Prince: She's new, actually.
Guard: Blimey, it's all go round here.

The prince will then take his friend upstairs, unless this takes place at Sandringham, in which case they shall both don gum boots and go out into the kitchen garden or stables. Leading the girl-friend by the hand the prince shall then say:

Prince: Hello, Mum, this is (*Here he shall use her name*) ...
Queen: I am pleased to meet you. How long have you been doing this sort of thing?
Prince: Mum! Please – we're not touring a factory now. Where's Dad?
Queen: I believe he's writing an introduction for a book about wildlife.
Prince: That's the spirit. Well, I'm just going to take (*here he shall use her name again*) for a spin in a helicopter.
Queen: Don't be late for dinner. Charles and Spike Milligan are dropping in again.

The prince shall then take the girl-friend up in a helicopter loaned by the RN where he shall turn to her and say:

Prince: I think she really liked you. You could tell by the way she let you help brush the dogs. Do you see those people in the potato field down there? They're photographers from the *Sun*. Did you know the *Sun* has more people covering Sandringham than the rest of the world put together? So Dad says.
Girl: I'm sorry – I can see your lips moving, but I can't hear a single word in this helicopter.
Prince: What?

The final part of the ceremony is known as Meeting the Press. This takes place outside the girl-friend's home at 8.15 a.m., as she leaves for work. When she opens the door, the press shall say:

Press: Blimey, girl, you took us by surprise, can you just go in again and then come out once more? Big smile, that's the way, lots of happiness, this is your big day, going out with the Prince and all that, hold it! Look this way, look that way, look this way again, come on love, you play ball with us and we'll play ball with you, what's he like then, have you met the Queen, is it wedding bells, just one more, that's it, now one more for luck.
Girl: Goodness – is it always like this?
Press: 'Fraid so, love.

The girl-friend then goes to work looking very thoughtful, reflecting that it's all going to be harder work than she thought, but that at least she's going to get the chance to meet in person people like Spike Milligan.

Irish story

Last Sunday morning I was standing at the end of the Giant's Causeway, on the topmost tip of Northern Ireland, watching the waves foam and crash over the blackened rocks, which was curious because the sea itself was dead calm. There was a little old man bent over the rocks, putting something into a white carrier bag, like a character in a nineteenth-century print.

'Seaweed,' he said, in response to my curiosity. 'Brown seaweed, very good for cooking. It only grows two months of the year, in winter, so you have to know where and when to look for it.'

He told me how to cook it. He told me how to recognize it. He told me that he had been born actually on the Causeway, in a house that was no longer there, and about the other six houses that were no longer there because they had been swept away, not by a storm, but by the National Trust, which had replaced them in safety on top of the cliff, and he would still be talking to this day if we hadn't had to move on to lunch near Ballycastle.

The people we were having lunch with were a pair we had met and taken to at a Belfast party last November. And a terrific lunch it was too, though the roast lamb seemed gamier than usual. 'That's because it's not lamb,' said Patrick. 'It's young goat, only we don't tell people that until after they've had a first helping, just in case they're prejudiced.'

Well, everyone's prejudiced about Northern Ireland, and one of the things you have to put up with if you live there is English people coming over and expecting the place to be like Beirut. It's nothing of the sort. Perhaps I'm just lucky, but when I think back to Northern Ireland, it's things like the old man on the Causeway, or roast goat at Ballycastle, that float into the mind. When we arrived at the Harbour Bar, five o'clock on Saturday, it was jam-packed, but by 6.30 it was nearly empty. 'It's the pattern,' said the barman. 'It fills up during the afternoon, then ebbs away. They'll all be back in an hour or so, ready for the evening. The place is open from 11.30 in the morning till 11 at night, when the doors close. All that closing and opening you get in England – it's an awful waste of time.'

That's the kind of fey logic which is at the heart of real Irish jokes, not the crude ersatz Irish jokes we've been fed in recent years. The Harbour Bar at Portrush itself is nothing much to look at – it's the cosy ambience which makes the place, the roar of talking and crackling laughter from the little rooms down the passage.

Northern Ireland is maybe like the Harbour Bar on a big scale – not very much to look at, but well worth getting inside. It's different there. For instance, did you notice that the barman said: '... till 11 at night, when the doors close'? In England he would have said: '... till 11 at night, when everybody goes home.' I think I'll pour myself another pint of stout.

Playing away

Who are Los Trios Paranormals?

Why are they causing such a tremendous fuss in the world of extra-sensory perception?

And an equal sensation in the world of rock music?

Because Los Trios Paranormals are the first living proof that

Arthur Koestler's theories about paranormal communications may hold water.

Los Trios Paranormals are three young men from Leeds who claim to play a concert in one town *while their audience sits in another place*. Last month they played for two hours in an empty concert hall in Leeds while an audience of 300 sat in an auditorium in Bradford. And many of that audience claimed to receive definite musical messages.

'I was sitting there in my seat concentrating,' says one member of the experimental audience, 'when all at once I start getting these atrocious headaches and feelings of claustrophobia, not to mention tight shoes. I only ever get these feelings in a rock concert. How do you explain that?'

'It was uncanny,' says another listener, Hazel, twenty-three, a temp secretary with the Mafia. 'I was sitting there, hearing vague far-off sounds of music in my head, when all at once I got the feeling that I was actually Paulene, fifty-six, an old Fats Domino fan. I mean, that's weird. After that I suddenly felt that in some previous existence I had been Russell Harty. Now that *was* weird. After that, I passed out. That was normal.'

What this all seems to prove is that the music played by Los Trios Paranormals is passed in some inexplicable way into the minds of people far out of earshot. Even if the wind blew from Leeds to Bradford on the night in question, there is no way that the audience could have heard the music physically as the group's PA refused to function.

Guitarist Poco Fernando, real name Les Thwaite: 'The PA just went dead on us. I mean, *we* couldn't hear what we were playing. But the punters in Bradford could. That's wild. And I'll tell you another thing. Rick, our bass player, was sick and couldn't make the gig. And nobody in Bradford said they could sense a bass player. If that doesn't prove it, I don't know what does.'

Enormous excitement has been caused in the paranormal world by the exploits of the group, according to the manager of the group, Alan Franks (no relation). He says that this puts the video revolution into the shade. What we've got here, he says, is something like telekarma, or perhaps cable telepathy, anyway it's big business and he's open to any offers, in writing only, sorry, no paranormal contracts.

But a note of caution has been struck in the rock world by Sam Price, Paranormal Adviser to the Musicians' Union.

'We cautiously welcome any advance in technology as long as it doesn't endanger jobs,' he says. 'And if, as seems possible, a group like Los Trios Paranormals can play in one place and be heard in another, this is good. Because it means that our members can fail to turn up for a gig and still get paid for it. Well, that's flipping fantastic.'

The big test for Los Trios Paranormals comes next month, when they are booked into the Odeon Hammersmith for a live gig, which they intend to play from a service area on the M1 near Northampton. A lot depends on how the critical London audience reacts to a completely absentee act. But Poco Fernando feels quietly confident.

'I feel quietly confident,' he told me from two hundred miles away, in his bedsit in Leeds. 'Frinstance, I'm not even using a phone at the moment. And yet you're hearing me. How do you explain that?'

Unemployment down by one

The managing director of Topscale Recycling felt good. He had looked out of his bedroom window in the morning and admired his garden, kept in tip-top shape by his gardener at an annual wage of £6,000. He had enjoyed his breakfast, prepared by his wife (about £7,000 a year). He had read his newspaper, delivered by a small boy for about 70p a year. And now he was being driven to work by his chauffeur for a paltry £8,000 a year.

He felt good because of all these people who were working for him. It couldn't be the money that made them do it (and that was paid by the company anyway). It must be because they liked him. That made him feel good. Yes, I'm quite a guy, thought the managing director of Topscale Recycling.

A quarter of a mile from his factory gates he made the chauffeur stop the car and get his folding bike out of the boot. He liked to arrive at work on a bike, not just because it impressed the workforce and because he could claim the bike against tax, but because it made him, in some way he couldn't define, feel good.

One thing especially made him feel extra-good on this bright morning. Topscale Recycling had recently expanded its operations to the extent of needing an extra store manager, and they had advertised the post nationally. This meant that they were making jobs. They were actually reducing unemployment. He felt as if he himself were the light at the end of the tunnel that people were always talking about. And today was the day on which they were to start sifting applications for the new post.

'Good morning, sir,' said the doorman whose job it was, apart from making difficulties for everyone entering the building, to park the managing director's bicycle when he arrived. The doorman personally thought it was silly to get a bike out of the boot four hundred yards from the factory gates, but he wasn't paid £12,000 a year to keep such thoughts to himself. He was paid £6,000 to do it. But he kept such thoughts to himself anyway.

'Right,' said the managing director, sweeping into his office and feeling extremely good. 'How many applications have we had for that job?'

His assistant decided not to beat about the bush.

'Three million,' he said.

'How many?' said the managing director.

'Three million,' said his assistant. This conversation was repeated several times until his boss realized he wasn't joking. He wasn't paid £9,000 a year to make jokes. They came extra.

'All I can assume, sir, is that every unemployed person in Britain has applied for this job,' said the assistant.

'Any idea why?' said the managing director.

'Yes, sir. The post carries a salary of £7,000 a year. There was a misprint in the advertisement and it came out at £70,000 a year.'

The managing director thought about this for a moment. He thought briefly of the hopes he had aroused in three million breasts. He thought secondly of the trouble they would have going through three million job applications. But most of all he thought of the wonderful amount of free waste paper that Topscale Recycling would get from three million unanswered letters. They had just made a fortune, simply by advertising a job.

'Make up another new job,' said the managing director, 'and

advertise it at £80,000 a year. And make sure there is no misprint this time.'

'Yes, sir,' said the assistant.

The managing director felt very good indeed.

They were about to make another fortune. Nobody had ever thought of recycling job application letters before. It was the biggest new growth industry in Britain.

This short story has been provided, free of charge, by Tory Central Office. Another one coming soon!

Announcing...
The Moreover Wine Club!

The Club for the people who can't be bothered with wine.

Did you know that two or three million people in Britain now have a pretty fair knowledge of the wines of the world, can tell you the bad and good years, and will inform you at the drop of a hat what wine goes with what bit of fish?

That leaves nearly fifty million who couldn't care less.

And it's at them that the Moreover Wine Club is aimed.

If you ever say one of the three following sentences, you're a Moreover Wine Club sort of person.

'Let's just order the house red, shall we?'

'I can never remember if it's red or white with chicken.'

'I prefer the stuff in plastic bottles, actually.'

With most wine clubs, it's like going back to school again. With the Moreover Wine Club, it's like drinking behind the classroom again. That's because the Moreover Wine Club has only one wine on offer!

Yes, it's true!

Whatever you write up for, we send you the same wine. Albanian Impexport Non-Vintage Vin de Table. Only £2.13 a bottle. £25 a case. Or £4,800 a lorry-load.

Albanian Impexport wine comes from the vine-wreathed north-facing slopes of the Qwexto hills of Albania, where nothing else grows. The reds are surly and slaty; the whites are thin and argumentative; the rosés are shy and retiring.

But they're ever so cheap.

And they come with our free labels!

Yes, we send you absolutely free of charge a vast selection of labels using words like Montrachet, Châteauneuf, Margaux, Spätlese, Frascati and Domaine. All you have to do is put the label you like on the wine we send you.

Namely, Albanian Impexport Non-Vintage Vin de Table.

Research shows that nothing makes more difference to a wine than the right label. Your guests will be tremendously impressed by the Muscadet or Côtes du Rhone you serve them, and there's no need to tell them that what they're actually drinking is Albanian Impexport plonko. Remember it's illegal to sell wrongly labelled wines – but there's no law against serving them to your friends or family!

And you can always pour yourself a drop of good stuff at the same time.

How can we make such a wonderful offer? Simple. We have recently come into possession of a huge shipment of Albanian wine, originally intended for the Chinese market. Don't ask how. Just believe us. It's ready for drinking now. In other words, if you lay it down, it's only going to get worse. If that's possible.

You've always wanted a wine to give to other people. Now you've got it.

So if you've ever said to yourself: this wine snobbery stuff is a load of compost; join the Moreover Wine Club at once. Be the first person in your street to lay down a tank of Albanian two-stroke alcohol. Send an SAE at once for full details.

You won't regret it. Only your guests will!

A car in a million

It's here at last. The car of the 1980s. And it's British!

The Moreover Magneto.

The car that fills the gap between the one you had last and the one you'll get next.

Motoring correspondents were flown from all over the world yesterday to the Pork Scratchings service area on the M1 to see Sir Richard Attenborough launch the car they're already describing as the chariot of fire.

The Moreover Magnolia.

Stylishly sculptured, with four wheels and windows on all sides, the Magnolia is not just a car. It's a way of getting from one place to another. With people inside. And luggage too, if you insist.

On the boot at the back you'll see the discreet figures 1700.

We put those figures there. Don't know why. They just looked nice.

But that's the sort of car it is.

The Moreover Montague.

It has features you thought you'd never see in a family saloon car.

You know how annoying it is when magazines and maps get under the front seat? We've thought of that. The Montagu has an under-seat map-ejector.

You know that moment when you reach for an extra strong mint and there aren't any left? We've thought of that too. There's a reserve extra strong mint canister.

There's a place for you to fix your football scarf to, so that it flies out of the window.

There's a clip-on back sash, to make it look as if you're wearing a safety-belt.

There's even an outside speaker for your cassette player, so that the passers-by can hear your Genesis tapes, while you inside are in total silence.

We've thought of everything in the new Moreover Malaprop.

When you set off in the Malaprop, there's a free glass of champagne for every passenger. Meals are served at three-hourly intervals, whether you want them or not. And there's a free selection of magazines and daily papers in the sick bag in front of you.

Travelling in the new Moreover Montaigne is rather like falling in love again. It's like looking across a crowded restaurant and meeting the eyes of the person you want more than anyone in the world. The waiter.

The Montaigne is not just an experience. It's birth, marriage and death, as well as a rather uncomfortable weekend with the in-laws. It's finding a parking space in Piccadilly. It's getting a seat on the

Friday evening train to Bristol. It's discovering oil in your back garden.

It's got an engine, too.

But we won't bore you with technicalities. Because there's only one question you want to ask, isn't there?

How much is the new Moreover Montgomery?

The answer is unbelievable.

£19,999½. (Batteries not included.)

How have we managed to price the new Montgomery so high – much higher than any comparable car?

Easy. We're trying to put it outside the range of everyone else, so that just *you* can buy a new model.

When you buy one, you know that you will be the only person on the roads with one. We can guarantee this. After all, we've only made one.

If sales are satisfactory, we might make another one. And there again, we might not.

That's the sort of car it is.

The Moreover Mintcake.

Order yours now.

Cash only.

Ta.

Unusual jobs: no. 5

Whenever we hear a recording of the proceedings in the House of Commons, we can hear behind the speaker a chorus of reaction from MPs, ranging from a quiet rhubarb to a rabble riot. But no matter how loud the chorus one voice always seems closer than the others. It belongs to Quentin Huckleby, SDP–Labour member for Crossover South.

'Like all great Parliamentary customs, it started by accident,' says Quentin, an affable self-employed conveyancer of about forty-five. 'I just happened to be sitting nearest the mike one day during a particularly boring debate on the renaming of the North Sea, and I was passed a note by the Speaker. "Please provide some reactions," it said, "or the radio audience will think there's no one here." Well, I could see what he meant, so I started harrumphing and groaning a bit, as we normally would do if Mrs Thatcher was speaking.

'Anyway, the Speaker came up to me afterwards and said I was a great success and could I go on doing it in future debates, so I always have. What he liked especially, I think, was that he couldn't tell from the noises I was making whether I supported the speaker or not. Of course, as a Labour–SDP member I often don't know myself, so I suppose I have without realizing evolved some non-committal but impassioned noises. I now have a special seat near the mike.'

Quentin Huckleby has not actually spoken in the house since winning his seat at the Election, but as he has grunted and groaned non-stop through every debate, he doesn't think he has to.

'People outside the Commons often think it's rude of me to interrupt and barrack speakers but they don't realize that the speakers love it. Mrs Thatcher raising her voice to soar over the rebellious crowd beneath her – well, she'd be lost if she didn't have that hubbub to fight. She'd certainly sound pretty stupid if she were shouting in a complete silence. When there's not enough noise, she actually signals to me to start the protest going.'

How does he get that distinctive 'Yah-yah' noise that only MPs seem capable of?

'It's not really "Yah-yah" if you listen closely. It's more like "Hear, hear" recorded at 45 r.p.m. and then played back at 33 r.p.m. It's got overtones of approval and disapproval at the same time. The same with what the press calls cries of "Oh! Oh! Oh!" This is really "Ho, ho, ho" slowed down and played back with more bass. And a touch of echo.'

Wouldn't Mr Huckleby admit that the Parliamentary chorus is rather like a secondary school class barracking a weak teacher?

'Not at all. I'd say it was more like a primary school, played back at half the speed.'

Isn't this all rather childish?

'Oh, definitely. That's why the public loves it. I know the critics say we sound like a pack of unruly passengers on a charabanc, but let's face it: that's what people identify with. Of course, as the prime mover I have to do a lot of rehearsing.'

Rehearsing? How can you rehearse crowd reactions?

'Easily. Sometimes I practise as a drinker who's just been told it's closing time – lots of MPs are well away, so that's fitting. Sometimes as an England forward being sent off in the French match, sometimes as Cecil Parkinson being found out.'

What would happen if he genuinely got angry about something being said in the Commons?

'Oh, we don't actually listen to what's being said, we just listen to the tone of the voice. I'm not sure what would happen if I found myself following the speeches. Drop off to sleep, I expect. The only time I got *really* angry was when I noticed Mrs Thatcher edging near the microphone during a Neil Kinnock explosion, and booing into it, rather like herself at half speed. Well, that's not her job, that's my job, and I rather told her off, I'm afraid.'

Can he remember exactly what he said to her?

'It doesn't really matter, does it? During a Neil Kinnock explosion, all you can hear is Welsh spit flying into outer space.'

The complete summer catalogue

The weather is turning cloudy and chilly, a sure sign that summer is on the way at last. And that means it's time to get out all those things you'll be needing in the garden this summer!

It doesn't matter where you keep them – in the garage, under the stairs, in that shed with the missing key – as long as you make sure that every single thing you need for the summer is there from last year. So use this handy checklist and tick off each item as you get it out.

One nearly complete barbecue kit.

A garden hose with four kinks in it, one fatal.

A kit for smoking your own food such as fish, plus one of last year's fish.

A deck chair which, when you sit in it, allows your bottom to touch the ground.

A croquet set containing more balls than mallets and more mallets than hoops.

A jar of something meant to speed up compost heaps, which seems to have leaked.

One Chinese kite assembly kit, which, when assembled, flies along the ground.

A pack of raspberry canes, which, when assembled, fall over.

Half a pair of garden shears, kept on the assumption that there must be a use for a shear.

A foot pump.

One stilt.

A lawn mower still awaiting its winter maintenance.

A net for playing deck tennis, badminton, or some similar game, carefully rolled up in such a way that it can never be unrolled again.

Not fewer than five table tennis balls, four with dents in and one with a crack in.

An empty soda siphon.

A complete set of instructions for the erection of a piece of garden furniture which has totally vanished.

A game involving a ball which you hit as hard as possible and which comes back at you immediately except that the rubber has gone.

A rake with as many gaps as teeth.

One unicycle, or rather half a bicycle.

A coil of rope with no beginning or end.

A flag belonging to no known country.

One home-made device for removing boots from feet, also capable of removing heels from boots.

One single oar, one single rowlock, but no visible boat. A racket for playing badminton, with an aperture in the racket to let the shuttlecock through.

A gym shoe which has been colonized by the insect world.

A pair of rubber swimming flippers, one with the heel perished.

Several copies of *Reader's Digest* from the late 1950s.

A quantity of old clothing which you put aside for Oxfam last year.

A quantity of green nylon netting left in such a way that when you pull at it, all the other objects listed above will come out as well.

Warning: new construction ahead

It always gives me a thrill when I spot a new usage creep into the language, like coypus infiltrating the hitherto uncoypued landscape of Norfolk, and I would like everyone to give a big hand to the hyphenated noun-plus-participle masquerading as an adjective.

If that sounds ugly, and it's meant to, let me give you an example. 'Index-linked pension'. A noun, a hyphen, a participle. We all know what it means. It means inflation-proof. Only to make it sound slightly grander, we say that it is linked to the cost-of-living index. It doesn't sound too bad, but then one coypu in the landscape is quite acceptable.

Another now common example is the description of diseases like cancer as 'smoking-related'. This is an adjective used by scientists who are perfectly certain that smoking causes cancer but haven't finally proved it, so are reduced to saying that it is linked to smoking. Quite unobjectionable, but two coypus in the countryside should cause no alarm.

When a third appears, I do begin to hear alarm bells. It appeared in the *Herald Tribune*, about a month ago. In the run-up to the elections in the Philippines, nearly a dozen people had been shot or otherwise done to death for their political beliefs, or ambitions, and the Trib had referred to these incidents as 'election-related deaths'. These linguistic coypus are obviously beginning to mate and have strange offspring.

The fourth coypu was duly sighted last week, again in the *Herald Tribune*. (Let nobody think I am criticizing this excellent paper, which is the first one I turn to every morning.) They printed a photograph of a man riding on horseback with water up to his knees, down the main street of a small American town. The presence of so much water, the caption explained, was due to 'rain-caused floods'.

Now, this is where we must start to call a halt, or to go out and shoot these pesky coypus before they take a hold. This little construction will become a bad habit, a reflex-linked action, before we know where we are. I suspect that we are dealing with an American-derived fad, which is why it is a *Tribune*-associated phenomenon, that Paris-domiciled newspaper being an expatriate-orientated publication though it is also a European-angled daily. That, if you didn't notice, was an example-stuffed sentence. I find the whole thing a nausea-operated topic.

The unwieldiness of it comes out best if we apply it to a well-known piece of writing. Here is a Wordsworth-derived stanza.

> I wandered like a care-linked cloud
> That floats on high o'er height-caused hills
> When all at once I saw a crowd
> Of bulb-connected daffodils
> Dancing 'neath the branch-formed trees
> In time with the waltz-tempoed breeze.

If the scientists and medics still think that there is a place for this construction in scientific language, I offer another version.

> I roamed in cloud-related gloom
> Through lake-associated hills
> When all at once I caught a rheum,
> A nasty go of damp-linked chills,
> Beside the acorn-started trees
> I shivered in the wind-caused breeze.

Gentlemen, my case rests. I adopt a coypu-opposed position.

New Orleans

The first few notes

When I first fell in love with jazz in the mid-1950s I knew that New Orleans was the place to go to. I also knew that I had left it far too late if jazz history was to be believed, which it sometimes is. Most of the best musicians had left the Crescent City by about 1920 to go on and make their names in Chicago, New York and the world. All that was left in New Orleans was a few old men barely keeping the tradition alive.

And now quite unexpectedly I have got to New Orleans at last, only to find that there is a great deal of jazz here, probably much more than there was in the 1950s. It isn't so much that it has revived here as that it has been brought back, mostly by young white players from America, Britain and Scandinavia, players who have so fallen in love with the music that they are prepared to lug their trumpets and clarinets half-way across the world to set up home here. Even in the traditional marching bands you will spot eager young white faces among the older black ones.

This is about as extraordinary a thing as it would be if London were rediscovered as the home of music hall, with pilgrims coming to London to search out the old singers and comedians, or if young Americans flocked to London to sing traditional music hall songs in East End pubs. What makes it odder still is that jazz is not central to the lives of most people in New Orleans.

It certainly doesn't play a central part in the life of the black community, from whence it came all those years ago. I had lunch yesterday at Buster Holmes, a small eating house on the edge of the French Quarter, which features red beans and rice, the dish beloved of Louis Armstrong. There were one or two jazz relics on the walls along with boxing posters and pictures of black celebrities but among the hundreds of records in the juke box there was only one by a jazz artist, Louis himself. All the rest were a rhythm 'n' blues, soul, modern rock, and even a few singles by British groups.

If you wander at night down Bourbon Street, the tourist strip of the French Quarter, you will hear – just as the guidebook says – music coming out of almost every doorway. A lot of it is young white jazz, but a lot of it is other stuff – country music, rock 'n' roll, strip club backing tracks and, at the 500 Club, some very good all-black rhythm 'n' blues bands. On the corner of St Peter's Street you come at last to a really classy black jazz artist, trumpeter Wallace Davenport. But ironically he isn't elderly and traditional enough to get a good crowd; the spectators are all round the corner at Preservation Hall.

This stark room, looking rather like a National Trust property before renovation has started, has been devoted for the last twenty years to giving the old guys a place to play. Impossible to tell how old some of them are, but over seventy and eighty is not uncommon. You pay a dollar to get in and you may not smoke, drink, eat or even sit – only listen in reverence to the survivors doing their thing, and doing it rather well, especially in the case of clarinetist Willie Humphrey. After forty minutes we give them a standing ovation, no other kind of ovation being possible, and we are ushered out in time for the next shift.

Authenticity is not just a key word, it is now a gimmick. It suddenly occurred to me, as I stood wedged between German students and a group from Wisconsin, that by dispensing with all tourist gimmicks these old guys had packed in more visitors than any of the clip joints on Bourbon Street. Two hundred of us at a dollar a head, a fresh house every sixty minutes. That is a lot of money. I certainly hope that most of it is going to the boys in the band. After a lifetime of being left behind by jazz history they deserve it.

Have a nice day in New Orleans

It's difficult to know where conversation stops in America and where slogans begin. Does 'Have a nice day' count as part of an exchange of ideas or just as a way of signing off a conversation? Even when it takes on a southern tinge and comes out as 'Y'all have a nice day' or 'Have a nice day, now, you hear?', you can't help feeling that it's a kind of recorded message. When my American visa was stamped into my passport, I was half disappointed they hadn't printed 'Have a nice trip' at the bottom.

It's now bigger than having a nice day. When I was queuing in the post office in Iberville Street, the clerk said to the woman in front of me: 'Have a nice day,' and the woman, instead of letting well alone, said: 'Thank you for serving me.' The clerk then said it was nice to do business with her, and I was seized with terror lest the woman said she would tell all her friends to come here, and the clerk said to do that very thing and I would never get to buy stamps. When I bought some typing paper ten minutes later at Woolworth's and the cashier said: 'Thank you for shopping at Woolworth's', I'm afraid I fled without replying.

Even inanimate objects sloganize at you. Trash cans in New Orleans sport a jocular sign saying: 'Throw something at me, Mister.' The museum which is preparing an exhibition on Louis XIV art objects has a banner which says: 'We're waiting for you, Louis!', which used to be said only by Louis Armstrong's English jazz fans. Even the New Orleans police cars have a quiet slogan on their back doors: 'To protect you and to serve you.' I know they don't really mean it, but if they ever throw me against a wall and frisk me, I feel sure I shall turn round and say: 'Thank you for protecting and serving me', and that this, somehow, is going to make things worse.

Another area rapidly being developed by Americans for graffiti is their left shoulder, or what we would call a lapel. The TWA air steward on the way over had inscribed very clearly on his shoulder the word 'Steve'. It was his name. Furthermore he invited us to call him Steve whenever we wanted something. We all felt vaguely inferior because we had forgotten to print our own names on our persons.

In New Orleans the art of writing on shoulders is well advanced. Waiters in big restaurants, employees of big stores, all have their names written on. But the most written-on people are those in hotel lifts, who have things like 'Georgia Board of Education' or 'American Trucking Association' inscribed on their shoulders. These are people going to or from conventions, which is what works outings are called when they involve more than one firm and more than four hundred people. Open any hotel door in New Orleans and you will find a convention going on behind it. Go into any lift and you will find silent people reading each other.

Things have not yet reached the state where you can be stopped by the police for not wearing something on your lapel but these are early days.

Yesterday, to escape from conventions, we went out into Audubon Park, a swathe of green occupied only by overweight joggers and bicyclists with headphones, and there mingled with a delightful picnic being held by two hundred people and children, complete with barbecue and Cajun band. Most of them had T-shirts reading 'Latter & Blum', which I took to be the name of the school holding a fund-raising event. Not so. It's the name of a big local real estate firm, who were holding their annual outdoor shindig. It was merely a convention in rolled up shirtsleeves. So we plunged on further into the park.

'Look at the squirrels!' said my companion. I wanted to but didn't. I wasn't prepared to take the risk of seeing a squirrel with a badge reading: 'Welcome to our park!'

It's wet but it burns well

People talk about the danger of Venice sinking below the sea. That's nothing. New Orleans has already sunk below the sea. Most parts of the city are about eight feet below sea level – always have been – and if you have ever dug a sand-castle in a low-lying part of the beach, you will know this creates a problem with seepage and inflow. In the case of New Orleans it causes $19M worth of problems every year, that being the money needed just to keep the city where it is, and dry.

It is all the fault of the French, of course, who built it in such soggy surroundings in the first place. So soggy that for a century or more it was thought lunacy to build any houses more than four storeys high. Even now the tall blocks in downtown New Orleans have to have huge concrete piers reaching way down into the earth before they even start to think of building the lobby, while the French Quarter next door preserves its old low European roofline, with church spires the highest things to be seen.

It seems odd that in such a wet place the biggest hazard is fire. Just before the place was sold to America by Napoleon there had been two enormous fires, claiming a thousand houses in all, and it was the Spaniards, owners of the city just before Napoleon, who did most of the rebuilding in brick instead of wood, which means that very little of the French Quarter is actually French. When the Americans started moving into their new property there was nothing to move into, the French Quarter being all the city there was and the French, as is their wont, not much disposed to make room for them.

So the Americans, as is their wont, started building with tremendous energy next door and for a while there was a French city with an American Quarter. That quarter grew into the Garden District, a stunning area of such grand houses in such a dizzy variety of styles that even the guide book gives up trying to describe them and settles for terms like 'Revived Greek Revival'. One house is a direct copy of Tara from *Gone With the Wind*. It is about the smallest house in the district, which, if the truth be known, is far grander and more impressive than the French Quarter.

The last big fire in the latter was ten or so years ago, when thirty-four people died in a bar on Chartres Street. There was another fire last week on Bourbon Street, when a T-shirt shop burnt out, and you can still smell the scent of autumn bonfires in the area. The firemen were able to control it quickly, because they have been trained to memorize the area's ramshackle geography, but as the local councilman said mysteriously: 'We were almost forced to learn a hard lesson there.'

Last week was, ironically, Fire Prevention Week; even more ironically it produced more fires than usual and the city fire chief is now investigating the theory that having a Fire Prevention week acts as a challenge to arsonists and pyromaniacs.

You might have thought it possible somehow to tap all that water just below the surface to create a city-wide system of fire sprinklers, especially now when all the streets in the French Quarter have been dug up for relaying. As one local magazine put it, the area has been ravished in preparation for next year's World's Fair, and, though I think they meant 'ravaged', they've captured the right mix of eagerness and dread with which the New Orleanians are greeting that event.

One of the houses I should hate most to see go is Gallier House, named after the architect who built it in 1857 with such modern gimmicks as hot and cold running water. Having finished his own house, he proceeded to build the French Opera House, which for decades was the centre of social life.

'It was still standing when I was a little girl,' said the old lady who took us round. 'I shall always remember it because my mother promised to take me to my first opera one Saturday, but I never got there.'

Why not?

'It burnt down the Wednesday before, 4 December 1919.'

Dans le quartier

The French Quarter of New Orleans is everything the name suggests; it's about one-quarter French. The rest is Spanish, American and Creole, and it adds up to the sort of place where you can wander through all day long without getting bored or repeating yourself.

I wasn't expecting this. I was expecting a few quaint street corners with a few quaint balconies, the whole scene set to music by a few quaint jazz bands – not an extensive township. The reason for this, I now realize, is that whereas some landmarks, such as the Giants' Causeway, look bigger and better in photographs than in real life, places like the French Quarter which depend on accidental town planning and a quiet scale never look very good in detail, just as it's impossible to photograph the back streets of Venice or Greenwich Village.

The balconies, for instance. They're different from other balconies not just because they're more ornate – although they are – but because they're bigger and therefore can actually be used for doing things on.

Most balconies on old houses in London are not for human occupancy – they're just about big enough for a couple of geraniums holding their breath – but you have to crunch your way around New Orleans for a while until you realize that people have on their balconies tropical plantations, barbecues, restaurant overflows, sunbathing areas, storage places and reading rooms.

They are also useful for sheltering under during New Orleans rainstorms, which fall by the inch rather than the raindrop. I always used to wonder why the men in New Orleans brass band parades were shown waving umbrellas as they danced crazily down the street. I now realize that lugging my oversize umbrella across the Atlantic, bringing strained smiles to the TWA stewardesses' faces, was the best thing I could have done.

The worst downpour we encountered defeated even the umbrella and we were blown indoors into a small bar called The Clinic, where a nurse was in attendance ready to pour healing liquids out of hundreds of different bottles.

'I'd like to try a typical New Orleans drink which isn't sweet,' I said. They have a fiendishly sweet tooth here. The Hurricane, the local cocktail, is as syrupy as tinned fruit salad, their Beignets are showered in icing sugar and the Ramos gin fizz is like shaving foam in texture and taste.

'Give him a Sazarec,' said a man at the counter.

'Honey,' said the nurse, 'I ain't never made a Sazarec. Whenever I'm asked for one I say I'm fresh out of the ingredients.'

'I'll show you,' said the man. 'Take some crushed ice...'

Between them they took ten minutes having fun working up a Sazarec. Then we all tasted it. Mmm. A bit liquoricey, but not bad. They spent another ten minutes telling us which restaurants to go to, another ten which restaurants not to go to, then the rain stopped and we set off into the steaming streets, crunching onwards. This was way off the beaten track, or, to put it another way, more than five minutes from Bourbon Street. The tourists don't like to venture very far from Bourbon Street, which leaves a lot of French Quarter for discerning people like you and me. There's a lot of Chelsea which isn't on the King's Road.

Today it's as hot and blue as a prize English summer day, and we've been using the balconies to get some shade, as we crunch our way into the deepest, unexplored French Quarter. I say crunch, because the infill they use for the roads here is not gravel or sand, it's seashells; piles of tiny white seashells like the outflow from an enormous fish restaurant. With oysters at 25p each and shrimps as common as dirt, you might be forgiven for thinking that New Orleans was an enormous fish restaurant. When asked to sum up life in New Orleans, one famous novelist and native of the city said she thought it was most like drowning very slowly under water. Well, perhaps it is, but what a way to go.

Election '84

When people out here learn I am British, they sometimes nudge me and say they hear that British politics is brightening up these days. I would like to think this meant that the wit and wisdom of Neil Kinnock is infiltrating the American public awareness. But of course they mean what I fear they mean, the Cecil Parkinson affair – that typically British business in which everyone seems to have tried to do everything for the best and ended up making a hash of it, and which is the only piece of British news reported here at all.

The most serious mistake made in the whole sorry story was the newspapers' decision to give it coverage, and that is why I left Britain a week ago, determined to stay in exile until it was all over.

I arrived in Louisiana to find the local politicians doing what politicians should really be doing: attempting to justify their re-election. At the top, they are looking for a new governor; at the bottom, they are looking for new dog-catchers and assistant deputy postmen, and by American law all these posts and everything in between are re-electable. When the inhabitants vote tomorrow they will have to fill in a form as long as an income-tax return, but at least they will then be able to get rid of all the posters which have festooned this fair state almost as badly as fringe posters swamp Edinburgh at Festival time, and you can't get worse than that.

Basically, these posters yield very little information about the candidate. They give the voters their surname, their best passport photograph, one of their nicknames (usually Bud) and the post they hope to be voted into. Political thought is limited to a slogan reading either 'Stand by your man' or 'Time for a change'. After a while I found myself hoping for a variant, such as maybe; 'Hi! I'm Cecil Parkinson! I'm new over here but very experienced!'

The battle to be governor is, for once, extremely interesting, especially as both candidates have been governors before. Ex-governor Edwards, a Democrat, was in office for two terms (eight years) and became very popular, having the kind of expansive personality that voters down here like and which tends to override any rumours of inefficiency or even corruption. Not being able to run for a third consecutive term he withdrew gracefully, but the ensuing scramble for his safe seat was so ungraceful and so clearly fixed that most of the Democrats did something unheard of: they rallied behind the Republican candidate, Treen, who became the first Republican governor since the Civil War.

Treen has been sober and industrious. He has also, unfortunately, presided over a collapse in the local oil industry so that the state finances, through no particular fault of his own, have slid from surplus to deficit. Now Edwards is fighting him to come back as governor and, although the polls show them neck-and-neck, there seems to be a feeling that the colourful Edwards can squeeze in ahead of the unflamboyant Treen.

Louisiana, remember, is the state that had the legendary Huey Long as governor in the 1930s. Everyone knew he was a crook and everyone seemed to love him. Going farther back, it is significant that under French domination Louisiana was inefficient, corrupt and cheerful, while as a Spanish possession it was very well run indeed in a quiet sort of way. What is significant about this is that the Spanish history is always played down, and that the French are given credit for almost everything the Spaniards did.

So have a look at the election result, come Sunday or Monday, and see whether Louisiana has gone back to its old colourful ways. Assuming, of course, that Mr Parkinson is not still dominating the headlines and crowding out the real news. If he has been relegated to yesterday's news, then I shall be able to come back. The trouble is out here that no British news ever gets through and I may be here for life. Actually, I'm not sure I'd mind that very much.

The Guinness Book of Louisiana

The Americans have the lovable habit of always claiming the biggest or deepest this or that, but in Louisiana it is at its most lovable. I'm writing these words in Baton Rouge, which has the tallest state capitol in America, built by Huey Long, who was probably the most colourful state governor of all time, and certainly the most interesting to be assassinated during 1935. As if this were not enough, the guidebook claims that 'while the Baton Rouge area is known for its petrochemical industries and the busy port, many people don't know that the city is also a producer of extra fine quality dirt', a reference to local gravel and not to Louisiana's politics.

Morgan City, on the edge of the Gulf of Mexico, does not look like an obvious tourist attraction, but this does not prevent the tour guide from telling you that 'Morgan City has it all: seafood, boats, oil and charm', which is another way of saying that it is an oil harbour with restaurants. It is the only city I have ever met which has an annual Shrimp and Petroleum Festival. It also has three world firsts to its credit – in 1947 it launched the very first offshore oil drill, in 1933 the first jumbo shrimp was landed here and in 1917 it was the location of the world's first Tarzan movie. Morgan City is the stuff of which quiz questions are made.

So is Thibodaux, a Cajun town which boasts America's largest volunteer fire department, with more than 500 voluntary firemen and, I would guess, not nearly enough fires to go round.

New Iberia, another Cajun town enriched by oil, has what seem to be the deepest salt deposits in the state, as well as the world's only tabasco sauce factory. But its most amazing possession is a Roman statue, fully 7 ft tall, of the Emperor Hadrian. Quite why the Iberia Savings & Loan Association decided to buy it is not entirely clear. But there he stands in a glass case, fully air-conditioned and surrounded by ferns. As the guidebook puts it, New Iberia boasts the only full-length statue of the Emperor Hadrian anywhere in the USA, a claim which is unlikely to be contested in our lifetime.

Some of Louisiana's claims are complicated by the American fondness for moving houses around the landscape. There is a house in north-east Louisiana which was built in 1722 and was believed to be the oldest structure in north-east Louisiana if not the whole of the Mississippi Basin. Last week its new owner moved it to New Iberia, so it is now the oldest house in south-west Louisiana, and the north-eastern record is held by some younger house.

Unfortunately, during the move the 60-tonne weight of the house proved too much for a small country bridge (weight limit $2\frac{1}{2}$ tonnes) and the bridge collapsed. For a while it was the oldest house sitting in a river anywhere in the world.

Personally, I am most impressed by Louisiana's drinking laws, which are not so well publicized in the guidebook. Whereas most states will take you out and have you shot if you have so much as an opened bottle in your car, the people of Louisiana can quite legally drink and drive at the same time, by which I mean with the wheel in one hand and a bottle in the other. Last Sunday an inhabitant was spotted driving home from the football game in New Orleans with a beer in one hand, the wheel in another and his left leg dangling out of the window. It was a good thing the New Orleans Saints lost. If they'd won he would have had both legs out of the window.

If you're not driving or you're too drunk to remember where your car is, it's also the only state where you can legally walk along the street night and day with a drink in your hand.

Even at Restaurant Jonathan, about the smartest and best eating place in New Orleans, the waiters' reaction to our failure to polish off a bottle of white wine was to offer us two 'go-cups' so we could finish the wine in the street. No wonder Louisiana likes to be known as 'the Dream State'. The only problem is where you'll be when you wake up.

Where did all the music go?

New Orleans may be the birthplace of jazz, but there are other, younger kinds of music to which it has given birth. There is a kind of rhythm 'n' blues which came out of this city in the 1950s and 1960s, lighter and more piano dominated than northern varieties, that commands as devoted adherents as New Orleans jazz ever did. The most famous practitioner is Fats Domino, but there are others, less worldwide, local stars such as the late Professor Longhair and a current hero, pianist James Booker, who managed to be spectacularly ill during a recent concert without losing any sound. When you tell the cognoscenti that you are off to New Orleans, it isn't the jazz they tell you to keep an eye on, it's the rhythm 'n' blues scene.

All, however, is not well. Fats Domino is virtually an exile from his own city. He touches base about once a year for a reunion concert with the faithful and spends the rest of the time more profitably on the road. And audiences at club performances by lesser men are not what they should or ever used to be; club owners now complain that there are very few groups who can fill a place even at weekends and that they have to hire two or even three groups on one evening to guarantee a sell-out.

Two of the city's most popular nightspots closed recently with financial problems; they put the blame in varying proportions on cable TV, lack of exposure on unadventurous local radio, new rock discos, the tendency of bands to price themselves out of the market and even on crime in the streets.

One of the top remaining spots is a bar called Tipitina's, a sweaty echoing kind of place with minimal decor, a kind of rock 'n' roll version of the 100 Club in Oxford Street, and when I went there to see the Radiators, a very good local rock 'n' roll band, the audience certainly didn't seem big enough to cover any kind of outlay and the band played correspondingly loud to fill the empty spaces. Only one or two bands, like the locally famous Neville Brothers, can be relied upon to get the place really full and steaming.

The biggest crowd I saw for any musical event here was a full turn-out in the huge Saenger Theatre for a blues evening featuring Bobby Bland, B.B. King and Millie Jackson. Among the several thousand people I saw only about a dozen white faces; this was the black community turning out to greet its heroes, yet it seemed to be a case of celebrating past achievements more than anything new. B.B. King played and sang well enough, but both he and Bland, whose name is extremely apt, looked like two middle-aged spreading gentlemen going through their past hits. There was much more clapping at the start of numbers than at the end. Millie Jackson, much younger, seemed intent mainly on proving that a woman can talk as dirty as a man, which seemed to go down well with most present except my neighbour, who shouted unavailingly: 'Wash your mouth out, girl!'

The only local radio station which can be relied upon to present a full range of adventurous music is WWOZ, which the other night claimed to have heard an excellent evening of Ethiopian reggae at Tipitina's. A pity there were so few people there, it said. And it may be that there are just too many kinds of music in this still very musical town to win all the audiences needed for survival. There is every kind of jazz, blues, rock 'n' roll, country music and reggae, which is known better in New Orleans than most parts of the USA.

One kind of music that seems on the increase is Cajun. This simple but attractive music, sung in French patois and dominated by violins and accordions, is creeping into the cities from the bayous, and sounds far better in the flesh than its repetitive image on record might suggest. Clifton Chenier, a black star of the music, filled Tipitina's last Saturday. On Thursday I heard Boure, a group named after a favourite Cajun card game, at the Maple Leaf, where they created a wonderful evening of hooting and dancing.

The impressive thing was that the band, apart from one grizzled fiddler, was very young, and that the equally young crowd were dancing correct steps – a kind of jive mixed with country two-step. Musically it can hardly be called a step forward, but it is hard not to be carried away by the stomping country rhythm and the lilting waltzes, not to mention the refreshing lack of decibels. The other day I even heard a Cajun version of 'When the Saints Come Marching In'. It was the first time in twenty years I had found myself enjoying this hammy old tune.

Alligators and Annie Miller

Before I ever left London, I was told to make sure I went on Annie Miller's swamp tour. In New Orleans they said I shouldn't miss Annie Miller's swamp tour. Now, in Houma, I've been on Annie Miller's swamp tour and I'm here to tell you not to miss it. Or, in the words of the man from Oklahoma sitting next to me in the boat: 'I've driven all round the States and this is the best thirty dollars' worth I've had anywhere, yes, sir.'

First, though, you have to get it into your head that Terrebonne parish, this last bit of America before you fall into the Gulf of Mexico, is wet, very wet indeed. Twenty-five per cent of the parish (elsewhere it would be called a county) is land. Seventy-five per cent is water: swampland, floating marshes, lakes, bogs. Through it all run the bayous, slow-moving rivers that flow down to the sea and which for a long time provided more reliable local highways than any road. Annie Miller, a veteran trapper, hunter, character, even commercial pilot, has two fast boats moored alongside her bayou home and makes a living showing people the recesses of the swamps that she knows better than anyone. Even the alligators come when they hear her voice, it's said, though this seems unlikely.

What makes Annie special as a guide is that she loves showing people her world, and gets excited each time she goes out. Late afternoon is the best time, when the birds are coming back from their feeding grounds – long-legged snowy egrets, spindly herons, hawks, exotic ibises – but she never knows quite what will turn up. Today she thinks it's just possible we might see a pair of bald eagles, more likely we'll spot a nutria. 'Nutria is a South American animal. A man near here brought seven back as pets, but they broke free during a hurricane and multiplied in the swamps. Everyone said they were a pest as they love eating the roots of sugar cane, but then they found they made good fur and now they're not a pest any more. There's a nest right up here that I know of.'

We glide past the nest. It's empty. But in the first tall trees back of the swamp we see bald eagles, enormous even a hundred yards away, sitting motionless like king and queen of the bayou beside their tree-top nest which looks as big as an exploded raft. You feel they haven't begun to recognize the arrival of man in their land.

'Although it's the national bird of America it's pretty rare now. They have a wingspan of about eight feet. They live about thirty years and once they choose a mate they keep together for life.'

'That makes it a mighty strange bird to choose as an American symbol,' says the cynical cameraman. We have a film crew on board, doing a last day's shooting on a swamp opera called *The Horror from Boogalusa Bayou* or some such. What they're looking for is shots of animals fleeing in terror. They'd like to fire a gun in the air to get the eagles going. Annie puts her foot firmly on that idea. Next, we pass some marsh birds very close to. The producer claps his hands while the camera turns, ready for the flight.

'Never saw those birds fly in my life,' Annie mutters to herself.

We shoot out from under the Spanish moss and past the beautiful lilac water hyacinths ('brought here in 1884 by a kindly Japanese visitor to the New Orleans World Cotton Fair,' says Annie, 'and been multiplying ever since – now their roots *are* a pest'), into an enormous canal about 300 ft across. It's the Intracoastal Waterway, taking ships of any size from Texas to New Jersey if that's where you want to go. We overtake a cortège of rusty barges, and plunge again into a small bayou, but then turn right into a forgotten lake, where to our surprise Annie stands up and starts calling: 'Baby! Baby!'

Several large alligators immediately swim up to the boat and, if they weren't such fierce creatures, you'd swear they were gamboling round it. Annie feeds them bits of raw chicken off a long stick, and they jump for it. The eyes of the film crew shine.

'Hey, Annie, could you get one to land and then have it run off in terror?'

'Sure, why not?'

We land on a soggy island. A six-foot alligator follows us, and the raw chicken, up the shore. It turns and goes in the water, but not terrified enough for the film crew.

The film crew give up and we go off to watch the return of the birds, who sure enough come wheeling in, white and mysterious, over the waste wetlands of the bayou. The sun goes down like a huge pumpkin, and dusk rolls in. You suddenly feel a million miles from anywhere, and a million years from today.

Me and Alvin Alcorn

'I see Count Basie is coming to town next week,' says Alvin Alcorn. 'I know the Count from way back. I knew him before he led his own band.'

Basie has been leading a band since about 1935, so that's quite a boast. Alvin Alcorn doesn't look old enough to have been playing trumpet since 1930 but he has; as New Orleans old-timers go, he's a young old-timer. He's small and dark and wears thick specs that don't hide mischievous eyes.

'Of course, Count is in a wheelchair now, and plays very sparingly. Leads in numbers, leads out numbers and shouts "One more time" in *April in Paris*, and that's about it. Jerry Adams here, he's our oldest member. Jerry, how about you get a wheelchair, too? Maybe have a wheelchair battle with Count next week, eh?'

Jerry Adams, laughing uproariously, fans his stubby fingers across his double bass as if they were as light as feathers. Jerry has been playing bass in New Orleans for close on a half-century. Thirty-five years ago he gave Clarence Ford, clarinettist and third and last member of the group, his first job. These guys have been playing at least 140 years between them and they are beyond a doubt the best group I have heard in New Orleans. They play every day from 4 to 7 p.m. in the lobby of the Marriott Hotel. A strange place to find them? Alcorn doesn't see why.

'Well, you won't find me playing down Bourbon Street any time. You won't find *anyone* good playing down there,' says Alcorn. 'All the bar owners and club managers think they know best and tell the bands to play tourist music, you know, fast all the time with a back beat. Got a request?'

Anything but 'Basin Street'. Anything but 'The Saints'. I name 'Fine and Dandy' for no good reason. I haven't thought about it for twenty years. They go straight into it, Clarence Ford playing long supple lines on the clarinet, Alcorn's trumpet so far behind the beat you wonder if he'll ever get back and Adams's bass dancing easily along. Some of the crowd at the lobby cocktail bar listen, some don't even know the music is there. When a pretty waitress passes by, Ford blows a dirty note on the clarinet and winks.

The Marriott is part of a huge American chain of hotels. In every bedroom you will find three books: a Gideon Bible, a Book of Mormon and the life of the founder, Mr Marriott. It still seems an unlikely place to find jazz, until you realize that the hotels in New

Orleans compete to buy the best jazz talent. The Hilton even has a floor named after the resident Pete Fountain.

'Haven't played "Fine and Dandy" in thirty years,' says Jerry Adams. 'Still remember it, though. Got any other challenges?'

'Jerry's brother, Placide, leads a band at the Hilton,' says Alcorn. 'My son, Sam, plays for the jazz brunch at Arnaud's Restaurant, *very* smart place. Yes, we've got relations all over. Stay here six months and you can be a relation.'

Although a New Orleans musician, Alcorn played in big bands most of his life and has no very fond memories of those days. One-night stands, hotels, buses, fatigue and not much money. Not much chance to make himself heard either, which may be why he has gone to the other extreme and relapsed into a trio, with no piano, drums or guitar.

'Don't need them. I can *hear* them all in my head. Funny thing is, when I play with drums now they sound too loud. I have been playing with this trio here at the Marriott for six years and I really like it – we play for the ones that listen, and the ones that don't listen, that doesn't bother me. Got any more requests?'

'"Some of These Days"?'

'OK,' says Jerry. 'We only played it three times already today. One more won't hurt any. And after that, seeing as you play bass, you can sit in for a couple of numbers.'

And I do, scared to death, and I survive the experience, and Alvin Alcorn says to be sure to carry his compliments to his old friends Chris Barber and Acker Bilk, and to come back to the Marriott next time I'm in Louisiana.

'Sure you'll be back in Louisiana. *Everyone* comes back to Louisiana.'

Farewell to New Orleans

'Unlawful to Litter the Highway', say the strict signs along the Louisiana roads. They could make a fortune out of fining the sugar industry then, because this time of year the highway is littered with sugar canes fallen from the huge farm trucks as the two-month-long sugar harvest begins. Some places it's so thick you seem to be driving on sugar matting. The canes are about nine foot high, but half of that is leaves, which are burnt off the fields...

Irate reader: Look, you've been writing non-stop about Louisiana for two weeks now. Can't you give it a rest? You're turning into Channel 4.

Me: Sorry, but it's a fascinating place. I wasn't expecting to find lizards all over New Orleans, or dragonflies flying down the middle of Canal Street, or to come face to face with alligators...

Irate reader: Don't tell me it's the alligator season too.

Me: No, that's just finished. Oddly enough, the alligator was a protected animal until two or three years ago, but now it's multiplying so much you can go out and shoot them in September. And then eat them. Fresh alligator meat is amazingly good – firm, white, meaty, with a vague tinge of fish.

Irate reader: Fat lot of good that is to a reader in London.

Point taken. The only answer is to go to Louisiana yourself, and see the acceptable face of America. A lady in Baton Rouge said sadly to me that she hated the way it was so much easier to export the junk side of the United States than the quality side; her heart had fallen when she arrived in London to find MacDonalds and Burger King all over the place, not classy Creole cooking, or indeed just plain good American home cooking.

She's right. I never expected to walk into a plain eating house like Gino's in a plain town like Houma, and sample in one meal fried alligator, huge frog legs, soft-shell crab (you eat the shell as well as the crab) and the best pizza in the world. It is Gino's own recipe for shrimp and crab pizza and it should be exported all over the world.

'We're working on it,' says Gino laconically. 'Had a Japanese customer in here once, and we now send a regular pizza order to Tokyo. It's a start, anyway.'

Nor had I expected Avery Island. Not an island now, but a small hill near New Iberia which sits on top of a salt deposit five miles deep. Here a hundred years ago Mr McIlhenny grew peppers, mixed them with salt for three years, added vinegar and called the result Tabasco sauce, and to this day all the Tabasco in the world comes from one factory on Avery Island. With his money McIlhenny turned the rest of the island into the most enchanting gardens you could imagine, full of bamboo, huge oaks, snowy egrets, camellias and, yes, alligators. I have never been anywhere quite so calm, in America or not.

Nor had I expected to encounter Nottoway, the biggest plantation home in the state, lovingly restored by two young men called Arlin Dease and Steve Saunders until it is now again the 64-room birthday cake staring at the Mississippi which was first completed in 1859, including a small ballroom for the daughters' use. I had not expected to meet Alex Patout, young chef at Patout's, a Cajun restaurant in New Iberia, and to find that a few months previously he had been up in Williamsburg cooking for the heads-of-state dinner which Mrs Thatcher was forced to miss 'due to the fact that she had to go home to be re-elected'. You missed a great dinner, Mrs T.

All these things, and many more, whether taking place against the cricket-loud Louisiana countryside or the soft nights of New Orleans where the crickets are replaced by music, would easily make an article each.

Irate reader: But you won't, will you? Back to humour next week, eh?

Me: All right. But I'll have to write about it somewhere. Louisiana is the sort of place you have to tell people about.

Irate reader: Believe me, I get the point.

Me: Thank you.

The Brillig Sleep

Interactive literature is the name of the new game: letting the reader rewrite a book in the author's words. As usual, Moreover Enterprises are one step ahead of the game – we're computing famous works in other *authors' words.*

Interested? Here's a small sample for you which the computer did in its sleep last night: Raymond Chandler's version of 'Jabberwocky'.

'Twas brillig. It had been that way all day, and it wasn't getting any cooler. I had loosened my neck-tie so many times that the knot had worked its way down to my navel. Outside in the street the first lights had come on and the slithy toves were doing whatever they do in the wabe. Some days they gyre, some days they gimble. It's no skin off my nose, but I wish they'd make their minds up, then we could all rest easy.

Five o'clock, and I still had no customer. The paper cup on my desk looked dry, so I eased some Bourbon into it. I heard a screech of brakes outside; some mome rath had decided to outgrabe and was paying for it. The pot of borogoves on my window-sill looked a little mimsy, so I poured half the Bourbon down my throat and the other half into the pot, figuring that it would be nice to share a drink with someone, even if only a borogove.

Then there was a knock at the door. I emerged from uffish thought and told the owner of the knock to come and join me. The door opened and there stood a young man with money written all over his face, the sort of nervous young man who has grown up in the shadow of a millionaire father and dreads the moment when Daddy tells him to take over.

'Mr Marlowe?'

I owned up. There was no law against being Mr Marlowe.

'I need your help. My father has asked me to deal with the Jabberwock, and I simply don't know how to go about it. You know the Jabberwock?'

Everyone knew the Jabberwock. It was a club on Ocean Parade, the sort where you went in rich and came out poor. They had a singer there called Jubjub who was reputed to eat men for breakfast and if being eaten for breakfast is your idea of a good time, then she was the girl to get in touch with. Personally, I prefer wrestling with anacondas.

'I'm engaged to be married to a girl called Jubjub. My father disapproves and ... do you know what this is?'

He put down a large gold coin on my desk. I looked at it. It was a large gold coin.

'It's a bandersnatch,' I said. 'Only a hundred are known to exist. They're very valuable, except when they're frumious, and then they're very valuable indeed. This one is frumious. What's it got to do with the Jabberwock?'

To cut a long story short, I went out to the Jabberwock that night, killed the owner, warned off Jubjub, did some burbling and went galumphing back. The young man wasn't best pleased by my solution, but his father seemed to like the way things had turned out. Frabjous, he called it. He even embraced his beamish boy, and you could tell from the latter's expression that this hadn't happened in a long while.

'I don't know how to thank you, Marlowe,' he said, chortling slightly.

'Don't bother,' I said. 'Just leave me the bandersnatch.'

He did, and they both left, hand in hand. It's always nice to reunite father and son, even if it means leaving old Marlowe alone with a pot of borogoves. I poured myself a measure of Bourbon and listened to the toves gyring outside. Maybe they were gimbling. It's hard to tell, especially when you don't give a damn either way. I ran a finger round my collar. 'Twas brillig. The borogoves looked mimsy on the window-sill. I gave them the ice and took all the Bourbon myself.

Unusual jobs: no. 6

X is a soft-spoken man of about forty. He works in the City, under a different name, as a stockbroker. About once a month he organizes and pulls off a bank raid. Afterwards, he gives all the money to charity.

'It started about four years ago,' he told me over a pint at the Marquis of X, a well-known pub in ECX. 'I was doing a stint for a local charity, holding a collecting tin in the High Street – Lifeboat Week, probably, as I seem to remember wearing a yellow cape. Anyway, I'd been there all morning when suddenly there was an armed raid at a nearby post office, so quick that I never saw a thing apart from a traffic warden being coshed over the head, but that's quite normal in the stockbroker belt.

'Anyway, I read afterwards that the thieves had got away with £50,000. And I couldn't help reflecting that my collecting tin had amassed a total of £16.70, including several Belgian francs and a luncheon voucher. The more I thought about the unfairness of this, and the more I thought what a lot of good £50,000 could do, the more I secretly found myself wondering about the possibility of switching from collecting tins to shotguns.'

X's first raid was on the local office of the X Building Society. He was quite nervous, but only because he often played golf with the building society manager and didn't want to be recognized. Otherwise he was totally calm.

'I think that if you know your crime is in a good cause, you do stay calm. You don't feel like a criminal. You collect the money and hand it over as soon as possible to a good cause, and then forget about it. That first time, I made the mistake of trying to keep things clean by signing a receipt for the money, because even building societies have to keep their books straight, but luckily I signed it X, and filled in a little box saying 'Does not want publicity', so they never connected it to me.

'The most dangerous bit, actually, is getting the money to the charity. Annually I donate about two million pounds more than I actually earn, so if it is linked with me there might be some awkward questions asked. For that reason I prefer to give the money anonymously. Whenever you read of some large sum given to buy a painting for Britain, or as a donation to an educational institution, and the donor prefers to remain unknown, that's usually me.'

X has never kept a penny of his proceeds except to cover the costs of stationery and parking fines. He has no qualms.

'The money I take from the banks would only be lent to Brazil or Poland and never be seen again. I like to think I am reinvesting the money wisely. Incidentally, where do they keep the cash at *The Times*?'

I said I didn't think they had any at *The Times*, made an excuse and left.

Come to lovely Vertigo!

Although after ten days in Spain my Spanish was coming back fast, the only person there I really understood well was a man with a cleft palate.

He lives on the cliff face at Ronda. Ronda, like its Welsh near namesake, is famous for its valley, which divides in half the 500 ft high sheer cliff on which the town stands, and if you can visualize somewhere like Chester coming right to the edge of Beachy Head, but surrounded by some Grampians instead of the sea, you begin to get the idea. If you can further visualize a man with a cleft palate and a vegetable garden living half-way down Beachy Head, then we're almost there.

The Ronda valley is spanned by a stone bridge 40 ft across and 500 ft up. The only time I ever saw my father on the Clifton Suspension Bridge he walked straight down the middle, preferring the risk of being run over to falling off, and I think I must have inherited his gift for vertigo, as I found myself walking from new Ronda to old Ronda across the bridge, among the cars. It's not that I'm afraid I'm going to fall off, just that I have this subconscious desire to jump off and fly like a bird.

'Let's take this path down the cliff,' said Caroline, pointing to a track which led into thin air. By the time I had disagreed she had already disappeared down it, so I followed and caught her up opposite a gate bearing a sign: '*Prohibido El Paso*'.

'Roughly translated,' I said, 'that means that walkers are advised to turn back here for fear of being tempted to launch themselves into space.'

Before my plan could take root, the little man with the cleft palate appeared on the other side of the gate and smilingly asked me if the senora with the camera would care to come through the gate and down his garden so that she could get a magnificent view of the bridge and the town. Amazed, I understood every word he said. This was because his cleft palate forced him to speak very slowly so that his fellow-Spaniards could understand him. As a result, he was the only person I met in Spain who spoke Spanish at the same speed as me.

His garden, which slopes rapidly to the edge of the void, grows lettuces, artichokes, almond trees and a small mad dog, tied up. I remember all this because I had a most detailed horticultural conversation with him in cleft Spanish. I wasn't sure, you see, whether he was just a nice old man getting lonely in his garden or a notorious assassin who lured travellers to the edge and pushed them over, descending later to remove their pesetas and cameras. So while Caroline leant on the brink and snapped away at the truly remarkable view of Ronda, I held him in debate, tensing myself for the moment when he would try to push her over.

It never came. Instead, I learnt that he had lived in this little house for sixty years, had been born there in fact. I learnt all about the best time to plant artichokes, and why. I learnt that nobody had ever fallen off the top of Ronda cliffs, but that plenty of people had jumped. No accidents, many suicides, he said. Why? *Estan locos*, he said, tapping his head. Nonsense, I thought – they all succumbed to a desire to fly. Not only did he speak the clearest Spanish I ever heard, he was less afraid of heights than any man I ever met.

He seemed sorry to see us go, and waved till we were out of sight. Later, from the bridge, we looked down on his house and garden stuck to the cliff like a house martin's nest, with the old man a mere dot in it, and I realized how close I had come to achieving flight. Still, at least I had learnt the Spanish word for artichoke and I used it proudly that very night in the restaurant, when ordering vegetables.

The waiter hadn't the faintest idea what I was talking about.

'I'm not surprised,' said Caroline. 'You're speaking the word with a cleft palate.'

The next day we visited la Cueva de Pileta, a deep cave reaching 500 metres into the hillside, full of prehistoric paintings, bats, amazing limestone formations and stone age camps. I recommend this cavern whole-heartedly. It's impossible to throw yourself off it.

Euroquiz

For those of you voting today for a Eurocandidate and still not quite sure what Europe is all about, or indeed quite where it is, here are all the facts you need to know.

Q. What is involved in voting for a Euro-MP?
A. It's exactly the same as voting for your normal MP.
Q. But I have no idea what a Euro-MP does, or what he is meant to do, or where he is when I need him.
A. As I said, it's just like voting for your normal MP.
Q. What is Europe?
A. Europe is a group of countries who have decided to make the regulations for the next war so hard to follow that it will probably never happen.
Q. What has been the result so far?
A. A lot of butter and a lot of paper.

Q. What is the butter for?

A. It is our main weapon against Russia. If the Soviet Union should ever declare war on us, they know we would drop a million tonnes of butter on them. This would ruin their diet and they would all die agonized, lingering deaths.

Q. What if Russia doesn't declare war?

A. We shall have to think of a new use for butter.

Q. When Greece joined the EEC, did they have any new ideas for butter?

A. No, but we now have a mount of olives.

Q. What is the basic idea behind the Treaty of Rome?

A. The idea, basically, is: when in Brussels, do as the Germans do.

Q. Why did Britain join the EEC?

A. To unite the French and Germans against us and make the next war impossible.

Q. I thought the answer was: to introduce a refreshing dollop of common sense and compromise.

A. Yes, but unfortunately Mrs Thatcher has spoilt all that.

Q. Why does Europe featherbed the farmers and not the industrialists?

A. Because farmers can at least produce butter, but all industry produces is acid rain.

Q. Couldn't you use the acid rain to get rid of the butter?

A. Not if it means Geoffrey Cannon writing an angry book about it.

Q. Has anyone ever left the Common Market?

A. Yes, Greenland.

Q. Was this a good or a bad thing?

A. Good, because we lost a blubber mountain. Bad, because the Common Market is now half the size it was and much easier for Russia to invade.

Q. Why on earth would Russia want to capture Europe?

A. As a nice going-away present for Mr Chernenko.

Q. Why wouldn't the EEC admit Britain under a committed European like Mr Heath?

A. Because when they heard him trying to speak French, they said: 'Mon dieu, if this is what a committed European from Britain sounds like, what must the others be like?'

Q. Why has Russia never invaded Europe?

A. Because they know all the roads would be blocked with French lorries.

Q. How much paper does the EEC produce every year?
A. Enough to wrap all the butter in Europe.
Q. Why is the EEC centre sometimes in Brussels, sometimes Luxembourg, Strasbourg or Rome, but never anywhere in Britain?
A. I'm not sure, I think it's something to do with our football supporters.
Q. Why should I vote for a Euro-MP today?
A. So you can say you were the only person in your town to do so.
Q. Which party should I vote for?
A. If you are against Europe, for Labour. If you are for Europe, for the Alliance. If you couldn't care less either way, for the Tories.
Q. And if I'm passionately pro-Europe?
A. Go out and buy some butter.

The numbers game

Have you noticed that there are some numbers that never change? Eleven million dollars, for instance. That is the amount for which Americans sue each other. When an American has an unhappy life and decides to sue his mother for it, or falls over and sues the man who invented pavements, it is always for $11M. Why this happens is unknown, especially as they never get any of the money.

Here are some other figures that never change.

Fifty thousand (50,000). The gap between the police estimate of the crowd at a protest rally and the estimate by the organizers.

Four (4). The number of years that elapse between the death of a very famous person and the appearance of a book revealing that he was murdered.

Six (6). The number of times, while sitting in an airport lounge, you take out your passport and ticket, to make sure they're still there, before you decide the whole thing is ridiculous and you put them in a special safe place.

Six (6). The increase in your pulse rate when you realize you've forgotten where the special safe place is.

Two (2). The number of years between an arrest and a trial.

Zero (0). The number of really interesting facts in a book written by a famous politician or a person who used to run any part of the BBC.

Thirteen (13). The number of players who drop out of an England football team before any game, owing to illness, injury, temperament, club commitments in the Far East or having just been sold to a club in Italy.

Ten (10). The number of days in a centenary year. Human beings seem incapable of celebrating a famous person for any longer. Even 1984, which was supposed to be a year-long scrutiny of George Orwell's novel, could hardly improve on this; there was no mention of George Orwell after late January.

Three (3). The number of serious candidates who present themselves for the post of Poet Laureate. One of these is always an elderly poet who would be perfect for the job if it were not that he has given up poetry long ago, and would not accept the job. One is the poets' choice, whom nobody else has ever heard of. And one is a light poet whom everyone wants to get the job, but is not given it for that very reason. The successful candidate is always a rank outsider.

One hundred (100). West Indian fast bowlers are always said to bowl at 100 m.p.h. Modern statisticians now suspect that they also take 100 paces in order to do so.

Three billion (3 and lots of noughts). The number of pounds by which any government spending estimate is exceeded.

Ten (10). The number of articles every year in *The Times* discussing how many noughts there are in a billion.

Two hundred thousand (200,000). The number of pounds sterling given to a departing executive as a reward for being no longer competent to run a company.

Two and a half thousand (2,500). The difference, in pounds sterling, between what you sell your house for and the money you have left afterwards.

Ten (10). The miles per hour by which average traffic flow exceeds any speed limit.

Seven hundred thousand (700,000). The sum which has to be raised in the next fortnight to prevent the export from Britain of a painting said to be part of the national heritage. (A painting is said to be part of the national heritage if it is previously unknown, has been hidden in a private house for 200 years, and was painted by an Italian.)

Nature Corner, with urban naturalist 'Bin Liner'

Today: the supermarket trolley

The supermarket trolley is a comparatively recent newcomer to our shores (writes Bin-Liner). Until about twenty years ago it was unknown, but a large-scale immigration pattern from the USA occurred until quickly it became a familiar sight in our supermarkets and larger groceries, where it was kept in captivity.

What has happened recently to alert naturalists' attention is that the trolley has started to break out of captivity and live in the wild. It is almost impossible these days to go for a walk in our suburbs or inner town areas without coming across one or more of these large creatures browsing quietly on a traffic island or just standing peacefully on the pavement. So far we have been totally baffled by this new behaviour pattern.

The phenomenon is quite common in old-fashioned rural nature studies, of course, where an import such as mink or coypu later escapes from captivity and inhabits vast stretches of East Anglia. But this is the first time it has happened to a purely urban creature. Nor has it happened to such close relations as the British Rail trolley or airport trolley, which very rarely stray far from their home. Only the supermarket trolley seems driven by the urge to escape.

Quite why it should want to do so is not clear, especially as it is totally unadapted to life in the wild. Its daily diet involves a considerable intake of washing powder boxes, packets of flour, frozen fish fingers, etc., and this it simply will not find out on our city streets. Many of them, I'm afraid to say, starve to death after only a few days and meet a tangled and rusty end, unless recaptured by their owners. And yet they persist in escaping.

Some larger stores such as Sainsbury's have tried a programme of keeping the trolleys chained up when not being taken for a walk yet even here they have met failure and have been forced to give up the idea, as if the trolley's drive to freedom is too strong for chains.

Professor Karelius, in *Urban Nature Studies*, Vol. XI, No. 6, puts forward the interesting theory that trolleys somehow develop a strong if temporary affection for visitors to supermarkets and try to follow them home. He even cites cases of families who have adopted a trolley as a pet and let it live in their house with them – in one or two cases the trolley has changed its diet entirely and takes only newspapers or the family laundry.

If this is so, however, it still does not explain why so many trolleys are found in the street, having patently not followed anyone home. He suggests that this may be because families grow tired of their demands or their great size compared with most household pets, and simply throw them out on the street as they might an unwanted dog or cat. If this is so, we certainly need more documented evidence than he provides.

My own personal theory is that the supermarket trolley's burst for freedom is prompted by an urge to inter-breed. If a well-known species such as a Tesco trolley finds itself surrounded entirely by other Tesco trolleys, it may well have an innate compulsion to search out and mate with, say, a Safeways or Fine Fare trolley, in order to keep the pedigree well mixed. Having said this, however, I must admit that I have no evidence to support it; I just happen to like the idea.

As a final postscript to these notes I must report a very rare sighting spotted last month: a fully operating, adult in-flight trolley seen in West London. These are normally only ever seen inside airplanes, where they have been trained to carry loads of miniature spirits, small hot lunches, duty-free cigarettes, etc. This trolley, spotted near West Drayton, had, perhaps predictably, lost all its load of drink and cigarettes. None of the hot lunches, however, had been touched.

Slow food special

At last!

A diet which really is different!

Yes, Moreover Laboratories have devised a new plan for eating and living which will put back the bloom on your cheeks, take pounds off your waist and make you wonder why your weighing machine seems to have gone wrong.

You don't have to count calories, refuse seconds or even cut down on fat.

All you have to do is stick to inconvenience foods.

What are inconvenience foods? Well, a packet of ready shelled peanuts is a convenience food, but a paper bag of peanuts in the shell is an inconvenience food. When you rip open a packet of peanuts, you can get through them in a couple of minutes. But when you have to shell each peanut individually, it takes far longer, you have much more fun – and you eat far fewer for the same satisfaction!

That's because you've given your stomach time to send back those signals which say: No more just now, thank you. Signals which the ready-to-munch packet of peanuts don't give the stomach time to send.

The Moreover Damn-Difficult-Diet chart tells you which foods will give you a hard time – and make you feel better for it. Pistachio nuts in the shell, for instance – you will spend most of your time trying to insert your finger-nail in a gap too small for it. Or Brazil nuts – hitting a nut with a hammer and then looking for the bits can't be fattening, can it?

Other high-quality inconvenience foods include all small game birds which contain more bones than meat (as a rough guide, anything beginning with p or q, such as quail, ptarmigan, pigeon or plover). All white fish which present a bone problem and which require hours of dissecting. All shellfish such as prawns or shrimps which, by the time you've got off the head, tail, outer casing and funny little bits inside, leave hardly anything to eat. Bigger shellfish like crabs and lobsters, which provide hours of fun with claws that yield nothing.

Vegetables like globe artichoke. Fruits like loquat or pomegranate – all that skin and seeds, and not much else. All these inconvenience foods have several things in common: they're a lot of fun, they're luxury exciting items and they provide precious little to eat. That's why the Moreover Damn-Difficult-Diet is the first one to make you thin while you're enjoying it. Here's a sample breakfast to show you in detail how it works.

Yoghurt and strawberries, followed by sardines on toast.

Make sure you have one of those small yoghurt pots which take ages to get the top off. Wipe the kitchen table after you've fought your way in. Into the remaining yoghurt put four strawberries, from which you have carefully removed the pips. Now, take one of those anonymous small sardine tins whose lid rolls back one centimetre and then refuses to budge. Throw away tin in fury. Eat anything that remains. NB: Wholemeal toast is very important, because the slice tends to remain jammed inside the toaster.

The principle of unwrapping difficulty is very important, by the way. The Moreover Damn-Difficult-Diet allows you to eat as much salt and pepper as you like, as long as you stick to those little airline packs of salt and pepper which have the names in four different languages and not much else, or the tiny cylindrical rolls which you tear the top off, taking most of the salt and pepper with it. And don't forget that this diet allows you to eat as many pork pies as you like, as long as you stick to pork pies wrapped in cellophane where it's impossible to find the outside edge to pull and open.

So send off *now* for your Moreover Damn-Difficult-Diet chart. The diet that puts the fun back into eating food – and takes the food out of it!

You know it makes sense.

Wimbledon – all the dirt

The Duke of Debenture, who won the Left-handed Men's Doubles title back in 1923 and ran Wimbledon for a short time in the 1930s, is still a familiar figure at the All-England Club during tournament fortnight. You can see him from 8 a.m. onwards outside the main gate, shouting: 'Who'll buy my tickets? Lovely tickets! Only ten times the normal price.' He then moves inside to manage his vast strawberry and cream business – all the strawberries sold at Wimbledon came from the Debenture estate – and then late at night stays to help count up the money.

'Don't get much of a chance to see any tennis,' says the 82-year-old Duke. 'Too busy with the money. But that's what tennis is all about – money. Money and rudeness. That's what tennis is about.'

Surely, though, tennis wasn't always about money and rudeness, was it?

'No, certainly not. It used to be about money, rudeness *and* silly clothes. Thank goodness we've eliminated the silly clothes – you know, when I won my title in 1923 I was wearing long trousers, stiff white shirt, bow-tie and white gloves, and the gals used to play in flowing ball-gowns, as I remember. Or am I thinking of the last night dance? Probably am.'

But did money and rudeness really play a part in the behaviour of prewar tennis stars? We have always been given the impression that they paid no attention to the profit motive or gamesmanship.

'Who said anything about the players, you silly little man? It was the officials and governors of the game who were obsessed with making money and keeping the players in their place. I remember an old uncle of mine who, when asked what his main source of income was, said: "Being on the committee at Wimbledon." He gave as his hobby: "Kicking out undesirables at Wimbledon."

'Anyway, this sort of obsession with money and rudeness was bound eventually to rub off on the players, and now it has. That chap McEnroe. Splendid fellow. Reminds me a lot of my uncle.'

The Duke of Debenture has an unusual explanation for the failure of British tennis players to win anything.

'They're not rude enough. When did we last have a player who went on court effing and blinding? They're not angry. All the good players these days go on court swinging at the line-judges with their racquets and aiming kicks at the ball-boys before they've even hit the ball – British players are far too good-mannered for that. They're damned good losers, of course, but they get more practice than anyone else.'

What does the Duke think of the British press's attempt to pry into tennis players' private lives?

'Don't be a little prig, man. You mean these rumours that half the women are lesbians? Doesn't worry me a bit. The more mannish players there are, the better. Can't stand these little blonde schoolgirls who come on court and hit the ball with their hand-bag. Give it a good clout, I say. As long as the lady champion lets the men's champion do all the leading in the last night waltz, I don't care what else she does.'

How, finally, does the Duke see Wimbledon developing in the year to come?

'More money, more rudeness. This year we've branched out a lot into fast food – fish and chips, pizza, that sort of thing. Next year I'm hoping to introduce Wimbledon's first drug stall, cocaine, heroin, etc. Someone's making a lot of money out of that and I would like it to be me. Which reminds me – my interview fee is £250 and I'd like it in used fivers, please.'

Startled, I intimated that my column's policy did not encourage paid interviews. With a speed and strength surprising in one his age, the elderly Duke picked up a tennis racquet and started beating me over the head with it.

Keep the grass off

Have you ever thought about grass? Probably not.

Most of us just take it for granted, like pavements or little old ladies. Yet grass is the most commonly grown crop in Britain.

Makes you think, doesn't it? And we're not just talking about fields full of grass. We're talking about lawns. All those bits of lawn up and down the country. Everyone's lawns. *Your* lawn.

We have added all those lawns together on a computer and they come to an area the size of Yorkshire and Lancashire, plus the Isle of Wight, not including Ventnor. The cricket pitches alone would stretch from London to Birmingham, if laid end to end. That's an awful lot of hectares in anyone's language.

Yet what do we do with these lawns? Unfortunately, what we do with them is cut the grass just when it looks like growing. Yes, every week during the summer we go out and harvest what little grass there is, then throw it away.

It doesn't make sense, does it? Do you see farmers in the wheat field going out once or twice a week to cut down the wheat, and then throw it away?

Nor do you see fruit farmers going out to the orchard just when the new apples are beginning to form, picking them off ruthlessly and chucking them on the compost heap.

So why do we do it to grass? Why do we turn over the major part of our gardens to the cultivation of a crop which we don't even bother to harvest?

The most common answer you hear is: 'To make the place look nice and have somewhere to walk.' Well, in an ideal world this would no doubt be answer enough.

Unfortunately, as you may have heard, this is not an ideal world and we all have to make sacrifices. The sad truth is that there really isn't room in modern Britain for lawns covering Yorkshire, Lancashire and the Isle of Wight (except Ventnor).

Under a new Common Market regulation lawns will gradually be phased out during the next five years and replaced by a crop capable of being harvested and sold at a profit. You will shortly, if you are a lawn-holder, receive a form through the post stating what crop you will grow, and where in Russia to send the harvest.

You must of course comply with this form, which applies to the whole of the EEC, but you do not have to wait for its arrival. You may, if you wish, plough up your lawn now and get it ready for recultivation.

As this scheme will take time to put into operation, many of you will not have to replant your lawn for another year or two. In the interim, however, you *must* resow your lawn with one of the two permitted Common Market grass species, either Megacompost or Tough Mediterranean Dune Grass.

The Megacompost is the growth preferred by the Russians, to whom we sell the bulk of our clippings mountain, and the Dune Grass requires no maintenance at all, being hard to tell from plastic.

From 1986 onwards there will be no more grass grown in Britain except in permitted areas such as traffic roundabouts and bowling greens. Cricket itself will not be banned but will have to be played on some other surface such as concrete or mud as it already is in some tropical countries.

We hope you will cooperate with this change. We hope to avoid all unpleasantness. Failure to comply will lead to huge fines. You have been warned.

An EEC pamphlet. No. 968584635423867564 (a). For extra copies, write to the Pamphlet Mountain, Brussels.

Sell all that you have, and send it to America

If I'd been in the Duke of Devonshire's place the other day, I too would have taken the chance of selling a few drawings for £21M – in fact, I *was* in the Duke of Devonshire's place the other day and that's what I tried to do. Sell a few of his drawings. I got chucked out of the place pretty quick, I can tell you.

Trouble is, I'm in the same boat as he is. I live in a house and have to find the money for the regular upkeep, without even being able to charge the public to come in. I found a chap wandering round my sitting-room yesterday, looking at things. I took him on a tour.

'This is the great drawing-room,' I said. 'This has been in constant use by the Kingtons since the mid-1970s. Note the fine upright piano. Note the first edition of Enid Blyton on the floor, keeping the piano upright. That will be 50p, please.'

'This place isn't worth 50p to look round,' he said. 'Anyway, you can't charge me. I live here.'

I looked closer. My son had grown another two inches overnight. No wonder I feel so poor – all my money goes on buying bits of cloth for him to sew on the end of his shirt-sleeves and make them longer.

'Anyway, if you're feeling skint,' he said, 'why not do what the Duke of Devonshire does, and sell some of the family art treasures.'

'What art treasures?' I said, glancing round the wall and seeing only wallpaper.

'He kept all his locked away in drawers. Why not have a look?'

So I did and Tom was right. We're sitting on a gold mine. I've hardly begun to catalogue it yet, but already things have emerged which I didn't even know I had. The following excerpt from my forthcoming sale gives you just a hint of the riches to come.

Lot 1. A portrait in pencil on paper, entitled 'My Dad', by Tom Kington. A very early work, signed by the artist and guaranteed genuine. 10 × 8 in fine condition, except for ballpoint pen scribbles, also by the artist.

Lot 2. Forty more similar portraits by the same artist, all *circa* 1974.

Lot 3. A genuine signed autographed letter, from the editor of a *very* famous national magazine, written on the stationery of the magazine. The message reads: 'This is not the article I had in mind at all. I am afraid I cannot print it.' It is signed by his secretary.

Lot 4. A genuine (?) letter from the managing director of the *Reader's Digest* (?) stating that I have a wonderful opportunity to win a fantastic prize if only I agree to take the *Reader's Digest* for the rest of my life, pending a medical examination (?).

Lot 5. A genuine letter from my daughter, signed, dated 5 May '84 and in perfect condition. It reads as follows: 'Some wally from the BBC phoned and said why didn't you turn up to the studio? They will have to fix another session. I could hear his ulcer over the phone. PS I won't be in for supper, OK? Soz.' Soz is W11 slang for Sorry, not my daughter's name.

Lot 6. A first edition of a well-known humorous book, also with a publisher's slip stating that this book must not be reviewed before 15 Oct. 1972. Guaranteed unread.

Lot 7. Another letter from my daughter, reading: 'That wally from the BBC phoned again and said, where is the script? PS Sorry I could not make supper last night. Hope to see you soon.'

Lot 8. The carbon copy of this article, with many spelling mistakes not preserved in the final version.

Lot 9. A final letter from my daughter. 'Sorry, but the BBC gremlin phoned again. He says they cannot wait any longer and are going to get Russell Davies instead. PS Where were you at supper last night?'

All this alone must be worth at least £3.50, and there is so much more to come. Why don't *you* look in your drawers tonight?

Does Lichfield really exist?

I waver violently between two opposite approaches to travelling to new places. Sometimes I dutifully do my homework in advance and arrive thoroughly educated, while at other times I arrive totally ignorant, or open-minded, and let first impressions educate me. The further I go afield, the more I tend to read up, so that when I reached Granada last month I felt I knew the place already. When this last weekend I found myself, unprepared, in Lichfield, it was as if I had come to a strange, exotic place.

Now that I've been there, it seems even more strange and exotic. Wandering round the outside of the blackish, reddish cathedral, I paused to stare up at a grotesque gargoyle, shrieking silently into space. 'If you're looking for strange creatures,' said a local, over my shoulder, 'you want to go round the other side. They are really weird there.' So they were – a whole menagerie of devils, griffins and lions, leering and eating smaller stone creatures. The Middle Ages may have been without television, but they had a good supply of exotic documentaries from the Church's natural history unit.

Inside the magnificent cathedral the accent was more on military matters. I do not recall having seen so many battle honours, regimental monuments, roll-calls of those dead in far-off places. India, mostly. The plaques of those who had passed away peacefully in bed seemed almost apologetic that they had not perished in battle.

Next to it was the strangest thing of all, a display board erected by Rackham's of Lichfield, local photographers, showing recent events in colour. A group of smiling Indian women in saris (India again), a great group of cricketers among whom I recognized Lord Lichfield, Ted Moult and Barry Norman and a crowd in front of the cathedral containing about forty double bass players *and an elephant* I never saw anything in Granada like this, nor can I think off-hand of any composer who wrote music for double basses and elephants.

I was in town to take part in a concert belonging to the Lichfield Festival, but our concert was not the main event of the evening. That was a concert given in the cathedral by sitarist Ravi Shankar – India again! The festival director told us that what he had heard of it had been magnificent and that two thirds of the large audience had been Indian.

It will come as no surprise to you to learn that when we looked round for somewhere to eat after our late concert, the three restaurants still open for business were Indian. And yet when we wandered round Lichfield on Sunday morning, admiring the trees and lakes in the middle of this admirable town of mystery, peering at the church-mason's quarter stretching away like some inland boatyard and inspecting the spot where the last public burning in England took place (1612), we didn't see a single Indian face. Where were all the Shankar fans, the sari ladies, the Indian chefs? Where was the elephant trainer? What curious cycle in history was it that took all those Lichfield people to India years ago and then brought all these Indian people to Lichfield?

As I say, a city of exotic strangeness. And I probably wouldn't have noticed if I had done the proper reading up in advance, but instead would now be babbling on about the bicentenary of the greatest Englishman of all time – as it is, this may be the first piece ever on Lichfield which hasn't bothered to mention Dr Johnson. Go to Lichfield and buy your Dr Johnson mugs if you like; I shall, till I am better instructed, think of it as an Indian city with parks and ornamental water, full of small palaces and dominated by the most enormous red fort, decorated with animals not found this side of Bombay.

More hearts and bazookas

Today Mills & Bang proudly presents another selection of new titles.

A Sporran for Shirley, by Alison Lurid

Sergeant McWhistler of the Black Watch had seen many things in his life. He had seen mobs in Aden, riots in Belfast and closing time in Perth. But he had never seen anything quite like Private Dundas's knees.

'Have you seen those two white things beneath Private Dundas's kilt?' he said to Captain Oliphant one day. 'I hate to say this about anyone, but I'm thinking that Dundas shaves his knees.'

'Private Dundas is a woman,' said Captain Oliphant briskly.

Three days later the sergeant had recovered his breath sufficiently to say to the captain: 'A *woman*?'

'Oh, come on, Sergeant. You know the new laws; we have to take good men even if they are women. And Private Dundas is a good man, even if she is a woman.'

'I will break her and mould her to my will,' thought the sergeant to himself. 'I will make her sorry she ever joined the Black Watch.' In which he was very wrong, for Shirley Dundas was more than a match for the hairy sergeant, and the night he challenged her to an eightsome reel was one he would never forget.

Desert Chase, by Gemma Raven

Africa, 1942. General Whitgift had pursued Rommel across the desert for 1,200 miles. One night his adjutant came to see him.

'General, you must stop chasing Rommel,' he said. 'All the men can see you're in love with him.'

The general's face went puce, purple, khaki, mottled and finally Harrods luggage colour.

'That is the most infernal lie,' he answered hoarsely. 'I just want to ask him out for the evening.'

But would he? Did he? The tension is terrific.

Molly in the Malvinas, by Thelma Webbing

Molly Mandeville, harum-scarum veterinary surgeon attached to the Falklands garrison, had almost grown tired of sheep. She never thought such a thing would happen to her. Then one day she looked up into the face of Major Trimfit. Heavens! His grizzled moustache, his white eyebrows, the patient bags under his eyes . . .

'Wow,' she whispered, 'but what a Southdown you'd make.'

'Pardon?' he said, puzzled.

'Never mind,' she thought. 'I won't mind counting sheep at night, if you're one of them.'

But she hadn't reckoned with the jealousy of Captain Stanley Merino, who was in charge of the sheepdog unit. The tension built up until sheep-dip day! Only one man could come back victorious. Which was it to be?

Pacific Patrol, by Eunice Binnacle

Hugo knew that the strangest things happened at sea. But he wasn't quite prepared to lift his eyes from the bridge of HMS *Impermeable* as they went round Cape Horn and see twelve dancing ladies tap their way across the foredeck.

'What the . . . ?' he said lamely.

'They're just rehearsing for the variety night in September,' said the bosun.

'But I ought to tell the captain!'

'If you like,' said the bosun. 'He's third from the right, in the blue dress. He likes to be known as Roberta.'

Suddenly Hugo knew that the voyage was not going to turn out quite as he had imagined. Little did he know he would be involved in the strangest marriage ceremony in Santiago . . .

Write for our complete list. You won't be disappointed.

Unusual jobs: no. 7

When Sam Kitteridge announces his job at parties, people tend to blink and ask him to repeat it. Did he say *sex* psychology?

'No, sock psychology, I say. They then ask me if I study the behaviour of people who *wear* socks. No, no, I tell them. I study the behaviour of socks themselves.'

The study is based on Kitteridge's profound conviction that socks behave in a way quite different from anything else in nature.

'You yourself must have noticed that if you put five pairs of socks into a washing machine for an ordinary wash cycle, you will almost always get either eleven socks out or nine. Now, where does that extra sock come from? And where does that missing sock disappear to?'

Kitteridge also studies the way in which single socks with no matching sock build up in a household till there are as many as twenty or thirty unmatched socks, some of them not claimed by any member of the house. One of them is almost always a long red towelling sock.

He is also intrigued by the way in which a pair can increase to a trio of identical socks, as well as by the curious phenomenon of the unknown name-tape.

'This simply means the way in which socks, usually grey school socks, can turn up with names sewn on them which do not match any of the family's names. Very often, these names are of people totally unknown to the family.'

This sort of study may seem useless to people not familiar with academic research, but Kitteridge is convinced he is on the edge of an amazing discovery. He believes that socks contain the secret to some form of energy which is totally unknown to science.

'I know it sounds odd, but the only explanation for all these happenings is that socks move around in a way which we do not yet understand, and if only we could crack this form of movement we might be able to harness it to more useful ends.

'You yourself must have noticed that if you hang up a wash-load of socks on a washing-line, say over the bath, then the next time you come back some of the socks are lying in the bath. They may even fall on top of you as you take a bath. *There is no way known to science in which those socks could move.*'

At the moment he is working on a theory that socks somehow derive energy from the spinning of the washing machines in which they find themselves.

His early research was done in a Milton Keynes launderette, but he was banned from there for using too many machines, and he has now set up his research lab with six machines, four basins and a complicated system of washing lines.

So far he has isolated a pair of black dinner socks and a large woollen Scottish stocking which seem to have unusual hidden energy, but it is still too early in the day to draw any conclusions.

'I have at last established that this behaviour is limited to socks. After exhaustive washing and drying of ties, pants, vests and hankies, I am convinced that they show no urge to move around at all. This is a sock-limited phenomenon, as we would say.

'Only last week I stored a single green sock away in a sock drawer for further testing. It turned up three days later on my *feet*, matched to a grey sock. A female colleague of mine claims that ladies' knickers have the same powers of movement, especially if there is a teenage daughter around, but this is unknown territory to me.'

Does he *really* feel he is pursuing a useful end?

'Most certainly. At least, compared to my colleagues. One of them has devoted his life to comparing different books written about Milton's poetry.

'If he finds any hidden source of energy there, I will eat my hat.'

Life, death and a bent wheel

Within the past fortnight, two things have happened to me which I never thought would: I was on a train where the communication cord was pulled, and I ran over somebody.

Both sobering experiences have combined to turn me from an outgoing extrovert into a sombre recluse, given to reflecting on the great questions of life and death.

To take the first first, I was sitting peacefully in the rear coach of the Bath–London express when the train came to a sudden halt outside Reading and a voice different from the honeyed voice of the buffet attendant came to the PA.

'If there is a doctor on board, could he come quickly to the second class?' The man opposite me groaned audibly, threw down his *Times* Portfolio card and disappeared for ten minutes.

After that time, during which we had all borrowed his card to check our shares, stared out of the window at the smoky countryside and failed to start even the slightest conversation, he returned.

One of us, braver than the rest, asked what was up. 'Difficult to say without my tools,' he said, 'but probably his heart. Anyway, they've phoned Reading and they'll take him off there.'

As we drew into Reading, sure enough, we saw a mobile stretcher rather like an upholstered supermarket trolley being propelled at speed along the platform by a two-person crew.

Shortly thereafter it came back bearing the patient who by this time had recovered enough to sit up and smile ruefully, scratching his head at his predicament like Stan Laurel having got himself into another fine mess.

The funny thing was that instead of us looking relieved that he had recovered, we all, I swear, felt silent resentment that our train had been delayed for a quarter of an hour by someone who didn't look too bad at all. We actually wanted him to look worse.

The same is true of the man I ran over. Well, considering that I was on a bicycle and he stepped out in front of me in Old Compton Street so that I went straight into him, it's not quite accurate to say I ran over him.

He being quite a tall person, it would be truer to say I ran under him. Nevertheless, I caught him quite a whack and my handlebar hit his hip-bone (I think it was his hip but these travelling diagnoses are tricky, as the railway doctor said) with a crunch.

'Are you all right?' I said.

'Yes. Are you all right?' he said guiltily.

'Fine. Are you really all right?'

'Yes, I'm all right. How about you?'

This could have gone on all day until one of us confessed to being all wrong, so I bade him farewell and rode off. It was only then that I discovered my front wheel was quite badly buckled.

I felt cross. Not just because he had done my bike an injury, but because he had been so blithe and unscathed about it.

We all feel a bit miffed when we accidentally stub a cigarette out on someone else's hand or karate chop his stomach when we only meant to execute a Gallic gesture, and he shows no pain at all.

So my conclusion after witnessing these scenes of drama and violence is this: if you or I are ever on the receiving end of an accident, for heaven's sake make the most of it.

As they bear you away on the express stretcher, screw your features up in agony and wave your arms about. As they rush you off the plane to the first aid post, roar with pain. When the bike strikes you amidriffs, collapse like Tom being sandbagged by Jerry.

You may feel silly overacting, but it will give the most enormous pleasure to everyone else concerned.

Trolleys: the amazing truth

The scientific curiosity of my readers never ceases to bemuse me. Recently I printed a survey on the behaviour of supermarket trolleys and related life-forms, which I thought had exhausted the subject. But I have already received several observations from readers which open up new horizons, such as that from James To of Balham who disagrees with our findings that British Rail trolleys seldom stir from their habitat. Working, as he does, near Victoria station, he observes that they flock in large numbers to local boarding houses and hotels, often quite far away, and especially to Victoria coach station. He believes that they are not taken there by families, but rather that the trolleys lead families where the trolleys want to go. What happens to the families is not known.

This ties in with a very exciting letter from F.E. Brodie of Caterham, who on a recent visit to Ostend Jet Foil terminal spotted there a trolley marked 'Not to be removed from Victoria Station'. 'I do hope,' he says, 'that more of these do not spread abroad in case the whole European continent is over-run following successful breeding.'

Mr Guy Beddington of Notting Hill would seem to agree, as like most of us he has tremendous difficulty in tearing two supermarket trolleys apart when they have been locked in embrace overnight, and he is apparently against breeding *tout court*; he backs this up with arguments not fit for a family newspaper.

But from Mr Vaughan Birbeck of Morecambe comes the most startling observation. Many things clamber ashore in Morecambe Bay, he says, including kipper boxes from the Isle of Man and – in mid-January – any amount of Christmas trees. Now they have been joined, all the year round, by supermarket trolleys landing on the shore. He goes on:

'It is unfortunate that the examples of trolley washed ashore are in poor physical condition (being encrusted with rust, seaweed and barnacles) and do not facilitate any detailed analysis. We do hope to persuade supermarkets to "ring" their trolleys, showing their place of origin and date of inception in order to learn more about this amphibious behaviour and possibly map their migration routes.'

I applaud that thought, and indeed all scientific fervour among my readers, such as that which came to the fore after an earlier report on sock psychology. Professor Kitteridge, you will remember, has been looking for the secret source of energy which enables socks to travel at night, multiply in washing machines and change colour behind your back. He tends to think that the energy derives from the machines. Mrs Smith of Coleshill thinks otherwise.

'My theory is that energy gets stored in a sock while being worn, and as the wearer discards it, the sock curls up into a ball and rolls off to an unknown place. If you find a sock and endeavour to uncurl it, it will have turned itself inside out.'

Hmm. More detail please, Mrs Smith. Adrian Hawksley of Twickenham writes simply to say that although socks in general may wander, there is one kind that never does. 'Hand-knitted socks (in my three-year survey these are grandmother's gifts to the family) rarely if ever get separated. Why is this?' Not having a grandmother, I cannot comment.

The fullest of all letters comes from Mr Hodge of Aldwych, who answers my question as to why some socks bear names known to no one in the family. Is it not possible, he asks, that they are the names *of the socks themselves*? 'I have always assumed that socks have the power of reproduction and that these names have been conferred upon the socks by the parents.' A simple but powerful thought.

He says: 'I have been told by a friend in New Zealand that if you leave wet socks lying in the bath there and return later, you find that they have moved upwards and are invariably hanging from the line over the bath. As is known, washing machines and spin driers in the southern hemisphere rotate in an opposite direction to that in which they rotate in the northern hemisphere.'

Of course. Finally, a submission from Alan Griffiths, a tutor of historical studies at University College, London, which suggests that sock migration is nothing new. It is a cutting from *The Times* which starts: 'Viking sock to go on display. An old woollen sock which was probably thrown away by a Viking warrior in the tenth century and survived because it lay for a thousand years in boggy ground in York...'

Dylan in the computer

Some readers who enjoyed our Raymond Chandler version of Jabberwocky *want to know if the computer has any other bits of interactive literature up its circuits.*

Yes, it has about 10,000. Here's an extract from its Dylan Thomas version of Meryl Streep: Under Silk Wood, *a radio play set in a small Welsh plutonium plant.*

Narrator: To begin very near the end of everything. It is night, no-nonsense, nuclear night in the small plant. Down the slow computer corridors nothing winks, except the little red lights on the square machines, dreaming in their sleep of going huntin', shootin', and fission. Nothing stirs, nothing shifts on night shift, only the sighing of the wind in the flag over the front door which says 'Plas Goch Plutonium' and the ghostly creaking of the kneejoints of Bill Bevan, night-watchman, fast asleep at his post.

Bevan: Who goes there? Come in and have a cup of tea.

Narrator: says Bill in his sleep, and his corned beef sandwich curls up and dies.

Listen. You can hear the people of Plas Goch breathing in and out, hoping to wake up tomorrow uncontaminated, but failing that, to wake up anyway. Under his solid lead bedspread Dai Geiger-Counter dreams of radio-activity, hoping to find a good programme.

Dai: Is that you, Radio Moscow? Hoping this finds you as it leaves us.

Narrator: Listen. Gwilym Thomas, retired MP, puts his arms round his wife and tries to strangle her, thinking she is Margaret Thatcher. She turns it into an embrace, as she does every night.

Thomas: Oh, Margaret! If only you weren't Tory. Couldn't you be Alliance, just for a little while?

Mrs Thomas: Be quiet, you old rogue, or I'll vote Plaid Cymru.

Narrator: And the ghosts of his past constituents float past him, worried, Welsh and wrinkled.

1st Constituent: Don't let them build it here, Gwilym.

2nd Constituent: We don't want plutonium drifting on the beaches, with the polystyrene cups and ice cream spoons.

3rd Constituent: We don't want boys building uranium sand castles.

1st Constituent: We don't want to bomb Moscow. We don't even know where it is.

Thomas: Boys, boys! This plant means jobs, money and Russian spies staying in the Cross Keys Hotel, buying rounds of vodka for everyone!

Constituents: All right – let them build it!

Narrator: Listen. In her neat room, hired from Mr Burton, the postman, and decorated with a poster of a pop group with huge haircuts and jeans too small, sleeps Karen, clutching her latest single. His name is Bob. She dreams of the plutonium plant where she works.

Karen: I don't want to work there. I don't want to work anywhere. I just want to ride on a big bus to London and meet a reggae man, with thighs like black puddings and hair like Welsh seaweed, who will dance with me all night and more besides.

Narrator: Listen. The sun comes up from behind the horizon, a huge astrodome in the sky. If you listen very carefully, you can hear it ticking its way through the early morning cloud, soft and sinister, shining down on Plas Goch graveyard, where the tombstones stand in lines like workers on the conveyor belt of death. Just listen...

The Glorious Twelfth

From Lord Disgusted

Sir, Many people mock the concept of grouse shooting as old-fashioned and behind the times. But this year you will have read that there are very few grouse left on the moors and that it will be a lucky shot who bags a pair, or pairs a bag, or whatever the expression is. This proves that grouse shooting does work. We *have* almost exterminated the little pests. Another year, and perhaps the Scottish highlands will at least be free from these cunning, evil-minded little blighters. Keep shooting!

From Lord Whortle

Sir, I read that as grouse are now so rare, many owners of grouse moors are thinking of turning their property over to forestry. As one who did so ten years ago, may I be permitted to comment?

Our experience is that, although people find it strange at first shooting at trees instead of grouse, they come to enjoy it very much. Foreign businessmen who have come to Scotland year after year without hitting a single grouse suddenly discover that shooting at and winging a tree is comparatively easy, and of course the tree does not die. Ignorant quarters say that hitting a stationary tree is not sportsmanlike; the truth is of course that on all but the calmest days the trees blow about a lot and it still requires skill to bring down a young larch or spruce.

Our season, too, starts on the twelfth, and we shall enjoy the usual race to be the first to bring the season's first pine needles to a London restaurant. Last year, by the way, I shot at and missed a young fir on the opening day, but brought down a pair of grouse sitting in the branches!

From Mr J. G. Lavoisier

Monsieur, As usual we shall be taking part in the race to be the first people to bring a London restaurant up to the Scottish moors to serve a grouse on the Glorious Twelfth. At midnight on the eleventh, we at the Petit Bistro de Chez Jean shall be air-lifting our little *boîte* by helicopter and flying it through the night to Scotland. By dawn we shall be in position in Glenbutler near Loch Rannoch and open to serve grouse all day. If no grouse are available, we shall be serving freshly shot trout and salmon. Looking forward to seeing you all!

From Colonel Wagpiper

Sir, I might have known it. Every year, as regular as clockwork, we get so-called satirical comments from such as your columnist Miles Kington (is that really his name?) about the noble sport of grouse shooting. How many times do I have to explain that without the dedicated breeding and conservation of those concerned, there would be hardly any grouse left? Shooting *is* conservation.

If you then ask me how it is that there are hardly any grouse left, my answer is: I do not know. But that is quite beside the point.

From Henry the Talking Avocet

Hello, darlings! Your old friend Henry here, half-way through his summer season at Lowestoft or Skegness or somewhere, and my goodness the crowds have been flocking this year to see me in my spectacular production of *Seagulls Over Sorrento*. But enough of me, I just wanted to reminisce briefly about the one time I got involved in the grouse shooting season.

In 1978 I was in Scotland to see a rather charming ptarmigan with whom I was conducting a passionate but short-lived *affaire scandaleuse*, and on 12 August we happened to be out on the moors when all hell broke loose. Not since a cabaret tour of the Lebanon had I felt so at risk.

Keeping my head, I infiltrated myself among the beaters and cried out in my best Knightsbridge accent: 'Aim at the trees over here, you chaps!' The result was gratifying. Six beaters shot, two winged and Lord Strathcomfrey driven round the bend. Yes, a good day's sport all round.

If a certain young quail named Yvonne should chance to read this, may I make it quite clear that all is over between us? You may keep the ring if you like. It is only from the top of a lager tin.

A TV star is born

'What is an easy chair?' said Professor Trevor Scrope. 'In what sense can a chair be said to be easy or hard? Is there such a thing as a moderately difficult chair? What is easiness – and what is chairness? Can we even expect an easy chair to be made out of a hard wood?'

He waited for the wave of light laughter to run round the lecture room and die down. He waited in vain – there was not even a ripple. Professor Scrope sighed. It was not much fun being Professor of Philosophy and Furniture Design at M4 University. The educational cuts had cut so deep that now they were not just firing people, they were combining two or more faculties under one person. He was lucky in a sense. His friend Butler had just become Professor of French Studies, Journalism and Naval History, and was being sued for libel to the tune of £500M by the Admiralty in Paris over a test paper he had set.

'Diogenes lived in a barrel, we are told,' continued Scrope doggedly. 'Was it, I wonder, an easy barrel? Did he ever think of building on an extension? If so, did he ever have trouble with the Vatman?'

Again, no laughter. Instead, to his amazement, the door burst open and a student entered shouting: 'Sir, sir, it's the BBC, they're on the phone, they want you to go to London and appear on...' By the time the student had finished his sentence, Scrope was already in his old Cortina and edging out on to the M4. The BBC! He moved up to 70 m.p.h. Was this the big one? He touched 80 m.p.h. Was fame just around the corner?

Well, not exactly, actually. The truth was that some famous furniture designer had just died and the BBC Tribute Department were putting together a tribute. What they mean by this is that they were digging out a clip from an old *Michael Parkinson Show*. To their unbelief they found that the bloke had never been on *Parkinson*, so they were grabbing the cheapest available professor instead.

'I'm appearing on a programme tonight,' said Scrope to the gatekeeper at TV Centre.

'We'll see about that,' said the gateman. 'Before I let you in, I'll need proof of identity, banker's references, letters from at least two TV stars, surety of £50...'

'It's all right,' said Roger Boothly, coming from nowhere. 'He's on my little prog tonight, doing a featurette.'

Trevor Scrope did it rather well. He was totally unafraid of the cameras, probably because he believed throughout that it was a radio interview, and finished his little chat in less than five minutes, which is the highest criterion the BBC can have. Afterwards in the hospitality room, over the Twiglets and Château Wenham, he waxed eloquent.

'I find the whole philosophical history of furniture terribly exciting...'

'I'm the barman,' said the barman. 'That's the producer over there.'

'I find the whole philosophical history of furniture tremendously exciting,' he told Roger Boothly. 'The way the history of thought is bound up with the way people sat, and what surrounded them while they thought. Descartes, on a chair, had abstract thoughts. Newton, on the bumpy ground under an apple tree, deduced practically that...'

'You may be the man we've been looking for,' said Boothly. 'Our pet experts at the BBC change slower than we sometimes realize. I mean, Magnus Pyke, Patrick Moore and Arthur Negus are all still terrific value, but...'

Scrope, who never watched TV, had no idea what he was talking about.

'...and there might even be a series in what you say. Furniture plus philosophy, eh? If we could think of a title...'

The oldest joke in Scrope's repertoire came to his mind.

'*The Seat of Learning?*' he suggested.

Boothly decided on the spot that the man was a genius and took him away to be signed up. Meanwhile, unaware that they would never see Professor Scrope again, his students were still sitting scribbling in his lecture room. They were filling in job application forms.

Unusual jobs: no. 8

Inspector Antelope is the only policeman I've ever met who calls everyone 'Darling'. He has long eyelashes and wears a T-shirt showing the badge of the Met, plus a slogan saying 'Met by Moonlight'. It's his job, among other things, to train policemen on decoy duty.

'Some of these young things they send off to West End clubs and Piccadilly Underground to entice males into soliciting them – well, it's pathetic. They flap their wrists and mince around and think they look attractive. One might as well send out Hinge and Brackett to get an arrest, darling. I have to shake all that nonsense out of them.

'It's my job to teach them that that stereotype is way, way out of date. Gay people today look terribly severe – short hair, perhaps the one ear-ring and those terribly depressing little moustaches which make you want to get your secateurs out and do some dead-heading. This sort of thing.'

He opened a small box marked Facial Fuzz and produced a small moustache. He whipped off his eyelashes and put it on, then stared at me till I felt uneasy.

'See? Sort of a tidied-up cowboy. Whereas *this* sort of moustache is heterosexual, bar-room rugby player's moustache – sort of cowboy run to fat.'

Adopting another moustache and letting his facial muscles relax, he turned before my very eyes into the sweaty, puffy kind of leering pub hearty that gives masculinity a bad name. He assaulted my ribs with his elbow and said: 'I picked up a right raver in the West End on Saturday – she was a goer and no mistake. So after a couple of pints...'

'Yes, yes,' I said hastily. 'But what about the actual drama coaching?'

'Depends what it's for,' said the inspector. 'West End gay work takes some time. Training a man as a drug addict is easier.'

'Why would you want to do that?'

'To trap a doctor into selling him drugs, of course. Then we might have to train him as a villain, a skinhead, a National Front member, or politician – one of the junior members of the Cabinet is a pupil of mine, and very useful he's been too. He always says that Mrs Thatcher could have gone straight to the top of our world.'

'As Commissioner of Police?'

'Well, no – as boss of the East End underworld, actually.'

Antelope's training programme started nearly twenty years ago, when police officers, infiltrated into pop festivals to check the drug scene, had to be turned into hippies. He dug into his box again and produced a long droopy moustache which he fondled nostalgically.

'This belongs to a bloke that I trained so well that when he got back on duty, he couldn't adjust. He used to arrest people and then let them go, saying: "That's cool, man – you do your thing and I'll do mine." Much more fun coaching people to be hippies than pickets.'

'The police are being trained as pickets?'

'Of course. If you see a miner on TV screaming at his colleagues to get the bastards in blue, odds are he's one of ours – one of mine, probably. What makes me weep is when you see a policeman using a truncheon on TV, beating a miner over the head. He doesn't realize he's probably bashing a colleague. Anyway, a policeman should never, *never* use a truncheon when cameras are around. He should use his boots instead.'

To my surprise he then put his eyelashes back on again and leant forward, putting a hand on my knee.

'But all this talk of shop is boring. Tell me something about yourself, darling, and the big glamorous world of Fleet Street.'

Luckily, I had already noticed the concealed mike, video camera and two-way mirror in the interview room. Not wishing to be trapped into anything, I slapped his wrist, made an excuse and ran for it.

Coke: it's nearly the real thing

It was one of those small chemist's shops which are scattered throughout Mayfair like poppies in a cornfield. Have you noticed, dear reader, how many there are? And yet they seem to have nothing on display but expensive sponges, delicate French soaps and elegant combs which are, I am glad to say, mostly made in England.

Do they survive entirely on well-heeled visitors from abroad who arrive at their Mayfair hotels, only to find they have left all their toiletry items at home, or had them flown on by a forgetful airline to Frankfurt? Can a chemist prosper merely on what happens in the bathroom?

It is a mystery which this little story hopes to clear up.

As I said, it was one of those respectable but small chemist's shops in the more fragrant reaches of W1. The door opened, and a tall handsome, stranger entered. His good looks derived partly from his well-cared-for silver locks and partly from his clothes, all chosen with care from *New Yorker* advertisements. He might have been a film star, a German magazine proprietor or a motor manufacturer from Detroit.

He was, in fact, an American lawyer specializing in homosexual divorce settlements, but the USA is a strange country and we must not judge him too harshly. No doubt somebody has to do the job.

'I would be extremely grateful if you could make up this prescription for me,' he said, waving a piece of paper at the proprietor much as a conductor might entrust a missing page to the star pianist. 'I shall need it for this evening,' he added.

The chemist looked at the formula. It meant nothing to him. He recognized all the normal requests – cures for over-indulgence, cures for a misspent youth, cures even for ordinary ailments – but this did not even begin to make sense.

'If you could tell me what is wrong with you,' said the chemist. 'In the most general terms, of course,' he added hastily, seeing a look of hauteur ripple across his customer's hand-chiselled and surgeon-polished features.

'There is nothing wrong with me. The medicine is restorative, rather than curative. It is – how shall I say? – an elixir prescribed for me.'

'Right you are, squire,' muttered the pharmaceutical technician, as five £10 notes magically appeared in the stranger's hand and landed safely in his own top overall pocket. 'Ready by 4.30.'

At 4.30 promptly the imposing stranger returned and was given the prepared nostrum. At 4.33 the silver-haired American was in his bathroom and preparing...

Let us baffle you no longer. The formula that the puzzled chemist had unwittingly prepared was a little-known recipe for producing a substance so like cocaine that the difference could only be noticed by an habitué, and hardly even by him. The American lawyer was about to ingest a powder which to you or me would seem to border on exoticism but to him was no more than the first cocktail of the evening.

The advantages of such a formula seem overwhelming. No need any longer to traipse quantities of cocaine through airport customs areas, where the action of a single ill-bred and over-curious officer might spoil one's social life. No further need to drag concealed portions of drugs from continent to continent, like furtive helpings of toothpaste. Instead, the freedom to arrive in a new country and have one's favourite sherbet made up at no risk and little expense by a reputable scientist.

What is this formula? What is the secret that has enabled our American friend and many like him to travel happily and freely across the world, seeing humanity everywhere through well-tinted lenses? And without going to the bother of setting up a motor factory in obscure parts of the United Kingdom?

The secret is open to all of you. All you need do is write to the Moreover Laboratories enclosing bank notes to the value of £500, plus SAE, and the formula will come to you by return of post.

Your name and address will immediately be forwarded to the Drug Squad at Scotland Yard as well, but we assume that you have lawyers that can take care of that sort of thing.

Let's hear from you, rich readers!

A Police Entrapment brochure, issued by Department X, c/o the CID.

Autumn and what to do about it

If you're out and about this Bank Holiday Monday (*writes Gull's Egg*) you'll probably notice that the season is beginning to change. Midsummer is turning to upper-midsummer, old man's beard is beginning to grow down over the collar and old men's noses are starting to go red. Swifts and swallows are gathering on telephone wires, twittering furiously and trying to get through to Cairo to reserve accommodation for the exodus which is almost upon us. Martins, too, are gathering in small crowds to descend upon villages and terrify the inhabitants in their fast sports cars; along with Martins you'll find Jeremys, Patricks, Colins and Rodneys.

This is the time when birds of passage make their fleeting appearance – in book fairs throughout the country you will see the second-hand Penguin in its distinctive green, orange, blue or Marc drawing, while the last of the summer ducks can still be spotted at Lord's. From Norway comes the bearded back-packer, from Sweden the blonde all-weather chick and from Germany the tufted scholar. If you are lucky, you may hear the unmistakable 'Hey-ha-hoo-oop-Lord-bless-us' of the Irish racing fan, stuck in the local hedgerow.

The days are beginning to draw in, the nights are beginning to draw out, the mornings are beginning to start after breakfast and the cocktail hour is creeping down to about 5.30, except in the Channel Isles where it never ends but it pours. Lighting up time is whenever you feel like it, as long as you read the health warning, and at close-down everything shrinks to a tiny dot, in the middle of the screen, and then vanishes.

Out in the shires, the fruits of old England are starting to ripen – medlars, quinces, burberries and alternating currants. Up on Blue Brie hill the fragrant cheddars are hanging low over the dry lymeswold walls, while the lone over-ripe stilton slowly makes its way home across the cheese board, home to solitude and to me. This is harvest time in the Cheddar Gorge, and it's welcome.

Meanwhile, the farmers are preparing the count-down to stubble-burning. Not much to begin with; the odd county burning end to end or the lone barbecue blazing merrily out of control in a deserted forest. But soon the flames will begin in earnest, and a whole series of beacons will burn from end to end of the country, bringing the age-old message: *The Farmers are Coming!* Wise countrymen will go indoors and hide their faces, while even wiser ones will pour water over their houses before going indoors. The friendly smoke will drift out across motorways and the letters column of *The Times* will be full of smouldering protests and burning indignation.

The last picnics are to be seen now, with their wonderful odour of crushed salad and wayside wasps' nests. I recommend chopped-up hard-boiled eggs, tossed in a dressing of mayonnaise and mixed with chives or thyme, then packed down and left to harden over winter to make a perfect picnic patio next year. Sloe gin is good too, but pasta is faster.

Now all the air a solemn spätlese holds, which should be very good when slightly chilled, or why not try a mixture of white wine, gooseberries, syllabub and Gloucestershire sauce? The first old potatoes are in the shops and so are the cheapest 1986 calendars you'll find. So why not turn everything into chutney, by boiling for three months with sugar then bottling? Better still, why not pluck the late-flowering crabtree and evelyn to simmer down into cakes of delicious bathroom soap, ideal with home-brewed nettle shampoo?

Better still, why not draw the curtains, pull up a bottle of foaming preventative and watch the glorious late summer shades of the Notting Hill carnival flicker alluringly across your TV screen? East, west, home's best, sitting in your old string vest, watching Channel 4 come and go, talking of Michelangelo. The next season will be along in a minute; meanwhile, here's a talk on TV's autumn schedules and how to guard against them.

Suffering in silence

No law exists to protect them. Every day of their life is misery. They are Britain's most persecuted minority, yet they receive no sympathy from the public or state.

They are people with telephone numbers almost exactly the same as that of a big organization. Day and night their phones ring with callers wanting help from the AA, trying to protest about TV programmes or simply asking to book a room. Mrs Jolly is an

82-year-old pensioner with a number very like that of a well-known newspaper. Recently she has almost gone out of her mind.

'If it's not people claiming to be millionaires, it's society people ringing up to talk to the gossip column. Sometimes they think I *am* the gossip column, and they say the most dreadful things about their friends. Other times it's journalists – I had one man dictate a 500-word piece on the miners' strike before I could persuade him I was a private address and then he was most awfully rude. Recently I had a man trying to buy the newspaper. I was very tempted to sell it to him.'

The biggest misery of the almost-correct-number people is that they think they are the only ones to suffer. Now all that has changed with the creation of an association to bring them together and help them to discuss their problem – the Almost Correct Number Exchange, or ACNE. At their first national meeting recently they elected as chairman the man who started it all, Reg Primrose. Although, by coincidence, his name incorporates two of the old London all-letter exchanges, he is, in fact, a Birmingham man with a number only one different from a big Midland hotel.

'I get ten, sometimes twenty, calls a day from people wanting to book rooms. At first, like most sufferers, I patiently gave them the right number, but then something in me rebelled, and I started taking bookings. I'd say: "Hold on, I'll put you through to reception," and then in a different voice I'd take their reservations. Some days I must have taken block bookings for more than fifty people, and if only I'd had my own hotel, I might be rich by now.'

As it was, the hotel was eventually forced by Reg's militancy to change its number. Emboldened by this victory, he started getting in touch with other sufferers and found overwhelming support for the idea of ACNE.

'British Telecom have the solution in their own hands,' says Reg. 'They must make sure that all big firms have similar numbers. For instance, the BBC TV number in London is 743 3000, but of course lots of people dial 734 8000 by mistake. What they get then is the Piccadilly Hotel, who are big enough to deal with wrong numbers – presumably they know that lots of their customers are ringing the Beeb by mistake. If all the big firms were grouped together, the small people wouldn't suffer.'

Until that day dawns, ACNE have decided on a policy of direct retribution. They have, for a start, secured a phone number for themselves very like a British Telecom Research Centre. When BT callers ring ACNE by mistake, ACNE tells them that BT has gone bankrupt.

They also have sufficient numbers to mount a programme of harassment against the worst offenders.

Recently they mounted a round-the-clock dialling offensive against an MI5 number which was giving one of their members a lot of trouble, being so like his. Eighty of them rang MI5 in succession, each asking for political asylum or to be put through to the mole. Now the MI5 number has mysteriously been changed.

So, if you suffer from this problem, Reg urges you to get in touch. He has only one word of advice. 'For heaven's sake write; don't phone, whatever you do.'

A clergyman for our time

The Rev. Jack Marsh had a pleasant smile, a small bald spot and three small churches to look after in a part of Hampshire much frequented by trout. He was also an accomplished bank robber, though no one knew this except the Bishop, with whom Jack had occasional confidential chats.

'Stands to reason, Bish,' said Jack the Rev., as he liked to think of himself. 'Out of all the clergyman in the C. of E., there is bound to be at least one into serious crime, right?'

'I suppose so,' said the Bishop, not happily.

'Well, that's me. Saves you worrying, don't you see? Now you don't have to agonize over which one it is – you know it's me. By the way, this is confidential, I take it?'

'Yes,' sighed the Bishop. 'I gave you my word, unfortunately. But look, when you're doing your ... bank raids, you won't hurt anyone, will you?'

'Lord bless you, Bish, not a hair on their head. What is it the Bible says? "Bash not the little sparrows on the head, or you will surely get thumped in the after-life."'

'Something like that,' said the Bishop, wondering fleetingly what

Jack Marsh's sermons were like. He need not have worried. They were racy, down-to-earth and very well attended.

'You know,' declaimed Jack Marsh that Sunday, 'I often think that life is a bit like a horse race. It's over before it's hardly started, and you've got no money at the end of it.'

The choir laughed and leant forward, listening for the tip which was to come.

'Take the 2.30 at Uttoxeter next week, for example. Fifteen horses all straining to come first, and yet knowing in their heart of hearts that only one of them can win. But who is to say that the first horse is any better than the last horse? If Dead Gladioli were to win, for example...'

'He's tipping Dead Gladioli,' muttered old Woodbridge, the gamekeeper, in the front row, and throughout the church there was a rustling of paper as people wrote the name down in their hymn books. After the service, the local rich farmers shook him warmly by the hand and drove off home to phone their bookies. There was quite a contrast between the big fat Volvos they drove and the Rev. Jack Marsh's little car. It was a Lamborghini.

'Darling,' said Mrs Marsh over Sunday lunch, 'there's a bit of talk in the countryside about you and your money. People are saying that ... well, that you're selling apples from the orchard in defiance of EEC regulations.'

Jack laughed. 'You just tell them that my wife runs the best-organized jumble sales south of Birmingham, and that anyone could make a fortune that way.'

That Tuesday there was a big bank hold-up in Basingstoke and the Bishop felt constrained to summon Jack.

'Your work, I take it, Jack?' said the Bishop, pointing to the local paper.

'"Local Man Crosses Sahara on Unicycle",' read out Jack. 'Yes, I did donate a few bottles of communion wine to keep him going.'

'These bank raids have to stop,' said the Bishop, ignoring him. 'For heaven's sake, Jack, anyone would think the Mafia was taking over the Church.'

'No blasted Catholics are muscling in on my racket, Bish,' said Jack angrily.

'All right, all right, I'm sorry, but remember: no more bank raids.'

Instead of answering, the Rev. Jack Marsh leant forward and

turned on the Bishop's TV set. A voice said: 'And the result; first, Dead Gladioli...'

'No more bank raids,' said Jack. 'I promise you that.'

The Bishop gazed fondly at the clean-cut, devil-may-care features of his favourite rural clergyman and wondered why, for all the heartaches he caused him, there weren't more vicars like him.

'What is it the Bible says, Bish?' said Jack. 'Blessed are the cool in heart, for they shall verily get away with the loot?'

'Something like that,' said the Bishop.

Magistrate versus the police (latest)

There were some very strange scenes indeed yesterday at the Magistrates' Court in Bow Street or somewhere like that. It was the first time that a man had been charged this century under the Impersonation of a Blind Person Act (1847). The magistrate in charge was Mrs Amanda Ferret; here is an extract from the hearing.

Ferret: I didn't know it was a crime to impersonate a blind person.
Police: Nor did we but we've looked it up. He was standing in Oxford Street, refusing to move on.
Ferret: Is that a crime too?
Police: Oh, yes – under the Refusal to Move On Act of 1867, amended 1890.
Ferret: Was he impersonating any special blind person? I mean, was he doing an imitation of Ray Charles or Stevie Wonder? If so, could we hear a number – I love Stevie Wonder!
Police: The defendant was not imitating a specific blind person, but was waving his white stick about, shouting: 'I am Mrs Thatcher and I will guide you to the end of the world!'
Ferret: Hmm. Was this intended as satire?
Police: Why not ask the defendant yourself, ma'am?

Ferret: Was your reference to Mrs Thatcher satirical in intent? (*Silence*.) There's no answer.

Police: We think he may be dumb as well.

Ferret: How could he be dumb if he was shouting about Mrs Thatcher, for heaven's sake?

Police: We hadn't thought of that. Perhaps he is deaf.

Ferret: Oh, this is ridiculous. Case dismissed.

Police: There is a further charge under the Trade Descriptions Act – that he did falsely describe himself as a blind man for the purposes of gain. He had a cap on the pavement.

Ferret: Is it a crime to have a cap on the pavement?

Police: If it's full of pound notes and cheques, yes. He was causing an obstruction.

Ferret: And making a few bob as well.

Police: That's probably because he was also pointing a machine-gun at the passers-by and making them put money in the cap. There is another charge against him, under the Firearms, Possession of, By Blind People Act (1914).

Ferret: Curious, certainly. But if he was a blind man he had no way of knowing it was a machine-gun. Case dismissed.

Police: We think he could see perfectly well and knew it was a gun all right.

Ferret: If he can see, you can't get him under the Firearms, Possession of, By Blind People Act.

Police: Damn. You got me there. Well, we have also charged him with unlawful possession of a white stick. There was a name on the stick and it wasn't his!

Ferret: What name was it?

Police: Josh Black of Whitechapel.

Ferret: They are a long-established firm of walking-stick makers, you dunderhead! Now get him out of here before I lose my temper.

Police: But we can't let a man go who has been waving guns around and might have shot somebody!

Ferret: Why not? I don't recall anyone arresting Willie Whitelaw. Now, unless you have any other charges against him...

Police: Only one more. Wasting police time by dressing up as an armed blind man, under the Police Wasting Time Act of 1943.

Defendant: Might I have a word with you, ma'am?

Ferret: Ah! You can speak!

Defendant: Yes, ma'am. I just wish to say that I cannot be guilty of wasting police time, because I am ... a police officer!

Police: Pull the other one, sunshine. Which police officer?

Defendant: I am Inspector Antelope, the Chief Police Drama Coach. I was out on a plainclothes exercise when I was arrested by this nincompoop, just as I was about to bust a very big ring of false blind musicians.

Ferret: You are the famous Inspector Antelope? But I have always wanted to meet you – this is wonderful! Oh, this calls for a party. Case dismissed. Court adjourned and let's all go over to the pub!

Police: It's outside hours, ma'am.

Ferret: Spoilsport to the last, eh? Believe me, I can get a drink over there any time I like.

The Northern Ireland solution (exclusive)

The last time I went to Northern Ireland I met two people who were working for the National Trust. One was engaged in restoration work, the other was busy devising future plans for National Trust property. Nothing odd about that, you might say. Ah, but there is. When did you last meet someone in England who was working for the National Trust?

Statistically it is most unlikely that I should meet more people in Northern Ireland working for the Trust than in the whole of the mother country. It suggests strongly that the Trust is much stronger on the ground over there than it is here. This is not the image we normally get of Northern Ireland, of course, which suggests that destruction is more the order of the day than preservation, but this image through the countless films and plays now surging from that beleaguered province is a misleading one, suggesting as it does that the place is inhabited entirely by TV film crews, psychopaths and weeping mothers, a sort of drizzly Beirut.

Anyway, so struck was I by the relative preponderance of National Trust people over there, even though based on a comparatively small cross-section, that I decided to look up a map of its properties in Northern Ireland. I was impressed. There are a lot of them, and many are sizeable – not just parkland and estates, but coastlines and stretches of country – so that a goodly percentage of the place is already Trust property.

I cannot remember when I first had my next thought, but the more I think about it, the more I think there may be something in it. We all know, do we not, that National Trust property is a haven from the hurly-burly of everyday nastiness? That nothing violent, or bad-tempered, even, takes place in those halls and rolling parkland? Did you ever see a brawl or an unpleasantness in a historic house, except those still occupied by the family?

Could it then be remotely possible that the National Trust of Northern Ireland is gradually taking over the whole province and that this is the long-awaited peace initiative?

It sounds unlikely, I know. All I can say is that it seems to be working. Just suppose that some brilliant boffin had said: 'OK, we can't stop people in Northern Ireland getting at each other, but what we can do is to restrict the places where they can do so. All we need to find is some non-sectarian, property-owning body which could gradually take over the whole place while nobody was looking ... Maybe one day the IRA and Loyalists would have nowhere left to fight.'

And what does all this lead up to? I'll tell you. Being uneasily aware that I am the only writer of my acquaintance who has never written a play about Northern Ireland, I am now working on a script about a family living in Co. Down. They have a hard life. Not a night passes without a BBC crew bursting in to get at the plugs for their lights, or an ITV crew breaking down the door to film their reactions and recharge their batteries. Upstairs in the attic they are hiding a refugee, a freelance cameraman who has no ACTT card and is frightened for his life.

The son is writing a play based on the family's problems in which Japanese TV have expressed a keen interest. The daughter is working nights at the Forum Hotel in Belfast, where she has been approached by an ITV director who wants to use her for a small part when all she wants is an affair with him. And then suddenly the unthinkable happens, the thing they never talk about: the man from the National Trust arrives to discuss buying their farmhouse for the nation.

It's a play with a difference. It even has a lot of laughs and a happy ending. It will disturb many people's ideas about that beleaguered province. And it blows open the Government's secret plans for Northern Ireland.

TV producers are invited to form an orderly queue outside my office door.

Dear God, not autumn again?

Autumn! Across the country the cricket season had come to an end, except in Scotland, where it had hardly started. Genial groundsmen everywhere set fire to the stubble disfiguring the pitch, watched the flames creep across the outfield, saw the pavilion burn down in a blaze of old pads and nets. The smell of forgotten sandwiches, barbecued, filled the air.

Autumn! The tiny Japanese and Belgian businessmen shrank in terror as the fierce gangs of grouse and pheasant closed in on them. One or two they winged with their guns, but then the hordes of hungry game-birds were upon them and, dropping their arms, they ran in terror. Not many lived to tell the tale.

'*Chéri*,' wrote one François to his loved one in Brussels, '*j'ai été terriblement mutilé par un petit ptarmigan et maintenant je porte un eye-patch. Je vais vous voir dans une semaine, mais pas très distinctement.*'

Autumn! The evenings are now beginning to draw in and leaves to fall, hem-lines are being worn lower, scarves are getting longer, clocks are being put forward and back again, prices are going up, the barometer is dropping against the dollar and I'm beginning to feel quite seasick.

Autumn! Time for the farmer to get the scarecrow out of the blazer and straw boater he has worn all the summer and into the sober tweed suiting which may not scare a single crow but should score a few points in the Best-Dressed Scarecrow Contest, organized annually by the second-hand clothes industry (patron Mr Michael Foot), whose finals are to be held in the Pork Scratchings Service Area on the M1 (entry forms from this address).

Autumn! Mad Johnnie Finlay, gamekeeper to the Perthshire nobility, buried the last poor Japanese businessman on the lonely moors above Spittoon and studied his bargain break brochure moodily. Two days in Tokyo sounded just fine. It was the three weeks' travelling there and back which could be a problem. He fingered the 50,000 yen he had found in the puir wee man's breeks and decided he could mebbe afford it.

Autumn! Schubert's Trout Quintet swam in from the sea and up the River Tay. Jings, but it was cold! With one accord they turned and swam out to sea again.

Autumn! Across our glorious countryside the leaves turned brown, then yellow, then a radiant red, followed by a mud-like khaki. If *you're* having trouble with your colour control, perhaps you have it tuned too high; alternatively, turn to Channel Four and find a programme for any colour you like.

Autumn! All over Scotland, old gentlemen brought out their kilts for the first Hunt Ball of the season. My God, they've been attacked by the Black Watch beetle! Next year, do remember to rub them all over with a gentle solution of one fifth blended whisky and four fifths malt, put moth-balls in your sporran, add a lump of ice and ask all the neighbours in.

Only three months to Hogmanay and here we are, still sober.

Autumn! A million bonfires throughout the Home Counties smelt of Lapsang Souchong and sent their raw smoke spiralling upwards until it all combined as acid rain and fell upon a boatload of Belgian businessmen drinking their way through the night back to Ostend.

Autumn! The first soused herrings of the season came ashore on the east coast of England and behaved dreadfully, terrorizing the small seaport. Until you've seen a soused herring on the loose, you've never seen a herring at all.

Autumn! A late swallow, missing the last migratory flight to Egypt, put on a false moustache and prepared to brazen out the winter as an elderly sparrow.

Autumn! A tough and lean Japanese businessman, feigning death on the Scottish grouse moors, had made his way across three counties disguised as a launderette engineer, moving only at night. Now he had reached the city of Dundee where he obtained temporary work as a roller-towel maintenance man. Little did he dream that he would meet a nice wee lassie and stay there for the rest of his life.

Autumn! A great year for mushrooms, all of which can be cooked and eaten. If in doubt, give to guests first. The greatest delicacy of all is the Double-Striped Death Cap, which causes reincarnation.

Autumn! A gobstopper of a season, a great striped humbug of a season, a big bouncy season blowing away the cobwebs of summer. If you'd like to know more about autumn, write to the British Autumn Board, enclosing an SAE, or failing that an old traveller's cheque you don't need any more. Mark your envelope 'Autumn!'

How I kicked the video habit

Today's piece may prove harrowing for some, ugly even. To others it may bring a message of hope. It is the story of how addiction can be fought and conquered, and how a family can come through darkness into the light beyond.

It is, in brief, the story of how I finally began to master the video habit.

It all began as a bit of a joke. Someone at work suggested I might want to review a couple of TV programmes. I had to be out that night, so he arranged for me to hire a VCR machine.

The first experience was delicious – no longer was I tied to the whim of the television companies and I could enjoy their offerings any time I liked.

I bought several tapes. I peeled all the adhesive labels off their backing and stuck them on to the tapes and their boxes. I even numbered the cassettes and indexed them in a little book. I displayed all the symptoms of what I now recognize as an addiction, though at the time I told myself I was controlling my TV intake.

My family began to get worried when I started recording *The Jewel in the Crown*. What worried them was that I didn't watch it, just taped it. I had to be out during the first two episodes, and by the time I was in for episode three, I hadn't got round to watching the first two, so there wasn't much point in watching number three. I taped it instead.

I got my son to tape subsequent episodes. I bought more tapes. And finally I had all twelve hours of *The Jewel in the Crown* stored away, with none of it watched.

I was particularly anxious to watch it, as I had missed all of

Brideshead Revisited and had thus been a social outcast for several months, unable to take part in conversations except with feeble bleats of: 'Well, I read Evelyn Waugh's novel when I was at school and I didn't think it was one of his funniest.' People would stare acidly at me without replying. I didn't want this to happen with *The Jewel*.

It happened, of course. Everyone started talking about the damned thing, and all I could say was: 'Well, I've got it on cassette and just as soon as I've watched it...'

Then Salman Rushdie attacked it and I didn't even know why he was attacking it. He went on TV one night to attack it and I taped his attack, knowing that I could see it after I'd seen the whole series and understand why he was attacking it.

You mustn't think, of course, that I was glued to the TV set during my period of addiction. I think I watched less than usual. It was just that I was taping more, creating a backlog of programmes.

Then last week I had to tape a BBC European football programme because my home team Wrexham, surging from the Fourth Division, were off to play Roma in the seething cauldron of the Roma FC stadium, and the BBC had promised to show the best bits.

But I had no tape available. My cassettes were all jammed with great movies, vintage film and early episodes of *The Young Ones*, some of which I had seen. I sank so low as to ask my son if he had a spare tape I could borrow.

'Dad,' he said, and I realized from the way he said it that I, his father, was being taken aside for a filial lecture; a sobering moment. 'Dad, we think it's time you started taping over *The Jewel in the Crown*.'

I thought about the unthinkable. The more I thought, the more a weight lifted from me. I had assumed that one night I would have to give myself a session of life in India.

I suddenly realized I didn't have to. I knew deep down that I would now never watch *The Jewel in the Crown*. I rushed over to the VCR machine and ordered it to wipe out the first two episodes.

So you see, if your family stands by you, you *can* beat it. I have begun to return to normal life. I have not taped anything since then. I haven't even seen Wrexham go down by 2–0 (but we'll beat you in the second leg, signore). I can even walk past the VCR machine without twitching.

Anyway, they're bound to repeat *The Jewel in the Crown* soon enough. I wouldn't mind seeing just ten minutes of it. If I'm out, I can always tape it.

Happy birthday, Ronnie

Ronnie Scott's Club was twenty-five years old in November 1984. It may not sound a lot, but in relative terms it's the equivalent of keeping a newspaper going for 400 years, a miners' strike for five years or an impromptu speech by Ronald Reagan for five minutes. Jazz clubs simply don't last that long. The only reason that Ronnie's (as everyone calls it) has lasted is the stubbornness of its two owners, Ronnie Scott and Pete King, so it was a privilege for me to be present on Tuesday at a birthday party for the club that everyone knew about except Scott and King.

They came blinking into the club at 3 p.m., expecting to be met by a small BBC TV crew. They found a hundred or more musicians, friends, employees, even journalists, waving glasses and cheering. Pushed to the microphone, they both made speeches which typified the two men. Ronnie looked round the audience and said: 'I don't know a single soul here.' Pete looked round them and said: 'I hope you all paid to come in.'

It has always been their custom to, respectively, insult and charge the customers, but they like to insult each other as well. Ronnie put his arm round Pete's shoulder and said: 'No, but to be serious for a moment, Pete King has been my friend and associate all these twenty-five years, and I can honestly say that without him it would have been a damned sight easier.'

Not a couple to whom sentimentality comes easily, but when I got Pete King in a corner later and twisted his arm, he admitted to being slightly overwhelmed. He had just come from what he described as a dressing down by the bank manager and needed cheering up. He also admitted that even after a quarter-century he still looked forward to getting to work at the club.

'I feel it most when I've been abroad in Europe or America, going to tremendous places and meeting lots of people, but the moment I get back into this room – well, it's like coming home. I don't know what I'd do without it.'

I can dimly understand his feelings, because I myself have spent more evenings in Ronnie's than anywhere else in the world except my own home. During my stint of a dozen years reviewing jazz for *The Times* I must have gone there two or three times a month and it never once felt like work. The hardest thing to do was avoiding over-praising Stan Tracey. For years and years he was the house pianist, accompanying all the incoming American stars, and quite often, to my ears, playing as well as or better than them. Stan himself was at the party, staggering under the impact of three major honours this year, including being made an honorary member of the Royal Academy of Music.

'Nice to have the badges,' he muttered, 'but they don't take them at Sainsbury's.' As I've hinted, jazz musicians are not a sentimental lot on top, and their self-deprecating sense of humour is the nearest anyone has ever come to rivalling Jewish humour.

Ronnie himself is famous for his deadpan jokes, which, on a good night, he will reel off in an endless stream. A week ago on television he was complaining that everyone called them bad jokes. They're not, he maintained; they're very good.

I agree. For instance, one night he was chatting to the audience when the bass player Ron Mathewson strolled on to the stand, wearing a hideous red plaid shirt and an equally garish pair of trousers in a different, clashing tartan. Ronnie stared at him in silence for ten seconds, then confided to the mike:

'Somewhere in London tonight there's a Ford Consul with no seat covers.'

But the joke of his I still like best is the one about the chef at the club who, claims Ronnie, is half black and half Japanese. Every 7 December he attacks Pearl Bailey. I hope somebody somewhere is getting his routine on film so that it is preserved for posterity, or, at the very least, so that it can be shown at the club's fiftieth anniversary.

Welcome back to 'Bin-Liner'

The leading expert on the natural history of the big city, 'Bin-Liner', has agreed to answer some of your queries about life outside the country.

For some time now there have been estate agents' placards on posts outside my block. I noticed yesterday that one of them was beginning to sprout small green shoots. What can this mean? P.H. of W11.

Bin-Liner writes: In a word, spring. You don't say how long the flats in your block have been unsold, but I imagine it must be four months or more, as it takes that long for a stake to put down its roots. If left to itself, the stake will grow into a healthy young tree and make an attractive green shade over the 'Double 2 Bed Flat' or whatever. Of course, it won't be left to itself, because an estate agent hates to admit his notice has been there long enough to grow, so he will come and replace it. I would advise taking cuttings now.

Can wildlife be neurotic? At dusk I have noticed a fox in my garden which, apparently, is subject to fits. If I didn't know better, I would say it was trying to do some disco dancing. G.D. of Croydon.

Bin-Liner writes: This is almost certainly what it is doing. The fox is under the impression that it is in Bristol, where the BBC Natural History Unit has made a speciality of films about urban foxes – I believe that auditions are now held monthly for foxes that can tap dance, sing a bit or do impressions of Russell Harty. If the animal is annoying you, it should be enough to open the window and shout: 'Thank you – we'll let you know!'

I have an elderly Morris Traveller car with the traditional half-timbered rear portion. Recently, I have noticed moss and lichen growing on the exposed sections of wood, which adds a certain bucolic charm, but I am uncertain about how to feed it. C.M. of Bath.

Bin-Liner writes: How nice to hear from someone prepared to preserve urban life; so many people would just spray their car with chemicals or root it out. The green on your car gets all the nutrition it needs from the air and from the wood, so do not worry. Have you considered planting mushrooms or wild fungi? They thrive on rotting organisms. If you go abroad by the way, you may have to scrub your car down, as sadly, your moss and lichen may offend regulations governing the export of living greenstuff.

I have noticed that many smart restaurants have bay trees in tubs outside their doors, which are chained up for fear of theft. Well, isn't this going to create a class structure among trees? I mean, if we deliberately divide trees into slaves and free trees – quite apart from the middle-class trees in parks with their railings round them – aren't we in danger of creating a revolutionary situation among trees, with all the conflict and strife that implies? Well, aren't we? M.S. of Liverpool.
   Bin-Liner writes: Get lost, you lefty loon.

As a hippy from Stockton-on-Tees, I have let my hair grow as I please, now three bullfinches appear to have made homes in my beard ... L.M. of Stockton.
   Bin-Liner writes: Those are not bullfinches, mate – they're fleas!

Banana skin republic

As this is the last piece I shall write before returning to my native Russia, I feel I must try to explain why I am taking this major step.

I first came to the West about twenty years ago as a very junior member of a humour and satire delegation, and stayed when the others went back. I did *not* defect. I just became lost at Heathrow, and spent days wandering around the airport, sometimes seeing my luggage going in the opposite direction. Instead of sinking into emotional despair, as many a Russian would, I sent an account of my experiences to *Punch* magazine, where it was published as an example of international domestic humour.

I soon found that I had many of the requisites of an English comic writer of the old school – that is, I was accident-prone, misread instructions on packages, had washing-machines that broke down, and went to the wrong place on holiday. The KGB made several attempts to kidnap me and take me back to Russia but, as I was always turning up at the wrong rendezvous, going home to the wrong house and getting into a bus going the wrong way, they soon gave up; they simply couldn't find me.

(It is my belief, by the way, that the West's major secret weapon against Communism is inefficiency. The Communist world can never believe that the West is capable of being as inefficient as they are.)

I duly changed my name from Milos Kontunov, acquired a family, house and Barclaycard, and even developed a tolerance to your almost unbearably mild winters. But I now realize that I have been bitterly unhappy the whole time I have been here. A Russian cut off from his mother soil is like a tree growing under water. Not a day has passed without my missing my sister and brother, Dacha and Lada, my parents, my friends and my little dog, who in my absence has grown up to be a big dog and, indeed has been dead since 1972. All these years I could have been close to them, writing humorous articles about them, using them as humorous fodder.

I miss everything about Russia. A Westerner cannot possibly understand how a Russian humorist misses the queues, the bureaucracy, the amiable corruption, the way Stalin pops in and out of favour. I miss the long winter nights, the snow in the trees, the warmth of the breath of a million vodka-drinkers. (Vodka, of course, does not smell. That is how we know when a man is drunk in Russia: his breath reeks of nothing.)

From time to time I have bumped into other Russians here and the aching nostalgia increases. I once encountered Svetlana Peters at Heathrow in 1976 (I was still looking for my luggage). She, of course, hated to be thought of as the daughter of Stalin, which was one reason she kept changing her name.

'You are Svetlana!' I greeted her. 'Daughter of the great tyrant, Joseph Peters!' She gave me an icy look and swept on. She was an American star by then, of course, a sort of Svetlana Turner. And who knows, I may meet her again in Moscow, at the place where we are trained for press conferences. For later today I am due to fly out of Britain and never see these shores again. So, it is farewell – and my parting message is: if you find my luggage, you can keep it.

Later: I have made a terrible mistake. I arrived at Heathrow on time. Unfortunately, the flight left from Gatwick. The KGB have sent me a message to say that I am a hopeless case, and no longer welcome. So please ignore this article: I shall be back here tomorrow as usual. Waiter, another vodka!

Athens v. Sparta – match abandoned

I bumped into the great palaeontologist from the East End of London, 'Cocker' Leakey, recently and discovered that he, like me, had been to Greece for the first time this year. Cocker, of course, is famous for his discovery of a fingernail millions of years old, which proves that originally man was not a hunter or nomad, but a football supporter.

In his definitive book, *Not Just a Pretty Skull*, he has established primitive man, or *Homo Millwallicus*, as a small dark fellow who stood upright, except on Saturday nights, and who would travel thousands of miles to support his team or, at least, to duff up another tribe.

But Greece, which symbolizes all that is most civilized in our history, is not the sort of place I imagined appealing to the down-to-earth Cocker. Didn't all those dignified remains make him uneasy? I put the question to him as we sat in the snug of the Skull and Trowel, his local, and he almost choked on his pork scratchings.

'Blimey, you're as bad as the rest of them. God save me from middle-class intellectuals. Look, the whole history of ancient Greece, if you can call a couple of thousand years ancient, has been written by nice bourgeois people with the occasional lord thrown in, so of *course* you all think it's very civilized. But you look through the history of Greece, and what were they doing most of the time?'

Thinking? Writing plays? Building temples?

'Do me a favour. They were fighting! They were always at it. Knocking each other's places down, ganging together, having another barney – strewth, it's like *Homo Millwallicus* had hardly evolved. Greece is the finest example of a football culture I've ever seen.'

But surely football isn't mentioned anywhere in Greek history?

'You don't actually have to have a football to have a football culture. Blimey, most of the football followers in this country never go to a match and, even if they do, it's the other supporters they've gone to deal with. No, look, what was the most significant development in Greek history?'

The city state? 'Right in one, sunshine! This was the first time that people had sorted out their rivalries on a proper town-club basis. And when they had their cities sorted out, what did they call their alliances?

Well, the Attic League and the Spartan League...

'There you are, *Leagues*! They'd sorted it all out into leagues, fixtures, home and away, seasons, everything. Look at the Trojan War as the first World Cup and you're home and dry. And all those buildings...'

The temples, and so on?

'*You* can call them temples if you like. Stone goalposts they look like to me. Listen, I was in the place only a fortnight, but I've never seen a clearer example of places being knocked to bits by a horde of infuriated fans.

'Gradually fell down over the years? Do me a favour! I've seen a football ground being done over which none of your flaming intellectuals has, and I've seen a Greek so-called temple, and believe me...'

But surely you can't ignore centuries of Greek scholarship?

'I'm not saying that. I'm not *saying* that. I'm saying you have to see it from a different angle. All those blokes writing screeds of philosophical rubbish, they existed, sure, but football always attracts your airy-fairy thinker – you have only to look at the Sunday papers or read Hans Keller on West Ham. It's one of the things that's killing football today. And do you know what the other is?'

Defensive play? 'Nah. Too many cups, that's what. Milk Cups and Tea Cups and UEAFA Cups and Cup-Losers Cups... And, tell me, what do you see most of in all those Greek museums?'

Well, vases and trophies, and large drinking cups...

'That's it! Cups and trophies! It killed the game in Greece, same as what it's killing it here. Blimey, it's thirsty work trying to knock the truth into your head. I'm ready for another beaker of the foaming Hippocrene, and it's your shout.'

Unusual jobs: no. 9

Les Handley entered his profession quite by accident. He trod on a cat one night. It was not badly hurt but it was limping, so he picked it up and then noticed it had a collar with a name and address on.

'Feeling a bit ashamed of myself, I went round to the owner's house to explain how it had got injured. They didn't want to know. As soon as they saw the cat, they fell on my neck, weeping and thanking me. Apparently the blessed thing had been missing for three weeks. But what set me off was the fact that they pressed a fiver on me.'

What he got, in fact, was a reward. It was then he started to notice the little signs plastered around London on trees (in middle-class areas) and lamp posts (in working-class and very posh areas), asking for the tracing and return of Tiddles.

'Now, there's not much point in looking for a missing cat to go and claim the reward with. There's one chance in a thousand you'd ever find it. No, what you've got to do is steal the cat first and *then* wait for the notice to go up. Generally speaking, that means you've got to steal cats with names and addresses on.'

Les generally waits a few days before he goes to claim the reward, as over-eagerness looks suspicious. The average reward these days is £10 to £15, and he reckons to clear at least a dozen cats a week, so he's on to £10,000 a year.

'That's not a fortune exactly, but it's tax-free. And I enjoy my work. That's the main thing. I love cats. To be quite honest, when the cats are with me I think they're often better looked after than at home.'

At any one time there are two or three dozen cats in his flat. In the early days this almost led to catastrophe.

'Thing was, there was a reward out in Bayswater for a small ginger cat. I had a small ginger cat, so I took it round. No, they said, it wasn't that small. An hour later I was back with another of my ginger cats, a bit bigger. Not that big, they said. I came back with one the right size, but – sadly – the wrong sex. Of course, me turning up with cat after cat made them suspicious, and the next time I turned up there was a police car lurking, so I just let the cat go and scarpered.'

Another near-disaster occurred when he found a cat collar lying in the street and matched it to a missing cat sign for a tabby called

Channel Four. He put the collar on a tabby at home and took it round.

'Unfortunately, I hadn't noticed when reading the ad that it was a Manx cat, so of course they were dumb-founded to see that their beloved Channel Four had grown a whole tail in four days.

'They knew it wasn't their cat. What they couldn't understand was why it was wearing their collar. Exit in double-quick time again. I'd strongly advise anyone thinking of taking up cat-stealing to read the notice *properly*.'

Doesn't Les ever worry about the heartache he brings to families who suddenly lose their familiar pet?

'Heartache? You've got to be joking. They haven't given their cat a second glance for years till it goes missing. Of course, they're a bit distraught when they can't find it, but that's nothing to the joy I bring them when I take it back. I treasure those moments. Some of these families have become firm friends of mine.'

A few of Les's cats are never claimed at all, and then he keeps them. He, in turn, puts collars on them with names and addresses and makes them part of the household. Recently a favourite tortoiseshell called Blue Cheese Dressing went missing and Les, somewhat ironically, found himself putting up Missing Cat notices.

'Blue Cheese was brought back inside four hours by a nice young couple, but there was something about the eager way they asked for the reward that alerted me. You rotten lot, I told them, you're just a pair of cat thieves! They shot off into the night. If any of your readers are thinking of becoming cat burglars, so to speak, I'd advise them very strongly *never* to mention the rewards. They'll always cough up.'

Les Handley, of all the people interviewed for this series, seemed to enjoy his work the most.

Skiing or the gentle art of leg-breaks

Hello, it's skiing time again! And we all know what that means, don't we? (*Writes Uncle Rudi, your unbearable guide to the piste.*)

Yes, snow, and pine trees, and blue skies, but above all – breaking your leg! That's what skiing is all about. You're out there, carelessly swooping down the lonely slope through the lovely trees when suddenly – crack! you're over and you have broken your leg.

Well, there's nobody in sight, because you've gone off on that lovely deserted run, and you've got to do something about it yourself, so I'm going to tell you now how to deal with it. Memorize this article immediately. Better still, take it with you and get it out when you've broken your leg.

Hello! Just broken your leg, have you? Don't panic. What you have got to do is straighten your leg as far as possible and then tie one ski to it as a splint. This will mean using your bootlaces to tie the ski on with. The other ski you can use as a crutch to hobble home with.

Unfortunately your boots will now fall off because you've taken the laces out. Also, the ski will be far too long to use as a splint, not to mention a crutch, so you will have to saw them down to the right length.

This means you should have brought with you spare boot laces, a saw and sandpaper. Did you? You didn't? Goodness, you are in trouble, aren't you? Perhaps we'd better bring in a real doctor.

Hello (*writes a hospital administrator*). Sorry we couldn't get a real doctor; he was out playing golf. Anyway, there you are with a broken leg on a deserted alp. The first question you ask yourself is: Am I properly insured? And did I bring the documents with me or did I leave them behind with the saw, boot laces and sandpaper?

The next question is: Is my injury serious enough to warrant getting a doctor out? You know, a lot of hospital time is wasted by people who really aren't ill, or who have a simple ailment that their chemist could deal with.

So before you get a doctor out to look at your leg and cause us endless trouble and rescheduling of appointments, have a chemist look at it. A lot of these chaps are very good. Don't bother us. Get a chemist. The French for chemist, by the way is *pharmacien*. Not at all. Glad to have helped. Cheers.

Cheers! (*Writes Jeremy, barman at the Coconut Glades.*) While you're lying there in agony, a drink would be the ideal thing to cheer you up, so I've devised a Glühwein Mexican Special for you – that's right, it's a wine plus tequila concoction.

Of course, you'll need four or five different bottles, plus a primus stove, and if you've left them behind with your documents, saw, boot laces etc., then I'm afraid I can't help you. You'll just have to wait for one of those dogs with brandy barrels to come along. Ciao.

Sorry I'm late (*writes a real doctor*), but I was out playing golf. And I'm afraid the bad news is that brandy is *out*. Alcohol opens the veins at the surface and gives you a feeling of warmth, but you know, it also takes away the blood from vital internal organs and then we're into heart attack country. What we need is something that closes the veins. And the only thing we've ever found like that is marijuana. Yes, odd isn't it? So get out a joint and light up.

Penalties for drug using are fairly stiff in Switzerland (*writes a lawyer*), and whatever the doctor says it's going to be pretty embarrassing if you're lying there with a broken leg, puffing away, and the first people to arrive are the Swiss Drug Squad, who have their own Mountain Drug Ring Busting team, and pretty efficient they are too. Hard men, as well. I can't say I'd relish the thought of being beaten up lying there in the snow with a bad leg. Still, it's up to you. That'll be £60 – I'll let you have the bill.

Well, that's it (*concludes Rudi*). There you are, lying in the snow, as the dusk descends and the stars come out – and what stars! They are particularly lovely at this time of year, and if you have your chart of the night sky with you, it will be an unforgettable experience. If you haven't, of course, it will be lost on you. So *do* remember when you go out skiing, always to have the following with you:

Boot laces, saw, sandpaper, insurance documents, mini-bar, primus stove, several marijuana joints and a night sky chart.

Have fun! Hope you survive!

A Christmas novel from Mills & Bang

A Falkland Passion, by Venetia Barnstraw

Chapter One

Georgia's first thought when she arrived in Port Stanley was that the shops were terribly drab. Oh, she knew that she was 7,000 miles from Bond Street, but really! Did everything have to be so provincial and boring? It was, after all, the week before Christmas and the nearest thing she could see to a Christmas present was an SAS balaclava helmet with holly stuck in it.

Then suddenly she realized it didn't matter. She had no one to buy presents for. She had come out here to the Falklands to start a new life and to forget Terry. For a moment, Terry's familiar crinkled face with its roguish smile swam in front of her, but she fought against the memory. She had to report to Falklands Stores HQ, where she was to act as secretary to one Captain Bolsover. They said that work made you forget...

Some soldiers were coming down the street, singing.

'Captain Bolsover?' said one of them, leering. 'Don't bother with him, love. You'll have a much better time with B Company, eh lads?'

Chapter Two

'Don't worry about the men,' said Captain Bolsover. 'They mean no harm. It's just that they haven't seen a pretty girl for years and you mustn't forget that men are brutes below the surface.'

'You too?' said Georgia, daringly. It was only her second day in the office, but already she felt she could trust his straight, Italianate features, so different from Terry's – damn! She mustn't think about Terry.

'I'm not a man,' said Bolsover. 'I'm an officer.' He laughed attractively. 'But seriously, you'd do well to keep away from the soldiers. And the construction workers. And the natives. I'm afraid that just leaves the sheep. But tell me, what *really* brings you here?'

'The end of an affair,' said Georgia, blushing. 'His name was Terry. I thought he loved me, but really he loved his boat more. And when he told me he was going to sail round the world...

Chapter Three

It had been a hard day for Dick Bolsover. As if it wasn't bad enough having Italianate features – his nickname among the men was Luigi, and the officers called him Rococo to his face – he had been out for a stroll among the hills and come across a soldier who had run amuck. Driven crazy by boredom and rain, the man had taken his rifle and started shooting sheep at random. Captain Bolsover had to arrest him, of course, but the big problem was the dead sheep. Could the men face roast mutton again?

'I know a rather good recipe for lamb marinaded in wine and garlic,' said Georgia later.

At supper that night there was a near-mutiny among them over what they called this foreign muck.

Is this love? he asked himself.

Chapter Four

> 'I'd rather be living in Argentina
> 'Than marching around for Sergeant Tina!'

The soldiers' song in the street outside floated up to the window of the room in downtown Port Stanley where Captain Bolsover and Georgia were working on the final details of the Christmas catering.

'Who's Sergeant Tina, Dick?' said Georgia.

'What? Oh, that's Sergeant Duckworth.'

'And why do they call him that?'

'Hard to say, really. Perhaps because the sergeant likes dressing up in frocks on his night off.

'We're in trouble, Georgie girl,' continued Bolsover briskly. 'The Hercules bringing in our entire shipment of Christmas puddings has come down in the Atlantic. Nobody's hurt, but they've reported a Christmas pudding slick two miles long, looking just like a minefield. Question is: what do we do for dessert now?'

'I've got a super recipe for instant Christmas plum duff,' said Georgia. 'I just need a ton of flour and a couple of lemons.'

'You're on!' said Dick. 'By the way, don't forget that tomorrow night is the officers' Christmas party. You're my guest.'

Chapter Five

Port Stanley was all decked out for Christmas. They had strung one streamer across the main street. Georgia had gone window shopping and was wondering whether Dick Bolsover would like a hand grenade or some barbed-wire cutters in his stocking.

Chapter Six

> 'Hark the herald angels sing
> '"White Christmas", as arranged by Bing,'

the soldiers sang. Dick Bolsover smiled at Georgia. 'Having a good time, Georgia? Forgotten about Terry now?'

Georgia, emboldened by a glass of sparkling Argentine white wine, smiled back, though she couldn't help wondering how far dear Terry had gone on his round-the-world trip.

'Come outside, Georgia,' said Dick thickly. 'There's something I have to ask you.'

Outside, the rain was falling harder than ever. Georgia suddenly realized, horrified, that Dick had put his arms round her.

'I love you,' said Dick hoarsely. 'I want to make my own conquest of Georgia!'

She shrank away, aghast. How could she have felt warm towards this man? Would no one rescue her? Suddenly, out of nowhere, came a form in yellow oilies and green boots. It was, unbelievably, Terry. He dispatched Dick Bolsover with one hook to the jaw and took Georgia in his arms.

'My darling,' he said, 'this is my first landfall on my voyage round the world and I fancy I have come just in time. I stopped for supplies and I found – you! Would you care to fill my extra berth?'

'I certainly would,' said Georgia. 'And while I'm at it, I'd like to rearrange the furniture on your boat and get it painted a nicer colour.'

If Terry had taken the hint, he would have gone on without her, but he didn't and that's another story.

Advertisement

When did you last think about rain?

Yes, that's right. Rain. The wet stuff that falls from the sky and later clears from the west. The liquid that comes in under doors or on dogs and cats. The magic stuff that makes taxis impossible to find. The only thing that can make cricketers run.

Rain.

Odds are you haven't thought about it for years, if ever. And even if you did, you thought to yourself: 'Oh God, it's raining again.'

We don't blame you. We'd like you to take rain for granted. Because that means we at the British Rain Bureau are doing our job properly.

What worries us (and we would be less than human if it didn't) is people who seem to think that one kind of rain is much like another. You couldn't be wronger! Drop for drop, British rain is the best in the world.

All right, so it isn't the most sensational in the world. There's nothing in Britain to rival the monsoons of India or the dramatic hurricanes of America. We can't rival those places in the world where the heavens majestically open and a sheet of water falls, until high streets are 6 ft deep in it and people go upstairs just to avoid drowning. There are no rain forests here and no raging torrents. Not even much in the way of rapids.

But would we really want things to be that way?

We at the British Rain Bureau think people would rather have rain that was dependable, regular and reliable. Rain that was soft and friendly. Rain you didn't feel threatened by.

British rain.

And don't go thinking that British rain is all the same. We are proud of our great regional varieties. The soft hanging rain that drifts across the Cotswolds. The tough, hard-wearing rain that swings in across Dartmoor. The lovely April showers that can arrive in any month, freshen up the landscape and be replaced by sun in ten minutes, as if Britain was going through some gigantic car wash. There are even people who think plain old drizzle has its charms!

Up in Scotland they have invented a special rain of their own called Scotch mist, which is so thin that it doesn't seem to be falling at all, but hovering.

Do you remember that old *Punch* cartoon in which the English lady is saying to the Scotsman: 'The rain seems to be clearing off at last, Sandy'? He says: 'Aye, I doot it's threatening to be dry.' (We have the original hanging in our Whitehall HQ.)

So next time you hear people singing the praises of foreign rain, give them the facts. Tell them that British rain is still the best in the world. That 100 per cent of the rain that falls in Britain is British-made, and that we import none of it. And that the British Rain Bureau is looking after your rain, night and day, so that grass may grow and rivers may run.

Don't accept any substitute for British rain.

This completely pointless advertisement was placed by the British Rain Bureau, and was paid for entirely out of your money. If you want to know more about the stuff that falls on the just and unjust alike, send off to the British Rain Bureau, the quango they forgot to kill off. We are here to serve you, also to spend our budget like mad before the end of the year so we can get even more money next year.

Write to us at Precipitation House, Whitehall, London. We'd love to hear from you. We'd love to hear from anybody.

Inside the Shed

'I'd shout for Chelsea, if I were you,' said Tim. 'It will look odd otherwise.'

'Right,' I said.

'And we might get murdered.'

'Right.'

There were 42,197 of us at Stamford Bridge last Saturday waiting to see Chelsea play Manchester United, most of us apparently standing in the Chelsea Shed. This is an imposing twentieth-century covered amphitheatre, heavily scented with fried onion. It looked out on a green field containing a set of goalposts and two little boys shooting balls at each other. One was rather worse than the other.

'He's rubbish!' shouted a man behind me. 'Remember to sell him in ten years time!'

'I'd laugh at their jokes, if I were you,' said Tim.

'Right,' I said.

It seems odd for 42,197 people to gather in one place to watch two eight-year-olds playing football, but this was ninety minutes before the match began and pre-match entertainment tends to come from the crowd rather than the pitch – the Chelsea Shed likes to gather early to practise their singing.

'Think I ought to join in with the singing, Tim?'

'Right.'

One song I especially liked went something like: '*We love you, Chelsea, we love you, we love you, Chelsea, yes we do, yes, we love you, Chelsea, yes, we do.*'

I may have missed out a few words, but that's the general gist. It was the only song I heard all afternoon without a four-letter word. The appearance of television cameras was greeted with another song entitled: '*Can you Hear us on The Box?*', interspersed with cries of '*Hello, mum!*' Football fans are all strangely convinced that their dear old mothers will switch on their tellies just to see their sons in the crowd.

With only forty minutes to go I had already read the programme five times. Half the programme was devoted to rejecting criticism of Chelsea supporters; the other half was devoted to criticizing Chelsea supporters for their behaviour at the last game. They had, apparently, jeered Chelsea for not winning.

But all this was forgotten when Chelsea finally ran out on the pitch and the fans cheered them wildly. And how superbly Chelsea performed! They passed, and sprinted, and shot unerringly, and the goalkeeper made fantastic saves, and everyone played like a genius, and the crowd loved them! They were wonderful!

Then Chelsea went back indoors again and it was still fifteen minutes to go to the game, because this was the pre-match warm-up.

'*Micky Thomas, Micky Thomas, There's only one Micky Thomas,*' sang the crowd.

I was glad to hear this. Micky Thomas started out playing for Wrexham, my home town. So did two other Chelsea players, Jones and Niedzwycki. In fact, John Neal the Chelsea manager used to manage Wrexham.

In fact, that's why I'd come to see Chelsea – it was probably the nearest I could get to seeing Wrexham, now languishing listlessly at the bottom of Division Four – and why I'd asked Tim, who is eighteen and thus knows more about football than I do, to take me.

Then the game started. There's little to report about it except that Manchester United won convincingly 3–1.

'Next time I'd shout for Chelsea if I were you,' said Tim.

'Didn't I?'

'No. You kept shouting "Come on Wrexham!"'

200 years of *Moreover* ...

In 1985 the 'Moreover ...' column celebrates its 200th anniversary, and many special events are being planned to mark this milestone. Ever since *The Times* was born 'Moreover ...' has been there too; it is probably a unique achievement in journalism for one column to have lasted 200 years, and we are proud to say that some of the jokes first used in 1785 are still being used today, as fresh as ever.

Like *The Times* itself, 'Moreover ...' has not always been known under that name. Its first rubric was 'A Droll Anecdote, Contributed by a Gentlemen Reader' – indeed, in those days the title was often longer than the joke itself. It came into its own during the Napoleonic Wars, when the writer of the column attacked both sides with equal savagery, which led to him being imprisoned on several occasions for sedition, by both sides. But he was at liberty at the time of the Battle of Waterloo and was the first journalist in Britain to report the result as a French victory, unfortunately, for which he was again sent to prison.

In those far-off days, of course, the new technology had not yet arrived, which meant that they could print things far more quickly and efficiently than we can today. The 2nd Lord Moreover, who wrote the column between 1823 and 1845 under the pseudonym of 'One Who Should Know Better', could post a joke to the paper in the afternoon and see it in print the next morning, without any of those infuriating misprints which nowadays cgtr%* finished three points down against the dollar *take in overmatter* and equalized in the last minute with a penalty which sent Drake the wrong way (cont p2 cpl 1).

During the next few weeks we shall be printing extracts from those early columns, such as the satirical verses on Queen Victoria's accession in 1837, which caused Lord Moreover to flee the country for two years, and the satirical attack on Metternich which caused him to flee back to England. When the Crimean War came, famous for its reporting by foreign correspondents, Moreover was exactly where you would expect him to be – back here in London. Indeed, the writer of the column in the 1850s (an illegitimate son of the 3rd Lord Moreover) managed to get through those years without mentioning the Crimea once; most of his columns were devoted to pursuing an affair with a wealthy widow, in code, and we shall be reprinting some of these as well.

The 3rd Lord Moreover, who had never shown any interest in the column, died in 1861 and there then ensued one of those inheritance trials so interesting to the public and so profitable to lawyers. No less than five different branches of the family claimed possession of the column and during the length of the trial (1862–7) it was written *in absentia* by *The Times*' Ecclesiastical Correspondent.

None of these columns (which were collected in book form as *Sermons in Lighter Vein*) will be reprinted.

Finally, in 1867, the so-called Moreover Claimant was exposed as an Australian adventurer and the column was restored to the 5th Lord Moreover, popularly known as Old Humourless. But during the 100th anniversary celebrations of 1885 his spendthrift son and heir, Sir Rodney Moreover, had the temerity to place the entire column on a hand of cards in a game organized by the Prince of Wales. He lost, and it passed out of the family for ever.

Nowadays the column is owned by the huge Moreover (Liechtenstein) Holdings, who make a fortune out of oil, TV, drugs and smuggling, and are thus enabled to stand the annual £2 million loss incurred by the column, mostly in the form of entertainment expenses. Our chairman is Lord Moreover (the title was a gift from Harold Wilson), who visits the office once a year incognito accompanied by his eight Libyan bodyguards. He has kindly agreed to let 1985 be a non-stop round of dinners, parties and celebratory outings for the column. Details of these will appear in due course, but the first one to put in your diary is the Moreover Man of the Year Award Ceremony on 15 January, at the M1 Pork Scratchings Service Area. The winner will again be Lord Moreover, but speculation over who will present the prize is bound to be feverish right up to the day itself. Don't miss it!

Parts of this column have previously appeared in 1892, 1904 and 1936.

Nature notes

Out and about with 'Crab Apple'

The lanes and tracks of England are rutted now with mud and manure (*writes Crab Apple*), which makes it treacherous underfoot. The branches stand stiffly against the sky and bitter wind brings the sheep huddling together for warmth; all in all, it's horrible weather and only a loony would be out and about, so I've stayed indoors ever since Christmas experimenting with my new cocktail-making kit.

Have you got one? Fun, aren't they? I went mad with Blue Curacao for a while, sploshing it into everything. Gave the wife a heart attack one morning, serving her blue porridge. Anyway, here's a new cocktail I've invented which I call 'Deadly Nightshade' ... (*'Crab Apple' has just been fired*, writes the *'Moreover ...'* Nature Editor. *We are pleased to announce that Nature Notes will in future be written by 'Sheepshank' of Country Life.*)

Out and about with 'Sheepshank'

Hello, everyone (*writes Sheepshank*). Well, there seems to have been some kind of mistake here because I was actually the knot-tying expert on *Country Life*, but nothing venture, nothing win. And when you're out on a country walk, there's nothing more important than fastening gates behind you. Most farmers now leave lengths of that orange-coloured twine all over the place, which is ideal for tying gates up with, and the knot I always recommended is a Bulgarian Flying Hitch.

Put a slip knot over the main gate post, then loop the string firmly round the nearest corner of the gate, bringing it up, back and down, as in a normal Flying Hitch. Leaving two loops, take the strings ... (*And 'Sheepshank' will be back at some unspecified future date with more knot news*, writes our Nature Editor. *Meanwhile, here are some special January Nature Notes from Boy George.*)

Out and about with Boy George

Hello, you beautiful people (*writes Boy George*). Of course, I'm not *that* Boy George. I'm just a Boy George look-alike who happens to have the same name. And believe me, it's very useful being mistaken for the Widow Twankey of pop music the whole time – you get the best seats in restaurants, the best rooms in hotels and free flights all over the world. Frinstance, I've just come back from Christmas on Montserrat, and believe me, nature is looking pretty good out there at the moment. Great sprays of hibiscus, frangipani and gardenia – and that's just what's in the waitresses' hair! No, seriously, if you have a palm tree that needs repotting, now is the time ... (*Today's guest star in Nature Notes*, writes our Nature Editor, *was someone called Boy George. And there I'm afraid I must leave you as I have just been fired personally by Lord Moreover on one of his rare visits to the office. Goodbye.*)

Out and about with Lord Moreover

As someone who already owns half of Norfolk (*writes Lord Moreover*), I can be said to be in pretty good touch with nature, especially intensively grown wheat. And my advice to you in 1986 is – deal direct with the Russians. No shilly-shallying about with Brussels and quotas and things with middlemen creaming everything off. Get on the hot line to the Kremlin, ask them how much they want, and when by. And insist they collect personally. As someone who owns half the ports in Norfolk, I think I know what I'm talking about.

Above all, cut out anything that isn't making a profit. This is nature's own lesson. The dodo wasn't making a return on investment, so nature ruthlessly cut him out. That's why, on my land, you won't find any trees, hedges, country churches or telephone kiosks. It's my way of getting back to nature.

Another example. This Nature Notes column has been running for years without attracting one single ad. I had no idea. A quite horrifying waste of money. I am closing it down today. If anyone wants to buy it, they're welcome.

A farewell to the pound

I can reveal that one of the most popular items in the British currency is to disappear. Yes, the pound itself is to be completely phased out during 1985 and replaced by the American dollar. The British Government's plans, which they had hoped to keep secret, are to wait till the pound sinks to the exact level of the dollar and then introduce the dollar instead of the pound.

The thinking behind this move is that it may effectively prevent the pound sinking *below* the value of the dollar. The Government concedes that it may be embarrassing to have an imported note as our main unit of currency, with a picture of George Washington on it, but their attitude is that most people in Britain couldn't tell you what was on the pound note anyway, and that a lot of us will automatically assume that the gent with white hair is Shakespeare or Gladstone.

They will be helped in their campaign by the fact that the new pound coin is so unpopular – indeed, it is suspected that they deliberately introduced the unpopular pound coin so that people would welcome its replacement by the dollar.

Be that as it may, the disappearance of the familiar quid is going to cause a lot of unrest. The pound has played a significant part in the history of these islands, as a tame historian was quick to confirm when we rang him up for an instant quote.

'My goodness, yes, it certainly has. You know, of course, that when the pound sterling was originally introduced by Edward III, it was made of solid gold, encrusted with gems and sold in its own velvet-lined case? In those days a pound could buy an army for a month, a small province in France or a quickie divorce from the Pope. Nowadays you can hardly buy a pint of beer with it. In 1389, if you bought a pint of beer with a pound, the charge was so minute they usually gave you the pound back.

'In Henry VIII's day the pound became made of silver and was renamed a sovereign, after Henry himself. It was also bigger, to get a full portrait of himself on one side and the complete words and music of 'Greensleeves' on the other. This was a clever move on his part, as it meant that every time a pound changed hands he got royalties as songwriter, lyricist and publisher.

'The first paper pound came in sometime in the eighteenth century – not like our paltry pound note, of course, but a small, well-bound booklet of some twenty pages, explaining the conditions under which it was sold and a 101 other uses to which it could be put, including the cleaning of pewter and use as a passport. People also used it as a substitute for chewing tobacco – do you remember that phrase about people shifting their quid from one cheek to the other?

'And did you know that in Victorian times they very nearly granted Charles Dickens permission to serialize a novel on the pound note, such was his popularity? Of course, I can't swear to all these facts, as my phone is the far end of the room from my reference books, but I don't suppose anyone will know any difference. And if you can pay me in dollars as usual ... Thanks.'

The implications are staggering. We have succumbed to American influence in many spheres – our English music tradition has been totally replaced by American sources, and our television is going the same way – but to surrender something as basic as the pound is akin to driving on the right or ordering a half-litre of best bitter. In fact, my sources tell me that the psychological risks involved may cause the Government to think again and to stick to the pound after all.

If that is the case, then we shall never hear the announcement of the switch to the dollar. And if that happens, remember that you didn't just read it here first, but you read it here last as well.

Blood by Heinz, names by Ordnance Survey

Opposite *Punch*, where I used to go to work, or at least used to go, there was a large office building called Temple Chambers. I must have passed that building at least 500 times before it occurred to me that the name Temple Chambers was wasted on a set of offices. It was the ideal name for a fictional detective of the old school. He probably wore a waistcoat and a bow-tie, had insufficiently cleaned brogues and always solved his cases in a library in the last chapter. He played the violin on the side, like Holmes, but in the style of Stephane Grappelli.

Other signs have occasionally yielded good names for characters. Max Headroom is one I favour for an upbeat hero, though for a downbeat hero I would prefer Matt Finish. A Dutch hero with aristocratic overtones could only be Hertz van Rental.

These names, though, have been hard to find over the years. Or at least they were till last year, when I was driving through the depths of the country dragging the double bass en route to some far-flung Instant Sunshine gig, and my companion cried out: 'Look! It's a tough American lawyer!'

Now, my companion is a sharp-eyed girl, but to spot an American lawyer in the English countryside, in pitch blackness, and to spot that he is a tough one, stretched the credulity. Yet she was right. Because we were passing through a village called Upton Scudamore, and if Upton Scudamore is not a tough American lawyer, I will eat my collected Raymond Chandler.

'Scudamore had hard eyes like diamonds, which he kept locked away behind bullet-proof spectacles. When his wife asked him if he had had a good day at the office, he probably charged her for the information. You get the feeling that if Upton Scudamore had been around in the Book of Genesis and offered his services to Adam and Eve, God would have ended up being evicted from the Garden of Eden, though all things considered, Upton would probably have preferred to act for the serpent...'

Yes, villages are the answer. What a wealth of fictional names lies there. Horsley Woodhouse, Haselbury Plucknett, Eccle Riggs, Morley Smithy, Hinton St George and Bubney Moor – all lying around on Ordnance Survey maps, just waiting for a passing Georgette Heyer Regency novel. I like the sound of Bushy Ruff, no doubt a moustachioed rascal with a heart of gold, good clean-living Christian Malford, affable lady-about-town Fenny Bridges and heart-stopping young beauty Honey Hill.

Don't imagine for a moment that all English village names make old-fashioned characters. There is a pair of villages near Shrewsbury called Wig Wig and Homer, who can only be villains out of Damon Runyon, and the same goes for Cutty Stubbs, Coole Pilate and Thick Withins. Thick Withins, I swear to you, is on the Buxton map, as are also Glutton Grange, Bumper Castle, Butchersick Farm and Dirty Gutter.

There is a village in Kent called Womenswold. Is this some kind of rural WI? I'm just off to the Womenswold – your supper is in the fridge. And is it related to another kind of gathering further north, the Nine Ladies Stone Circle? Which early jazz band did Bix Bottom play with? Did Auton Dolwells change his name when he came from

Hungary? Why is there a village in Dorset called Barpark Corner and is it related to one in Sussex called The Mens? And will Lydiard Millicent ever get engaged to the village next door, Clyffe Pypard?

This morning I was passing a lingerie shop and cried out, pointing at a label: 'Look – it's an English village!' The label said 'Cotton Gussets'. My companion led me away, but only as far as next door, where I saw another village name: Lloyds Nightsafe.

'It's all right, dear,' she said. 'It's not a village name.' She's right. Lloyds Nightsafe is obviously a wild flower.

Short is beautiful

Although there was a time when I knew the entire works of Byron, Wordsworth and Allen Ginsberg off by heart, I find now that the poems that have stayed with me longest are those taught me by my father. Here is one classic I learnt from him:

> I wish I were a cassowary
> On the plains of Timbuctoo
> Then I'd eat a missionary
> Boots and hat, and hymn book too

His favourite poetry book, and mine too, was a little anthology of the works of Harry Graham entitled *Ruthless Rhymes for Heartless Homes*. The most sentimental poem in it went as follows:

> Father heard his children scream,
> So he threw them in the stream,
> Saying, as he drowned the third,
> 'Children should be seen, *not* heard.'

One cannot stay with four-line poems all one's life. There comes a time when one has to admit that there are other, more valid forms. But instead of looking for longer verses, I have found myself gravitating towards the even terser two-line poem. Who was it who wrote this one?

> I know two things about the horse,

> And one of them is rather coarse.

I have no idea, but he was a master of form. As was the author of this classic:

> Roses are red, and violets are blueish;
> If it wasn't for Jesus, we'd all be Jewish.

The trouble, it seems to me, is that the great poets have never recognized the supremacy of the two-line epic. Or if they have, their publishers have swiftly dissuaded them from adopting it, with the result that Tennyson and Pope never left behind any two-line classics.

All that will be changed in the forthcoming *Moreover Book of Condensed Verse*, in which the Moreover computer has reduced the works of all the great poets to two lines each, preserving in each case the essence and quiddity of their thought. Here, for instance, is what he has made of Milton.

> When I consider how my life is spent
> I find that most has gone on rent.

And W. H. Davies:

> What is this life if, full of care,
> We cannot dance like Fred Astaire?

Who can deny the deep philosophy contained in these two-line nuggets? Who would not breathe a sigh of relief if all the poets were reduced to such a rich basic stock? Does not Coleridge appear much clearer when his verse becomes:

> It is an ancient batsman,
> And he stoppeth one of three?

The only poet that the computer has had problems with so far is Wordsworth, whose thought is too woolly to allow of clear interpretation. Not content with this Wordsworthian trope:

> I wandered lonely as a cloud
> And ended up, quite skint, in Stroud

the computer has also produced:

> The child is father of the man,
> And I am my great-uncle, Anne.

But we are convinced that the *Moreover Book of Condensed Verse* will be a smash-hit best-seller. In the words of Alexander Pope:

> A little learning is a dangerous thing;
> Two CSEs will fit you to be King.

As true today as it was then. Order your copy now.

The wheels of India

If you thought there were a lot of bicycles in Oxford and Cambridge, you should see Delhi, Hyderabad and other civilized Indian towns. Last month I was constantly being urged to buy silks and saris and silverware, and I bought enough to fill a washbag, but what I really secretly wanted was an Indian bicycle. Not many frills about them, except for the occasional spray of fresh flowers and strange shock-absorbers which seem to back up the forks, but how solid they are, how easily they take a couple of people on the back. Try sitting a friend on the back of an English bike and you wouldn't have any bike left.

Especially I wanted a bicycle rickshaw, which is a pedalling version of a horse and trap. I've never hankered after a chauffeur-driven car, only after a chauffeur-pedalled tandem, with him sitting in front and me behind with the *Financial Times*, and my *Times* inside the *FT*. The trouble is that on a tandem you have to do some work wherever you sit. Not so with an Indian rickshaw, where you sit enthroned and let him do all the work, and just as soon as I own a daily newspaper, that is how I will travel to it.

Or even an auto-rickshaw, which is a moped version of a pony and trap, and this time the driver gets cover from the rain as well, so as a democratic newspaper proprietor I suppose I ought to get one of those. Indian city streets swarm with all of them, as well as cars and taxis, so a main crossing where the lights are about to turn green is a fearsome sight – bikes in front, rickshaws breathing down their neck, auto-rickshaws revving up to burst through them – it's like watching the whole Welsh XV about to charge from a drop-out. Miraculously, once under way they all seem to avoid one another. The only sign of an accident I saw was a man rubbing his wife's bottom.

'She has no doubt just fallen off his moped,' I was informed. 'When you are wearing a sari you can only ride side-saddle, and this has its attendant risks.'

I once saw an attempt to segregate the traffic. On the main bridge in Hyderabad there are four lanes going either way, separated by concrete ridges. The inner one is for pedestrians; the next for bikes; the next for auto-rickshaws and bullock carts, the other for four-wheeled vehicles. Cows can go in any lane. This bridge apart, the rest of India, as far as I can tell, relies on what we would call road sense and what they call hooting all the time. Indian drivers do not hoot in anger, but use hooting as a language ... 'I am coming up your off-side ...' 'If you do not give way, I will take your off-side ...' '... I have just taken your off-side.'

As an encouragement, most Indian vehicles have a sign on the back saying 'HORN PLEASE'. One auto-rickshaw I hired in Hyderabad was actually stopped by a policeman, who shouted at my driver: 'You've got a horn, haven't you? Use it!' Never before have I seen a motorist cautioned for *not* hooting. As to how good Indian drivers are, I would say that the ones who are still alive are very good. I did have one very bad driver, but the one I had the next day was brilliant. He had previously been in the Indian army, driving tanks for fifteen years. When he got me home after a two-hour drive, he said: 'Perhaps I should not tell you this, sir, but for the last twenty miles we are having no brakes. Gears only.' And I never noticed.

The oddest cyclist I met was, perhaps predictably, English. He was a young lad who had come out to see all five Test matches, and to cycle from one to the next. He had averaged about 100 miles a day and found it no problem, except for the first few days when he had dysentery. The thing that Indians had found most unusual about his bike was its eighteen gears; their surprise was understandable, as Indian bikes have no gears. Their riders pedal stolidly along in the equivalent of middle gear, knees splayed out slightly and using the sole of the feet to push, never the ball or toes. Perhaps this calms the stomach and avoids dysentery.

But the fact that he was bicycling they did not find odd at all. Quite right. In a civilized country like India the bicycle is given its rightful place – there are even, at intervals along the main boulevards, little boys under shady trees ready to mend punctures for you. Why does this not happen in London? As soon as I own a paper, I shall campaign vigorously for it.

When a Russian leader dies...

So, Konstantin Chernenko is dead. The man they called the president of Soviet Russia is dead. The ruler of the most powerful nation outside America has passed to his forefathers. The big cheese has snuffed it. Yes, the leader whose word was law from Moscow to Manchuria has gone to the great retirement home in the sky. And now a thousand hack writers are busy at work churning out their obligatory valedictory articles around the globe.

What was he like, this arbiter of Communism whose hand was on the tiller which controlled the course of the Soviet empire? This ruthless party machine boss who held the threads which controlled the actions of millions of Russian citizens, what was he like? The simple answer is that, apart from the fact that he coughed a lot, we simply don't know. His finger was on the button of the mightiest war machine the world has ever seen, yet there isn't a damned thing to say about him. It is almost as if the man himself never actually existed in real life.

So what are they like, these thousand hacks who have been commanded to write their wise words about the late Konstantin Chernenko, the man whose passing is being honoured today by one of the greatest turn-outs of dark suits the world has seen since Yuri Andropov kicked the bucket? They are frightened men, these syndicated columnists desperately trying to put a few words together. The editor is screaming for their articles, yet already they have reached paragraph three and can't think of anything else to say. No wonder they reach for their bottle of Scotch and send the messenger boy out for another packet of cigarettes.

But this much is certain. When all else fails, they will begin a paragraph saying: 'But this much is certain.' After that, perhaps they will say: 'The world can never be quite the same again.' Then they will look at what they have written and say: 'That's ridiculous; the world will be exactly the same, because Mr Gorbachev is no different, only a bit younger.' Then they will delete this paragraph and try another one, starting: 'Who can honestly know what goes on in the Kremlin power game?'

Who can honestly know what goes on in the Kremlin power game? Certainly not the thousand hacks who wouldn't know a power game if it beat them over the head with a rolled-up *Financial Times*. Certainly not the editor who is screaming for their copy while trying to choose the best photo of the VIPs arriving in Moscow, preferably one with David Owen trying to upstage Neil Kinnock. Probably not even the messenger boy who has just come back with a packet of the wrong cigarettes, for God's sake you know I smoke Wild Strawberry Filters!

So what is he like, this messenger boy who has just had to go out for the second time to the kiosk on the corner and change the twenty Gitanes for Wild Strawberry Filters? Well, this much is certain. He doesn't give a damn who runs Russia. All he knows is that he has to waste his time running around for the big-shot columnist, who has to waste his time churning out his thousand words for the editor, who has to waste his time screaming for copy in order to satisfy the proprietor, who has to waste his time doing whatever it is that newspaper proprietors do.

A bit like the Kremlin, really. Lots of people running round buying cigarettes and screaming at each other, with someone at the top wondering what to do next. But this much is certain, Mikhail Gorbachev is now the most powerful man in Soviet Russia, the man with a thousand messengers at his beck and call, ready to get a thousand packets of cigarettes, also to destroy the USA if necessary.

So what is he like, this young, dynamic, balding new Red supremo? Well, we've no idea, really. But that doesn't prevent us churning out another thousand words of copy and somehow miraculously, amazingly, getting within reach of the final paragraph of our article which will, almost certainly, start with the words: 'What of the future?'

What of the future? Will Gorbachev change the rules of the power game? Or will he hew close to the traditional image of the Soviet leader? Will there be a loosening of the Communist structure or will it be business as usual? Isn't it nice asking all these questions? Doesn't it sound as if we know what we're talking about? When, in fact, we don't have the faintest idea what we're talking about and only time will tell?

So what of the future? Well, only time will tell. But this much is certain. The world can never be quite the same again. Thanks – how much do I owe you for the cigarettes?

An ABC of new diseases

In all the excitement over Aids, it is often forgotten that many other perfectly valid though less sensational ailments are being discovered by science all the time, and sometimes being invented by it as well. Here is an A to Z of the most recent.

Agoraphobia: the fear of Greek marketplaces, from 'agora' meaning a Greek marketplace and 'phobia', meaning a tendency to shut yourself up in your bedroom for weeks on end. Agora is also a small piece of Israeli money, and doctors have occasionally reported people who have a real fear of small Israeli coins. Only one case has been fatal – that of a person who was handed small Israeli coins in a Greek marketplace.

Biographia Nervosa: a compulsive desire on the part of actors and actresses to list every production they have ever been in for a theatre programme, without ever mentioning their date of birth.

Croydon Bends, The: an irrational feeling that one is on the wrong train, usually accompanied by a feeling that even if one is on the right train, it won't stop at the right station.

Dyslexia Personalis: an inability to master names. This usually takes the form of calling one's children by one's pets' names, or addressing present spouse by name of previous spouse, or not being able to remember which Lloyd-Webber is which.

Einstein's Fallacy: the persistent tendency to set out for an appointment at the very time one is meant to be there. In extreme cases the patient does not set out at all, but rings up to say he is ill.

Elevated Vision: the tendency to go around looking up. This is caused by having been harnessed, as a baby, in one of those carriers strapped to the parent's chest, so that you could see nothing except upwards. This also produces **Heartbeat Deficiency**.

Facsimilitis: the irrational belief that the nice pictures of people stuck up outside passport photo booths were actually taken in that booth.

Geneva Block: the chronic inability to understand why Ronald Reagan thinks it will help disarmament talks if he makes many more weapons first.

Heartbeat Deficiency: many babies, if they have been strapped close to their parent's chest, where they can hear their parent's heart beating, grow up convinced they need two heartbeats. This leads them to wear a personal stereo system, with the drummer playing the part of their missing mother. See **Personal Stereoitis**.

Infomania: the compulsion to stay behind in a cinema and read the credits to the bitter end.

Jacket Fallacy, The: the deluded belief that the photograph on a book jacket resembles the writer of the book, or indeed that the blurb resembles the contents.

Kington's Syndrome: the tendency to put passport, visa and tickets in a safe place and then mislay the safe place.

Labelitis: chronic over-moistening of the tongue, causing stamps to fall off envelopes.

Maggielomania: the delusion that everything one says is right.

Neil's Disease: the delusion that everything someone else says is wrong.

Owen's Syndrome: a pathological combination of the previous two.

Personal Stereoitis: the compulsion to wear personal stereos in trains and the belief that nobody else can hear them. The only cure is to throw the patient out of the train.

Questionitis: the compulsive belief that Magnus Magnusson already knew the answers to all the questions he asks on *Mastermind*, that Robert Robinson uses all the *Call My Bluff* words in everyday conversation, etc.

Rampant Paradoxia: the urge to leave Fire Doors wedged open, to leave ashtrays in rooms containing No Smoking signs, to put Pull signs on doors which open both ways, etc., etc.

Stapler's Sickness: injury caused by the repeated removal of staples with fingernail, leading to infection, gangrene, death and even possible loss of clerical job.

Tequila Eye: injury to the retina caused by cocktail parasols.

Undistributed Middle: abdominal swelling caused by vanity, i.e. a belt or pair of trousers several sizes smaller than your waistline.

Viking Syndrome: a compulsive urge to prove that America was discovered far earlier than anyone suspects.

Water on the Thigh: an unpleasant rash caused by Perrier-sodden napkin.

X-Ray Syndrome: persistent over-excitement at being searched by airport security officials.

Yelling Fever: total breakdown of nervous system following humiliating failure to open a packet of crisps.

Zeditis: paranoia and depression caused by inability of list-makers to think of anything beginning with Z.

The ancestry racket

'Get your ancestors here! Get your ancestors here!'

The cry came from a raggedy old man, pushing his barrow up the Bayswater Road one Sunday morning. Stranger, have you ever been up the Bayswater Road on a Sunday morning? If you have, it's a hundred to one you were a stranger, because the only folk you get up there at that time are people from Suffolk hanging paintings on the railings for people from Arabia to buy.

'Get your ancestors here! Lovely, fresh ancestors!'

I peered into the old man's barrow. It was full of dusty, cracked old volumes – Burke's *Landed Loonies*, Debrett's *Guide to Dead People*, that sort of thing. He noticed my interest and was on to me like a flash.

'You've got a kindly face, sir. Cross my palm with traveller's cheques and I'll find you an ancestry you'll be proud of for the rest of your life.'

Something in the old man's face, some vestige of nobility, told me he had not always been employed thus. Gently, with the help of a 5p coin, I eased his life story out of him.

''Twas not always thus, sir. Until yesterday I was head of the College of Arms. Norman Herald, I was called. And now you see me like this, selling the odd stranger a scrap of his own family history. 'Tis pitiful, sir.'

A street cleaner came past at that moment, filling his own barrow with plane leaves, ice cream wrappers and old VAT returns. My man was on to him in a moment, clasping his wrist.

'Tell me your name, sir, and I'll tell you your fortune.'

'My name is Patel,' said the street cleaner. Unusual to find a Patel who did not own a supermarket, I thought.

'Patel!' said the old man. 'A lucky name. A fine old name.' He flicked through a book whose name I could not see. 'Yes, here we are – your family emigrated to the state of Gujarat 300 years ago, but before that you wandered across the huge landmass of Europe for many centuries, your original home being the land we now call Scotland. And by great good fortune I have here a piece of your old family property!'

Saying which, he drew out of the recesses of his barrow a filthy bit of tartan cloth which even I could recognize as Hunting MacGregor.

'You old rascal,' I said. 'You know as well as I do that tartans were not even given family significance until after 1760. The whole kilt thing is a modern invention.'

'Bless my soul,' said the ancestry salesman, 'but you're a knowing young fellow. Cross my palm with Krugerrands and tell me your name.'

Something in the old man's eyes prompted me to tell the truth. I ignored the feeling.

'Maxwell,' I said.

'Maxwell! A grand old English name. The Maxwells of Derbyshire have flourished for many years in Wiltshire, and vice versa. By the greatest good fortune I have a piece of the old family tapestry here.'

And so saying, he drew out the piece of filthy MacGregor once more. He blew his nose on it and offered it to me, together with the title deeds to a disused railway line in Clackmannanshire.

'You are now Honorary Lord of the Station of Newtonmuir, and Porter Extraordinary of Gaskhorn. God bless you, sire! That will be seventy-five guineas.'

'You're a grand old fraud,' I said. 'As you well know, the titles of the London, Midlands, Lake District and Clackmannan Railway died with their holders. They are not transferable, like their platform tickets.'

He looked at me suspiciously.

'Quite the little know-all, aren't we, sir? May I ask how you come by this knowledge?'

'Certainly,' I said, flashing my badge. 'Ancestry Fraud Squad. I must ask you to accompany me to the station. I believe you are the Mr Big we have been looking for.'

A look of pride came into the old man's eyes.

'Mr Big of that Ilk, if you *don't* mind,' he said. 'Remember our family motto: *Ego numquam factus sum.*'

'Meaning?'

'I've never been done for nothing.'

But how wrong he turned out to be. Don't be like Mr Big of that Ilk – leave the selling of our heritage to the appropriate government department. A message from the Ancestry Fraud Squad.

You are tuned to Radio 4. Please don't leave us

Hello. This is Radio 4 and here is the news.

An expert says that Radio 4 can damage the brain. Princess Diana wears a pink dress and tiara to the opening of a fashion show. It will be a cool, showery day over most of Britain. Now the news in detail.

Last night a communications expert, Dr Brian Throughput, attacked the BBC for its news coverage on Radio 4, saying that very often one item could be expanded in such a way as to fill almost a whole news bulletin. He went on to say that this created expectations in a listener which were not fulfilled, causing what he called a mental equivalent of an empty stomach.

Here with a special report on Dr Throughput's extraordinary attack is our communications correspondent, Brian Hasgood.

'Uninformative. Repetitive. Mind-rotting. Repetitive. Boring. Repetitive. These are just some of the adjectives used by Dr Brian Throughput, Professor of Communications at Bunuel University, to describe the Radio 4 news format. He said last night that the Radio 4 habit of taking one news item and repeating it in as many different forms as possible created an impression that the listener was being given fresh information, whereas he was just being given the same bit of news over and over again.

'Dr Throughput, who has been at Bunuel University for almost three years, said that one typical trick was to introduce different voices on to the programme. After the newsreader had read the item twice, an expert might be called in, and then an on-the-spot recording of someone involved in the news item would follow.'

Dr Throughput backed up his accusations with a detailed breakdown of what he called the Radio 4 mentality. Here's an on-the-spot interview with the professor, made after last night's attack on the media.

'Radio 3 on the whole presents very good news bulletins, and of course the World Service's are admirable. Radios 1 and 2 really don't have long enough news bulletins to allow repetition. It's Radio 4 which is the main culprit, with endless repetition of whatever trivial item has been allowed to stray into the number one spot. It's so hypnotic that we don't really realize it's happening.

'And just when you think you might be coming to the end of the item at last, the BBC springs another surprise, like introducing someone with a contrary viewpoint.'

Here, to defend the BBC against the charges, is the Producer-General, Bruce Denim.

'Of course there is a certain amount of repetition, but only enough to bring the facts home to the listener. In my opinion we are getting the balance just about right. I think Dr Throughput has got it all wrong.'

Bruce Denim. Now the rest of the news. Princess Diana appeared at a fashion show last night in Italy wearing a stunning pink dress and tiara. Here's our fashion correspondent, Dominique Harrod.

'Wearing a stunning pink dress with matching tiara, Princess Diana last night was the star of a top Italian show of new fashions, which she had been invited to open. Here is part of her speech.'

'Hello. I am Princess Diana and I am wearing this stunning pink dress with tiara. It gives me great pleasure to declare this fashion show open. Now back to the studio.'

Princess Diana. Forecasters say it will be a cool and showery day over most of Britain, and here's a forecaster to say it.

'Hello, there. What we can expect today, I think, is a cool day over most of Britain. This means it will be less warm than usual. If there are showers as well, and we expect there will be, it will also be wetter than usual. And the outlook, I'm afraid, is much the same.'

Now the headlines again. An expert, wearing a pink suit and tiara, says that Radio 4 can ruin the brain. Princess Diana, looking cool and showery, opens an Italian fashion show. And the forecast? Much the same, I'm afraid. Now the headlines again. A cool pink expert has said that too many weather forecasts can give the mind damp rot. In Italy, Princess Diana said much the same, I'm afraid. Now it's ten past eight and time for a real programme.

From mighty acorns tiny oak trees grow

There seems to come a moment in the history of all organizations when the people in charge look at each other and say: 'Why don't we branch out a little?' Up to that moment they have been specializing in one thing, selling postage stamps for example, but one day they have this brilliant idea: Why don't we do dog licences as well! After that they move on to pensions, parcels and postal orders and before you know where you are you have long, maddening queues in every post office in the country.

(After that they have another brilliant idea, namely closing down post offices where there are no long queues, but that's another story.)

The example most familiar to everyone is that of milk floats. Once upon a time they just sold milk. Then cream crept in. Then yoghurt. Now you can stop a milk float and buy fruit juice, potatoes and oven-ready chickens.

I expect economists have thought of a name for the tendency to branch out a bit (perhaps it's called capitalism, unless I'm thinking of something else) but I never read economists so I don't know. Newspapers, of course, branch out a lot. Once they just sold news. Now it's magazines, bingo, free holidays, and personal fortunes of a million pounds. Of course they don't actually sell those, they just give them away. Perhaps that's why so many papers are in trouble, but not being an economist, I wouldn't know.

What I do know is that there is a receptionist in a provincial TV company who sells eggs. I think she keeps hens at home, or knows an economist who keeps chickens, something like that, but anyway one day last year eggs appeared on her desk, and now people say to her: 'I've come to see the Head of Heavy Entertainment and could I have a dozen brown, please?' And towards Christmas a sign appeared on her desk: 'Please order your turkeys for Christmas now.' She is, let's face it, branching out.

My local bike shop has taken to selling eggs.

Many garages now sell potatoes in big sacks.

If you have a Barclaycard, your bill now arrives with a mail order catalogue.

Everyone is branching out, with the sole and rather tragic exception of evening paper-sellers. When I first came to London, you had a choice of three evening papers and now you only have a choice of one. I expect economists call this branching in. If I were an evening paper-seller, I would sell free-range eggs, then move on to potatoes and milk.

I am not an evening paper-seller, though. I am a columnist. And it suddenly occurred to me the other day that all I do is sell my column. Here I sit, on this valuable bit of real estate within a stone's throw of the fashionable *Times* letter page, and I am committing commercial suicide *because I haven't branched out*. Economists would think me an idiot.

All that is now going to change. I propose in future to offer a valuable range of services in this space. The following are the ones I am most seriously considering. It would be a great help to my marketing division if you could spare the time to tick the ones you most need and send the form back to me.

☐ Offering help with *The Times* crossword.

☐ Advising on choice of names for babies.

☐ Translating recherché menus.

☐ Getting a good price for your valuables by making false and malicious bids at Sotheby's.

☐ Recommending trouble-free back-street routes into London.

☐ Explaining why personal computers are unnecessary.

☐ Printing lists of post offices without queues.

☐ Listing banks which open on Saturday afternoon.

☐ Explaining why waiters laugh at you in Japanese restaurants.

☐ Giving you a list of ten intelligent remarks to make at the interval of a new play which you haven't understood a word of.

☐ Showing you how to whistle with two fingers in your mouth.

☐ Helping you to memorize your postcode.

☐ Revealing how to extricate freesias which have been put by your florist in polythene bags the wrong way round.

☐ Translating estate agents' language into English.

☐ Telling you what to say when you have lost all your money and family, and a TV interviewer asks you: 'How do you feel?'

☐ Selling eggs.

I look forward to hearing from you.

President Roy of Bolivia

The tale I am about to relate to you is absolutely true, and I must ask you to believe that I have made up nothing.

In 1980 I was sent to Peru by the BBC to make a film in their series *Great Railway Journeys of the World*. This was because I spoke O-level Spanish and did not mind being on trains that arrived late. The lighting man in the BBC crew was called Roy and, although old enough to have a hefty beard, he had never been out of Britain before. So chary was he of foreign places that during our entire month there he never changed his watch from British time.

So, having typed Roy as the kind of man who paid little attention to overseas goings-on, I was amazed when he drew me aside after a week and said to me: 'I haven't told anyone else, Miles, but I am out here on a mission. I am the next president of Bolivia. As you know, our last two days filming are in La Paz, and my people are waiting for me to arrive.'

This placed me in a quandary. Should I keep Roy's secret and cash in on his coming promotion? Should I alternatively go secretly to the producer and tell him that the lighting man had gone bananas? Luckily, I decided to keep quiet. Luckily, because after another week Roy drew me aside and said:

'I have good news for you, Miles. I have decided to make you my minister of finance.'

'Why me, Roy?'

'Because you are the only person I can trust. I am surrounded by enemies.'

Four days later, high up in the Andes, there was a further development. Roy came to me with a very heavy face and told me to prepare myself for bad news.

'What is it, Roy?'

'After you have been in office for a month, I am going to have you shot.'

'Why so, Roy? I thought you trusted me.'

'I do, I do. But I have to blame someone for the mess I have got the country in.'

As we drew nearer and nearer to Bolivia, Roy's machinations got darker and deeper, and I believe that on the day before we entered the promised land I was due to be in charge of five ministries, and be executed in four of them.

The extraordinary thing was that on the day we entered Bolivia there was a coup, and the government fell. The military announced that an announcement would be made later. People everywhere gathered round their transistor sets for the next development.

'My people know I am here,' murmured Roy to me, as he set up his lights for the next shot. 'I am waiting for the moment.'

The next thing I can remember is being holed up in a hotel in La Paz with Roy, being shot at by government troops across the road. I told him I didn't think much of his command of the situation. 'I have resigned, Miles,' said Roy gravely. 'This country is not yet ready for a man like me.'

And so, unbeknown to the historians, a great moment passed. I didn't see Roy again, though I sometimes got postcards from around the globe signed 'El ex-presidente de Bolivia'. I didn't see him again, in fact, until recently when I entered a delightful hotel called El Balcon de España near Tarifa and found a BBC crew who had just finished filming Laurie Lee's *As I Walked Out Early One Morning*, the story of his travels across Spain in 1935.

'Hello, Miles,' said the lighting man Roy.

'Hello, presidente,' I said without thinking.

'Ssh,' he said. 'The others don't know. It is best they should not know. By the way, I have good news for you. Things are very restless in Bolivia and I may well be recalled. Only yesterday I had to disband the army and start forming a new one. How would you like to be Inspector General of the armed forces?'

I hesitated.

'I will double your salary.'

How could I resist? With a leader like Roy, it is very hard not to follow. Meanwhile, he has instructed me to continue this column until it is time to take office. It will all be good experience, as he has promised me the editorship of the seven government papers he intends to set up. I could not help noticing, by the way, that Roy's watch was now on Bolivian time.

MORE ABOUT PENGUINS, PELICANS, PEREGRINES AND PUFFINS

For further information about books available from Penguins please write to Dept EP, Penguin Books Ltd, Harmondsworth, Middlesex UB7 0DA.

In the U.S.A.: For a complete list of books available from Penguins in the United States write to Dept DG, Penguin Books, 299 Murray Hill Parkway, East Rutherford, New Jersey 07073.

In Canada: For a complete list of books available from Penguins in Canada write to Penguin Books Canada Ltd, 2801 John Street, Markham, Ontario L3R 1B4.

In Australia: For a complete list of books available from Penguins in Australia write to the Marketing Department, Penguin Books Australia Ltd, P.O. Box 257, Ringwood, Victoria 3134.

In New Zealand: For a complete list of books available from Penguins in New Zealand write to the Marketing Department, Penguin Books (N.Z.) Ltd, Private Bag, Takapuna, Auckland 9.

In India: For a complete list of books available from Penguins in India write to Penguin Overseas Ltd, 706 Eros Apartments, 56 Nehru Place, New Delhi 110019.